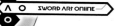

REKI KAWAHARA ABEC bee-pee

SWORD ART ONLINE
kiss and fly

SWORD ART ONLINE

"...Wh-what's the point of *you* comin' up *here*?!"

Argo § The mysterious and flighty info dealer of Aincrad. She has high agility and fights with claws. Her nickname is Argo the Rat.

"Hiya. It's been a while."

"Mmm...I...feel it..."

Asuna § Kirito's girlfriend. In *ALO*, she plays an undine magician, but her rapier skills from *SAO* are still as sharp as ever.

"Haaah...Then it seems like your BSIS level really is normal..."

Kirito § The Black Swordsman, who saved everyone trapped inside *SAO*, the game of death. In *ALO*, he plays a spriggan.

"Let go, Kirito!"

Lisbeth
The girl who forged Kirito's swords in both *SAO* and *ALO.* In *ALO*, she is a leprechaun blacksmith.

"That's right, Big Brother. I don't think you're supposed to grab that branch!"

Leafa
Kirito's sister. Real name: Suguha. She plays a magic fighter sylph in *ALO*.

"Um, Kirito...?! I feel like... you aren't meant to do that—!"

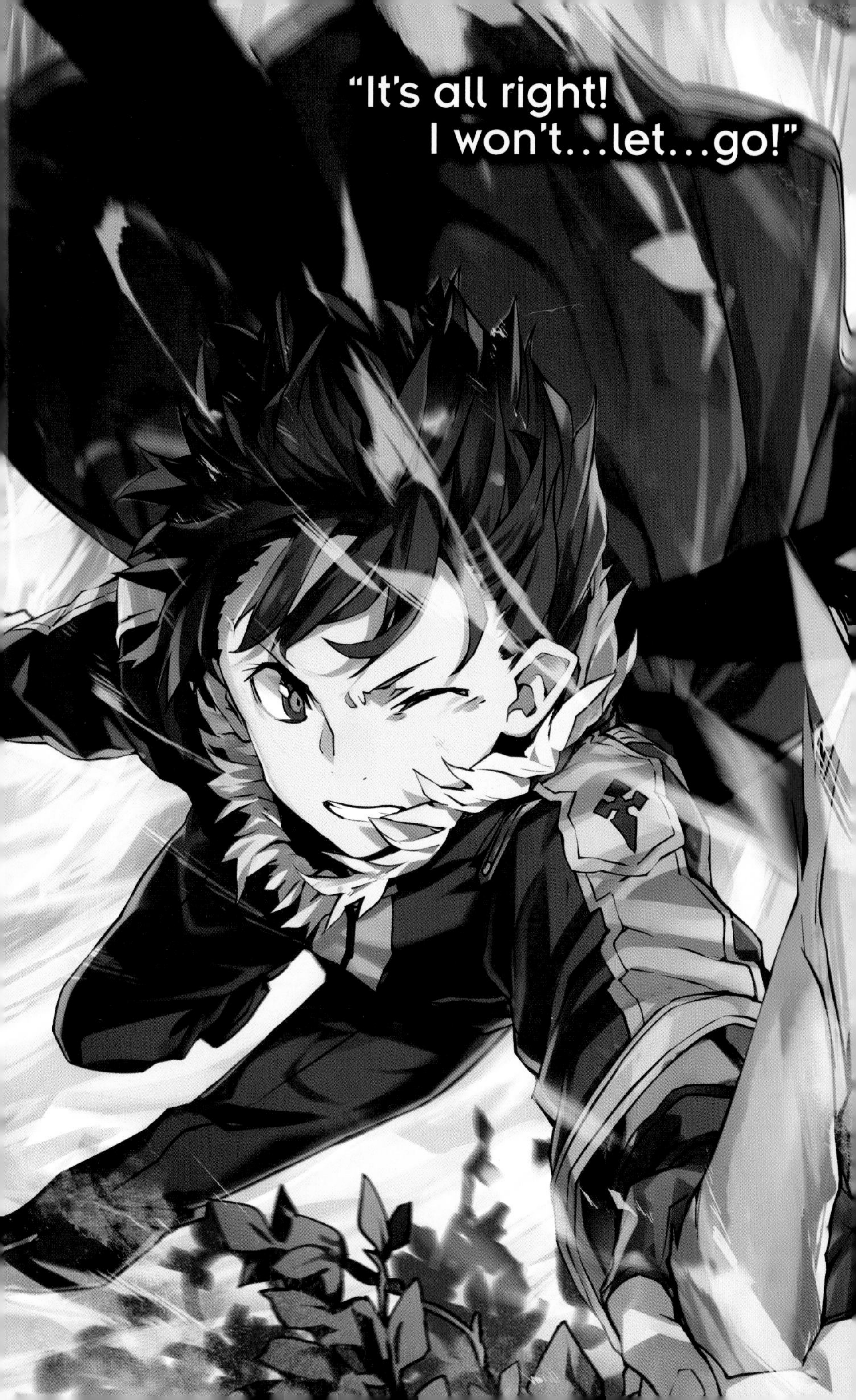
"It's all right!
I won't...let...go!"

"You see?
You're perfectly in sync!"

Merida § Member of the Sleeping Knights.
Invited Yuuki and Ran to play the
VRMMORPG *Asuka Empire.*

"I-I'm just swinging my katana around. Sis is the one who times everything to match me..."

Yuuki § A player known as the Absolute Sword for her incredible skill in swordsmanship. Started the Sleeping Knights with Ran and Merida.

"I'm just casting spells from the back, so I have a good view of Yuu..."

Ran § Yuuki's identical twin sister. The elder of the two. The original leader of the Sleeping Knights.

Legendary Weapons

The strongest class of weapons in *ALfheim Online*—as Unique items, supposedly only one of each exists on the server at a time. Some known legendary weapons include the Holy Sword Excalibur; the Demon Blade Gram; the Spirit Katana Kagutsuchi; the Bow of Light Shekinah; and the Hammer of Lightning Mjölnir.

Crest of Yggdrasil

A legendary weapon made from the highest branch of the World Tree, which Kirito snapped off and took with him. It looks like a narrow branch that measures over four feet long, but it is classified as a Two-Handed Staff and commands incredibly high stats worthy of a Unique. In the story "Calibur" from Volume 8 of *Sword Art Online* and later on in this volume, Asuna uses it as her main weapon to aid her role as a healer.

SWORD ART ONLINE
kiss and fly

VOLUME 22

Reki Kawahara

abec

bee-pee

NEW YORK

SWORD ART ONLINE, Volume 22: KISS AND FLY
REKI KAWAHARA

Translation by Stephen Paul
Cover art by abec

SWORD ART ONLINE Vol.22
©Reki Kawahara 2019
Edited by Dengeki Bunko
First published in Japan in 2019 by KADOKAWA CORPORATION, Tokyo.
English translation rights arranged with KADOKAWA CORPORATION, Tokyo, through Tuttle-Mori Agency, Inc., Tokyo.

English translation © 2021 by Yen Press, LLC

Yen On
150 30th Street, 19th Floor
New York, NY 10001

Visit us at yenpress.com
facebook.com/yenpress
twitter.com/yenpress
yenpress.tumblr.com
instagram.com/yenpress

First Yen On Edition: June 2021

Yen On is an imprint of Yen Press, LLC.
The Yen On name and logo are trademarks of Yen Press, LLC.

Library of Congress Cataloging-in-Publication Data
Names: Kawahara, Reki, author. | Abec, 1985– illustrator. | Paul, Stephen, translator.
Title: Sword art online / Reki Kawahara, abec ; translation, Stephen Paul.
Description: First Yen On edition. | New York, NY : Yen On, 2014–
Identifiers: LCCN 2014001175 | ISBN 9780316371247 (v. 1 : pbk.) |
    ISBN 9780316376815 (v. 2 : pbk.) | ISBN 9780316296427 (v. 3 : pbk.) |
    ISBN 9780316296434 (v. 4 : pbk.) | ISBN 9780316296441 (v. 5 : pbk.) |
    ISBN 9780316296458 (v. 6 : pbk.) | ISBN 9780316390408 (v. 7 : pbk.) |
    ISBN 9780316390415 (v. 8 : pbk.) | ISBN 9780316390422 (v. 9 : pbk.) |
    ISBN 9780316390439 (v. 10 : pbk.) | ISBN 9780316390446 (v. 11 : pbk.) |
    ISBN 9780316390453 (v. 12 : pbk.) | ISBN 9780316390460 (v. 13 : pbk.) |
    ISBN 9780316390484 (v. 14 : pbk.) | ISBN 9780316390491 (v. 15 : pbk.) |
    ISBN 9781975304188 (v. 16 : pbk.) | ISBN 9781975356972 (v. 17 : pbk.) |
    ISBN 9781975356996 (v. 18 : pbk.) | ISBN 9781975357016 (v. 19 : pbk.) |
    ISBN 9781975357030 (v. 20 : pbk.) | ISBN 9781975315955 (v. 21 : pbk.) |
    ISBN 9781975321741 (v. 22 : pbk.)
Subjects: CYAC: Science fiction. | BISAC: FICTION / Science Fiction / Adventure.
Classification: pz7.K1755Ain 2014 | DDC [Fic]—dc23
LC record available at https://lccn.loc.gov/2014001175

ISBNs: 978-1-9753-2174-1 (paperback)
       978-1-9753-2175-8 (ebook)

10 9 8 7 6 5 4 3 2 1

LSC-C

Printed in the United States of America

"THIS MIGHT BE A GAME, BUT IT'S NOT SOMETHING YOU PLAY."

—Akihiko Kayaba, *Sword Art Online* programmer

SWORD ART Online
kiss and fly

Reki Kawahara

abec

bee-pee

022-01

The Day Before

§ 22nd Floor of Aincrad
October 2024

1

Nine PM, October 23rd, 2024, Aincrad Standard Time.

I, Kirito, the level-96 swordsman, proposed to Asuna, the level-94 fencer, and she accepted.

This was only within the VRMMORPG called *Sword Art Online*, of course. In the real world, Asuna and I had never seen each other in person, and I wasn't old enough to be legally wed—although maybe Asuna was.

I'm not sure what the first online game to incorporate a marriage system was, but for the last twenty years at least, weddings between characters had been a popular feature of MMOs. In most games, there was a bonus given to the married couple, so many players chose to do it for practical reasons, while others got married as a result of role-playing. There were even examples of people getting married in-game and then going on to get married in real life afterward. I imagine that if you surveyed all the MMO players in the entire world and asked if they'd ever had an in-game marriage, over half of them would say yes.

But unfortunately (or perhaps fortunately) for me, of all the MMORPGs I'd played, I had never been married to another player.

The reason why, aside from my total lack of communication

skills, was because I felt completely unsure of what it meant to be "married in a game." If I, Kazuto Kirigaya, playing the male avatar Kirito, was married to the female character Random-ko, played by someone somewhere in the real world (who quite possibly could have been male or female), should I consider myself to be in a permanent party with Random-ko forever? Should I also assume that I had paired up in some way with the real person playing Random-ko…?

To be completely honest, it wasn't as though I'd never received an invitation to get married from female players on my friends list or in my guild in games I played before *SAO*. But every single time I was asked, I froze up in front of my monitor, sweating profusely, and just made things awkward for them.

I was an overthinking, overly timid coward, and I knew it.

But the entire reason I was so enthralled with MMOs was because they were worlds where nothing was real. Behind every character was an unfamiliar player of uncertain gender and age. There was no point in wondering, *Who is this person anyway?* Everyone, including me, was not actually their in-game character.

However, there was something about the marriage system that collided headfirst with this perception of mine. Even if it was just in a game, there was something about having a unique relationship with another person that I couldn't get past. I couldn't help but be conscious of that person in the real world, sitting at their computer with a mouse and keyboard.

So I avoided ever becoming permanent partners with other online players, and that carried over into *Sword Art Online* after it turned into a death game. In fact, I might have kept my distance from others even more, since our avatars' looks and bodies were essentially our own.

But there was one person who slowly but surely melted away that alienation, that fear of mine—Asuna.

In the nearly two years we spent trapped inside that deadly game, she occupied different positions, but she never left my field of view. She started off as an impromptu party member, then eventually joined the Knights of the Blood guild and also took part in our boss raids. Sometimes she helped investigate mysterious safe-zone murders, and sometimes she cooked S-ranked ingredients into meals for me. It was through my experiences with Asuna that I learned a valuable lesson.

In this world—and in the real world, too—and maybe even in the old-school MMOs I played on a desktop, it was my choice to decide if the person I stood across from was really *them* or not. If I doubted them and kept them at a distance, they would be false. If I trusted them and drew closer, they would be real.

And with me now, right here, was a warrior named Asuna.

It was fun to be with her. Asuna fighting, Asuna laughing, Asuna sulking—they all stirred powerful emotions in me. I wanted her to always be within arm's length, and I wanted a tangible connection to her. When I looked at Asuna, I no longer wondered who she really was, even for a moment.

That was why I proposed to her.

It was not as though all my doubts were gone. I couldn't be completely certain that my desire for Asuna's presence was truly what you'd call *love*. I kept at a distance from my family in the real world and maintained my stance as a solo player in this world. It made me wonder if I was truly capable of loving another person.

But I felt sure that if I stuck around with Asuna long enough, I would learn the answer to that last question.

That was the mental side of getting married in *SAO*, as I had come to feel about it.

On the other hand, even in a game, that still left the physical side of getting married—or more concretely, the question of our domestic situation.

After we were married, we would be living together, of course. The back-alley room where I slept in Algade on the fiftieth floor was much too small for the both of us, and even Asuna's maisonette in Selmburg on the sixty-first floor wasn't quite up to size. And aside from the space issue, there was another reason we couldn't continue living in the same places.

Asuna the Flash, subleader of the Knights of the Blood, was essentially the most popular player in all of Aincrad at the moment.

The newspapers printed and sold by info dealers featured popularity polls, where she regularly placed first by a mile. She had multiple fan clubs. The owner of a chain of general stores offered her a deal to record not CDs, but RCs—recording crystals—but they'd backed off when she pulled her rapier on them.

She was worlds different from the player I remembered at the start of all this, when she wore a hooded cape like Little Red Riding Hood. All the same, if word got out that the game's sweetheart was married, it'd be front-page news.

If all her many fans mourned the change, and their energy eventually morphed into curse-type attacks aimed at me, her marriage partner, then my real-life luck was sure to plummet. Well, fine, maybe that wasn't really a concern, but we couldn't enjoy our new life together if people tried to interview her about it all the time, so we wanted to keep it a secret for as long as we could.

Naturally, we'd be telling her many—and my few—friends, so the secret wouldn't last for that long, but we couldn't enjoy the honeymoon forever, anyway. Only four days had passed since we toppled the Gleameyes, the boss of the seventy-fourth floor, so it would still be several days before players discovered the boss chamber on the seventy-fifth. But even if Asuna and I didn't take part in mapping the labyrinth tower, we had to be there to fight the boss.

So before then, we had to find a home in a nice, peaceful place where we would spend time together for at least ten days...or maybe two weeks...or even more.

As far as finances went, if Asuna and I sold off all the items we'd collected that no longer served any real purpose, we would have enough col to purchase a single-story home in the safe zone, near a town. But within that same day, the info dealers would sniff us out. Ideally, we'd want a home on one of the forgotten floors long past, in a discreet, out-of-the-way location but with a comfortable amount of space.

That was a difficult set of conditions to meet, but as a matter of fact, I'd had my eye on such a place before I proposed.

The twenty-second floor of Aincrad hadn't been the frontier of player progress in a year and a half. Being lower on the conical flying castle, it was therefore a larger floor, but nearly all of it was covered by deep forests and grasslands—a beautiful floor that was low on interesting features to most players. There hadn't been any memorable quests or field bosses, either. The advancement group made a beeline to the labyrinth from the main town of Corral, rushed through the mildly difficult tower, and beat the boss in a number of days that was significantly fewer than average. At this point, the only players who would visit the twenty-second floor were fishermen heading for one of its many lakes and woodcrafters gathering lumber from its forests.

I hadn't visited it for a long time, either, but there was a sight that had stuck with me for a long time that I just couldn't forget:

On the day the twenty-second-floor boss was defeated, I rushed back to Corral alone to clean out all the quests I'd left unfinished.

Near the banks of a crystal clear blue lake, I found a tiny footpath that was nearly invisible until you were right on it. It didn't seem related to any quests, but I walked down it anyway, climbed a hill, and found myself at a single log cabin sitting quietly in the midst of a dense pine forest.

Moss dotted the log walls, and there were two or three saplings growing from the roof, but it wasn't dilapidated at all. If anything, it had a kind of natural beauty, like a house built by elves that blended in with the trees around it.

I opened the wooden gate (the fact that I could do this was proof no other player owned the home) and used my Search skill to survey the interior (it was empty, meaning no NPC lived there, either) before approaching the front terrace. At last, hanging from the doorknob, I found the wooden FOR SALE sign.

At the time, I was still under level-40, so I used my finger to count the digits of the number on the sign, then exhaled and turned to leave—though I couldn't help but look back over my shoulder several times with longing. In my head were visions of being rich enough that the col I'd need to buy the house overflowed from my packed inventory.

As a matter of fact, by the time I was level-70-something at the end of the fiftieth floor, I could have scraped together enough to buy it. But as a member of the frontline team, I couldn't make my base of operations a house that was a twenty-minute walk from the nearest teleport gate. Ultimately, I chose a little roost in Algade on the fiftieth floor, and I'd been spending my nights there until just a few days ago.

It had been a year and a half ago that I found that little log cabin in the woods—but when I made up my mind to propose to Asuna and wondered where we would live, that was the first image that popped into my mind. Frankly, to me, there was no other choice.

To propose to her, I'd brought up the information on the log cabin, suggested we move there together, and lastly, said, "Let's get married."

Asuna had said yes without a moment of hesitation. I'd like to think that the log cabin played some small part in that.

2

So with that out of the way...

The day after my proposal, at two in the afternoon on October 24th, Asuna and I visited the twenty-second floor.

The day before, we went to the Knights of the Blood headquarters in Grandzam on the fifty-fifth floor and submitted our notice for a temporary leave of absence. Temporary or not, it technically meant leaving the guild at the system level, so the red cross of the guild's insignia no longer showed up on our player cursors.

We traveled through the teleport gate in Corral and began walking toward a large lake to the southwest. I asked Asuna, "How long has it been since you joined the KoB?"

"Well...," the fencer replied, inclining her head and sending her chestnut-brown hair swaying, "the commander recruited me last December...so it's been over a year already. It was just after the boss fight on the twenty-fifth floor..."

"Oh, right...The KoB started up after the Army got decimated..."

I glanced at the bottom of the floor above us.

Just three floors from here, the twenty-fifth floor of Aincrad had been the greatest test for the best players since the very first floor.

Immediately after a player left the main town, it became clear that the monsters on the twenty-fifth floor were significantly tougher than on the previous one. The layout of the landscape was complex and mazelike, and a number of players died just getting to the next town. NPCs did not offer much information, and there were numerous traps like poison swamps and pits. By the time we had finished exploring the floor and reached the labyrinth tower, the frontline group as a whole was exhausted.

The person who was responsible for whipping us back into shape and energizing us for the tower was Kibaou, the leader of the guild known as the Aincrad Liberation Squad—at this time, they were not yet called the Army. He hurled insults at the group with his characteristic Kansai dialect until we were all furious enough to be back on our feet and ready for action.

However, just before we rushed into the boss chamber to fight the floor boss, someone fed Kibaou, the unquestioned leader of the frontline group, some false info. They rushed into the chamber with only forty-plus guild members, much less than a full raid party. Over half the ALS died in that battle. It was only when the main force of the advancement group arrived, including me and Asuna, that we managed to topple the horrific boss, despite more deaths.

But nobody could openly celebrate passing the quarter mark of Aincrad. Not when Kibaou's furious screams of grief were echoing off the walls of the chamber.

From there, he parted ways with the frontline players, taking his surviving comrades all the way back down to the first floor. There, they teamed up with a mutual aid group called MMO Today, and that alliance formed the foundation of the Army.

"The mood of the entire advancement group was dire back then…Suddenly we'd lost a third of our numbers—and it was possibly because of an intentional trap. I suppose it's no surprise things felt raw. People were downcast even at the meeting to beat the field boss on the twenty-sixth floor…but that was when the new KoB guild showed up. Everyone all decked out in custom white-and-red gear…it left quite an impact," I said, going over the old memories as we walked along the lakeside. My partner was very quiet, so I glanced over and saw Asuna, with her cheeks red, turning away for some reason.

Catching on, I feigned ignorance and continued, "But especially, it was the sight of the vice commander that caught my eye...and Klein's, and even Agil's. But *her*, well! She went from plain-looking equipment to the total opposite, with a pure-white no-sleeve bodice, a bright-red miniskirt, and then those white knee-high stockings...If you ask me, it felt like the scattered remnants of the group all came together as one—"

Wham! There was a bludgeon attack on my left shoulder just short of causing actual damage, cutting my thoughts short. I turned my head and saw the vice commander herself, face beet red, holding a fist.

"Ugh! You know how embarrassed I was to be seen like that! I assumed the commander would stand at the fore, but then he just says, 'The effect will be greater if you stand at the front, Asuna,' so I did it out of sheer resignation!"

"Um...I see...By the way, I assume that had to be a custom uniform, right? Who designed it?"

"...All the other officers held numerous design meetings in secret, leaving me out. When they showed the uniform to me, I said, 'I'm not wearing that!' But then Daizen got tears in his eyes and claimed, 'You wouldn't believe how much it cost us just to produce this one outfit!' So again, out of sheer resignation..."

"Ah...I see."

The Knights of the Blood were known today for their iron-clad rules and strict discipline, but it sounded like their early days were rather jovial. At any rate, the KoB's arrival certainly gave the frontline group a big morale boost, and they had stood at the front line of the deadly game ever since. Even at this very moment, on the newly opened seventy-fifth floor, red-and-white parties were battling furiously...

Once again, I glanced up at the bottom of the upper floor. That gesture was enough for Asuna to read my mind. She unclenched her fist and gently grabbed my hand.

"You basically beat the seventy-fourth-floor boss all by yourself. It only had two or three pixels left on its HP bar. Nobody's going to complain if you take a little break from the usual activities."

"...But they'll all complain if they learn *why* I want a break," I replied with a smirk, squeezing her hand back. The vice commander looked like she wasn't sure whether to be angry or embarrassed, but she settled on a chuckle.

By the time we'd gone halfway around the huge lake, which was probably half a mile across, there was a coniferous tree that looked like a cedar, looming higher than the others. At its massive roots was a faint, tiny footpath that broke off from the trail leading around the lake and headed southwest.

"...So you found this path? You're always so keen when it comes to finding these hidden routes," Asuna said, which I chose to take as a compliment.

"And I didn't have the Detection mod on my Search skill at the time, so it was all pure eyesight and intuition," I boasted. "Once we get over that hill, you'll see the house right away."

Now it was Asuna's turn to light up with excitement. "Ooh, I can't wait to find out what it's like! Let's go!"

"...Um, Asuna, it's...just a typical log cabin, so I don't want you to get your hopes up too high."

"When I was a little girl, I often dreamed of living in a log cabin. As long as there's a proper hearth and a rocking chair to sit in, I'll be over the moon!" she crowed, hurrying up the hill. I hustled after her.

A rocking chair could be bought at a furniture shop, but I couldn't remember if there had been a hearth or not. But at this point, I had to assume there was one. I found this cabin a year and a half ago for the purpose of this very day. If fate had been guiding me properly, there would be a hearth.

Praying that we'd see a chimney on the roof of the cabin, I crested the hill a few steps behind Asuna and stood next to her, scanning desperately for a chimney.

But—

It wasn't there.

There was no chimney.

We were looking at a circular space covered in green under-growth, with not a single man-made object there…and certainly not any houses.

3

It was the wrong place.

That was the most logical explanation. So I apologized to Asuna, went back down the hill, and rushed around the area for the next two hours, searching.

But not only were there no log cabins, I couldn't even find another footpath branching off. Stunned, I returned to the original hill and examined what I could see from there.

"This is it. This is definitely the place…?" I murmured to myself.

The spacious grass yard (just an empty lot now with no house there), the thick coniferous woods behind it, the looming pillars supporting the outer aperture of Aincrad in the distance, and the endless expanse of sky behind it all. I could vividly recall each of these details from my memory of being here a year and a half ago.

But the most important thing of all, the log cabin, was not here. Just to be sure, I went into the clearing, even walked to the very center, but the house did not suddenly pop into being.

Shocked and rooted to the spot, I heard footsteps marching across the grass behind me until they stopped very close by.

I couldn't turn around. The suggestion to move into the log cabin on the twenty-second floor *was* my marriage proposal.

Now that the house wasn't there, my proposal had essentially been rendered false.

"Asuna…it's true. There was a cabin. Right here," I murmured, face downcast.

She circled around directly in front of me, patted my shoulders, then cupped my cheeks with her hands and lifted my head. Those hazel-brown eyes were as kind and soft as they ever were.

"I believe you. Of course I believe you," she said, let go, and took a few steps back. "I'm sure it got removed for some systemic reason. It's a shame, but even without the house, it's a beautiful place. I'm very happy to have come here with you."

She stood atop the green grass and spun in place, skirt twirling. The sun dappling through the trees and gleaming off her long hair, her platinum breastplate, and the sheath of her rapier, Lambent Light, were so beautiful they could be used for promotional videos.

Obviously, Asuna couldn't read my mind, but she stopped and faced me anyway, patting the belt pouch on her right side.

"Hey, since we're here, let's take a photo to commemorate the occasion. I brought a photo crystal."

"Oh…um, sure…" I smiled, but Asuna could tell from my voice and expression that something was wrong.

"Was this really such a shock to you?" she asked. "That the house is gone…?"

"Er, no, not a shock, necessarily," I claimed, shaking my head and hands, but Asuna still seemed worried for me. It was going to be impossible to dispel that notion from her at this point, so I fessed up.

"The thing is…I had a whole plan regarding what I was going to do here today. And it can't happen if the house isn't here…"

"Hmm? What did you want to do?"

It was hard to explain with her big, beautiful eyes staring at me, but after proposing to her, I couldn't be shy about it now. I cleared my throat and started by explaining how the system worked.

"Well, here's the thing. Getting married in *SAO* is pretty simple in terms of how it works. You start from the main menu, go to the communication tab, then go down the list of requests to the very bottom, where the MARRIAGE button is. Then press it, select your target…and if they hit OK, it's all done. No need to submit any forms to any offices…"

"And you don't have to visit my parents and say, 'I'm asking for your daughter's hand in marriage!' either," Asuna interjected with a smirk.

I couldn't help but imagine that unavoidable cutscene (with Commander Heathcliff from the KoB playing her father, for some reason), and it made me shiver. The daughter—er, Asuna giggled at the sight of me.

I cleared my throat. "A-at any rate! Because the process only takes, like, five seconds, I wanted, you know, to do it in a way that would be more memorable for you. Unfortunately, we can't have some big, huge wedding ceremony, so I thought the best method of all would be to buy our new house and have something in front of it…"

By the end, I had craned my neck down toward the ground and started mumbling awkwardly, but I managed to finish my thought successfully and exhaled with relief.

And then I took a high-speed body tackle.

Or rather, one had come for me. I hadn't been bracing for it, so I landed hard on my back in the grass.

Fortunately, Asuna wasn't trying to pound my face with knuckle sandwiches. Her warmth just leaned against my chest as she whispered, "That's…wonderful."

"Er, I mean, it was just a spur-of-the-moment idea—"

"But that's what makes it so wonderful. You thought so hard about making things nice for us, and you even looked all over for a house…"

Up close, just inches away, I could see that tears were brimming in Asuna's eyes. That hit me deeply, and I enclosed her slender body in my arms.

For a while, the two of us lay there on the grass, feeling the breeze. In time, Asuna's voice whispered in my ear.

"It's enough."

"Huh...?"

"I'm already happy enough. So shall we do the marriage process and go back for today? We can look for a home some other time."

The stone bottom of the floor above us was dyed yellow with the sunlight of afternoon. The sun would be down in just another hour or two.

"Yeah...good idea."

I straightened up, still embracing my fiancée, and glanced around the empty circle in the midst of the coniferous forest.

If we were patient and thorough about looking for modestly sized buildings that were outside of town, had no monsters spawning nearby, and were remote enough that other players were unlikely to wander by, we would surely find something. There was also the option of asking Argo the info dealer for help. Surely the Rat wouldn't sell the coordinates of our new home to anyone else. *Surely*.

So like Asuna said, there was no need to be fixated on the cabin. The little grassy knoll was striking enough, and the memory of our marriage ceremony here would surely remain in Asuna's memory—and mine—long after *SAO* was beaten, if it happened.

......And yet.

That was all well and good. But there was something about this experience, unrelated to our eloping, that itched at the back of my mind, eating away at me. It was like an unfinished quest that I'd gotten stuck on and abandoned, sitting at the bottom of my quest log. Taunting me.

"...Kirito?"

The sound of my name brought me back to my senses with a start. Asuna's face was close; she wore an expression that said she could see everything. I froze up again.

"Y-yes?"

"...I bet you're thinking, 'That's all well and good, and yet...'"

I nearly made a guilty *erk* expression but managed to hide it with a poker face just in the nick of time. "Um, wh-whatever do you mean?"

"I can tell these things, you know. You're wondering why the house isn't here anymore and want to get to the bottom of it."

Okay, so my poker face wasn't that great. That was useful to know. I'd learned from experience that continuing to deny it would only make it more painful, so I fessed up and admitted it:

"Ummm, well…yes. B-but I mean! It just doesn't make sense that a player home would disappear like this. You mentioned some kind of system-level issue, but *SAO* doesn't have any GMs, so I can't imagine that it was manually removed by an admin. Even if the cause was from a program, houses have infinite durability—they don't go bad. And there are no earthquakes or wildfires in Aincrad, so the only other possibility I can imagine is…uhhh…"

I started going into heavy deduction mode until Asuna pressed her index finger against my mouth.

"All right, stop right there! Look, I've known you for long enough. I know you're not the kind of person who can just turn off that part of his brain…" She sighed with resignation.

I undid the pause before she had even taken her next breath. "W-well, I know our time off is valuable, but I can use part of it to figure this out…can't I?"

Asuna grumbled under her breath that she'd had a feeling this would happen and that it wasn't the point of our vacation, but in the end, she took a deep breath and announced, "The window for investigation opens and closes tonight!"

4

Over 99 percent of the countless terrain objects that populated Aincrad's many floors were classified as indestructible. All natural features, aside from standing trees, and all man-made objects, like buildings and walls, were impervious to any kind of attempted destruction.

In some dungeons, depending on the design, there were breakable walls, and every now and then, you found breakable rocks and soft earth in the environment, but I had never heard of a house that could be broken down. What if you bought a house that could be destroyed? Just imagine being asleep in bed when a huge hole smashed into the wall, and a guild of orange criminal players came storming inside... You'd be living in the world of the Three Little Pigs.

So right off the bat, I knew that my missing dream home could not have been destroyed by players.

"...Well, I agree with you there." Asuna nodded when I finished my explanation. "That is, assuming there isn't some extra skill like Land Speculation or something."

"B-but what would be the point of driving up land prices here? They'd do it along the lake in Selmburg or something."

"Ah yes. Property along the lake there is expensive. It would cost three times as much as my place...But I guess if we can't find the house here, we might spring for a place there."

"Er, I dunno…M-might be a little tough on my income," I stammered, going pale. Asuna gave me a big smile and reassured me that she was joking.

She quickly moved back into strategic-officer mode and stared at the empty space of the little glen. "Well, let's eliminate the possibility that someone destroyed the house…And just to be certain, the customization of player homes doesn't extend to outer walls and roofs, right?"

"Uh, what do you mean?"

"I mean, when you buy a house, there's a customization menu for the owner to play around with, right? Where you can decide which fixtures you want to remove?"

At last, I understood the point Asuna was making. "Ahhh," I said, nodding, "so you mean someone might have bought the house, used the customization menu to remove the walls, roof, and floor, and turned it into a blank lot. Hmm…I've only ever lived in little places like apartments, so I've never seen the customization options on a house…"

"Same goes for me. Hey…let's ask Liz!" Asuna suggested, opening her menu to type a quick message to her good friend Lisbeth the blacksmith.

I was on good terms with Liz, too. She was the one who'd forged my sword, Dark Repulser, so she was one of the few people on the list we would inform about our marriage. After purchasing the house today and completing the marriage process, we'd intended to send off a message to a dozen or so people promptly, including Liz. But now the order of events had changed, and we were going to be asking her about real estate.

The reply came back within moments. Asuna read over the message on a screen that only she could see, and she bobbed her head.

"She says you can't remove or rearrange the exterior walls and roof. If you pay up, you can change the color or add bay windows and flower beds and options like that, but that's it…"

"…And I'm guessing one of those color options isn't 'invisible.'"

More important, Asuna and I had walked all over the empty

lot and found no traces of the building. If it were there but invisible, I would have smacked my face on the front door.

"Then…is there another option? Like outfitting it to be able to sink underground?" Asuna wondered, tapping at the ground with the toe of her boot.

I couldn't help but smirk. "Ha-ha, it's not going to be like some supervillain's secret base. Besides, if you dug a hole in Aincrad deep enough to fit an entire house inside, you'd pop through the bottom and fall down to the next floor."

"Awww, that sounds so lovely, though. Like a gnome's house."

"I thought those were dug into the *side* of a hill…Wouldn't it be a dwarf's house if it's underground? You remember that huge dwarven citadel with at least a dozen floors, right?"

"Ew, I hated that place. It was so dank and had all those bug monsters…Besides, even that 'underground' castle was just on the inside of a mountain on the floor map."

"It's a structural flaw of Aincrad, isn't it? Since there's a limit to how thick the ground can be, you don't get those classic RPG sprawling underground dungeons."

"I'm fine with that!" Asuna snapped. "But do you really want to just stand around chatting? I mean, I'm having fun, but…"

I glanced at the sky to the sides. The trailing wisps of clouds in the sky were colored orange. The sun would be down in just two more hours.

"G-good point. Well, if it's not invisible or a secret underground base, then…is it a moving fortress? No, that would make it too easy to march straight from the main city to the labyrinth tower. And that would rule out a flying fortress, too…"

I was getting further from likely possibilities and deeper into wild fantasies, much to Asuna's chagrin. She glanced upward, while I hung my head, folded my arms, and thought.

"So it doesn't seem likely that it was obliterated with the customization menu. Plus, that would mean another player has already bought it…I have a feeling that whatever caused this wasn't player related…"

"......Hey."

"But does that mean...a field boss with the ability to destroy terrain objects...? No, even the Geocrawler on the fifty-sixth floor couldn't break the gate to the village. If there was a boss that crazy on the twenty-second floor, we would have had to put together a whole raid party..."

"Hey, Kirito."

I felt a tugging on my coat sleeve and interrupted myself to look at Asuna.

"...What?"

"......Look."

She lifted one of her white-gloved hands and pointed. I followed the angle of her finger up into the sky.

It was there, in the sky, directly above the largest cedar tree, beyond the north side of the empty clearing.

Floating high in the air, nearly touching the bottom of the floor above us, was a house. Because of the angle from the ground, you could only see the bottom, but the combination of massive logs made it clear that this was the cabin I'd been searching for.

I was so stunned that I couldn't feel happy about spotting it—just shocked that it was floating over 250 feet overhead.

In a daze, I murmured, "Wh-why...is the house...flying...?"

"......You mentioned a flying-fortress option...It's not that, is it...?" Asuna asked. I squinted to get a better look at the tiny feature far overhead, but I couldn't see anything like wings or balloons or propellers.

But thanks to my skill-enhanced vision, I spotted two things I hadn't noticed before:

First, there was a swirl of air below the house, flickering like heat haze. It was probably flying on top of something like a whirlwind fixed in place.

Second, sticking out of the south-facing window of the house and waving wildly at us all the way down on the ground was a person.

"S-someone's in there," I pointed out to Asuna's surprise.

She craned her head farther and said, "Y-you're right. From this distance, I can't tell if it's an NPC or a player, though…"

The visual clue that distinguished a player from an NPC was the color of the cursor. But this distance was much too far for the cursor to display.

I had no idea why the house was flying, but if the figure inside was a player rather than an NPC, we couldn't just leave them up there. If the house fell from that distance, it would easily kill them.

"Wh-which is it…?"

Asuna and I watched with bated breath—when the figure suddenly pulled in its waving arm, then stuck it out again. It let go of some object that fell, glittering in the sunlight. The angle was so straight that it seemed to move slowly, heading directly toward the clearing where we stood.

"Oh…oh…oh…"

I took four steps to the right, then three steps forward, and caught the little object with both hands. Asuna rushed over so we could examine it.

"An empty…potion bottle…?" she said. I nodded, then looked back up at the floating cabin in the sky.

"It's a player!" I shouted. An empty bottle after the potion's contents had been drunk would soon disintegrate and disappear. To prevent that and keep the bottle, you had to put it away in a bag or in your virtual inventory menu. NPCs wouldn't do something like that, so having an empty bottle was a sign that it was a player trapped in that floating house up there.

"W-we've got to save them," I said, holding the bottle.

But Asuna, as ever, posed the proper question: "H-how?!"

"……"

That was indeed the question. As a general rule, there was no way for a player to fly in *SAO*. After all, then you could simply fly up to the next floor and bypass the labyrinth tower and boss—or go all the way up to the hundredth floor, the goal.

A few months ago, Asuna, I, and the blacksmith Lisbeth had

flown briefly when we held on to the tail of a white dragon. But there was no choosing our destination then, there were no dragons on this floor, and I *certainly* didn't want to repeat that experience.

"......W-well, let's head to the spot right under the house," I suggested without any better options. Asuna gave me a funny look but agreed.

When we walked out of the clearing and into the forest, the carpet of branches overhead blocked the sight of the flying house. But I used my special real-life skill Direct Line Intuition to maintain my bearings. It was surprisingly difficult in a forest, where you couldn't see into the distance. I had tried explaining it to Asuna once, that you had to treat your legs like they were autorunning, but she just looked at me like my head was on fire.

But my intuition was correct, and after two or three minutes, the especially large cedar tree appeared. It was definitely positioned directly under the house. I looked up as I approached the trunk, and through the many branches, I could see the tiny floating shadow high above.

"So...what now? Climbing to the very top of that tree isn't going to get us close to reaching the house," Asuna observed, walking forward with her face pointed skyward.

I took the same pose and replied, "I was thinking that if we were directly below, we might be within shouting range...but that doesn't seem likely, either..."

"Ahhh. If we could talk to one another, we could learn how that happened. Should we climb the tree, then? Maybe being up in the branches will make it possible to hear."

"The problem is, these pine trees are harder to climb...Might be too hard without the use of the Acrobat skill..."

We were just within fifteen feet of the massive cedar tree when there was a roar from close by, like that of a monster, causing us both to jump with fright.

"Arf! Harrrf-harf-harf!!"

On pure instinct, I reached behind my back for the hilt of

Elucidator but paused there. The howling was coming from a quadrupedal creature no more than sixteen inches long…Something I would normally call…

A dog.

It had longish fur in a light-brown color, with big bright eyes and a fluffy tail with a blue ribbon attached to it. The color cursor was yellow, indicating that it was either an NPC, a beast-tamer's pet, or a nonactive monster that wasn't in an aggro state.

"Ooh, it's so cute!" squealed Asuna. She crouched down and reached out a hand, but I quickly held her back.

"N-no! Wait!"

"How come? It's so cute."

"It c-could be some kind of trap! For one thing, it's weird that there's just a dog hanging out on the map. What if it transforms into a direwolf the moment you touch it?"

"It'll be fine. Look at how its tail is wagging."

In the meantime, the little dog was hopping and spinning around in front of Asuna, practically begging her to pick it up. I maintained a tight hold on Asuna's sword belt so she couldn't squat down, and I stared at the mutt to check its cursor. The name that appeared was *Toto.*

"…Toto? That's not a species name…So is that its given name…?"

"Awww! Even its *name* is cute! C'mere, Toto! Here, boy!"

"I told you to stay back…"

Asuna had already been hit by the Charmed negative status effect, clearly. I dragged her back with all my strength and gazed into the big, deep eyes of the mutt named Toto, seeking signs of wicked cunning within them.

Belatedly, I spotted a new detail. Floating about eight inches above the dog's round head was a little ? icon.

"What…? A quest symbol?!" I shouted. "But why is it already in progress…?"

Asuna noticed it as well, and the pulling against my grip lessened. "You're right…It's got a quest…"

Each floor of Aincrad contained so many quests, you could barely hope to complete them all. Most of them came from NPCs with ! symbols over their heads, and when the quests were already active, the symbols turned to ?.

Meaning this doggy was a key person—er, animal—to a quest in progress. But the problem was that neither I nor presumably Asuna had accepted any quests relating to a dog…

"Oh! That's it!" Asuna shouted. Startled, I let go of her belt. The fencer spun around and fixed me with a deadly serious look. "We're usually occupied with taking out the labyrinth tower and floor boss, so we don't usually take on the side quests, right? It's been our blind spot. Whenever there's some phenomenon that doesn't seem to make sense, it's got something to do with a quest. Such as…a flying house!"

"……Hmm," I hummed, agreeing. Asuna spun back to face the little pup, who was still in a state of great agitation.

"And that means, in order to find the cause of why the house is flying…we need to make contact with little Toto here! You understand, don't you, Kirito? We don't have a *choice!*" she said, making it sound like a great personal sacrifice. Before I could stop her yet again, she crouched and reached for the furball.

"Arf-arf-arf!" the little brown dog barked happily and leaped into her arms. Its tail wagged furiously as it licked her face.

"Ha-ha-ha! Oh, that tickles! Awww, you're so cuuute! I've always wanted to have a dog just like this!"

Fortunately, Toto did not turn into a giant man-eating wolf.

But what *did* happen next surpassed anything I expected by at least three light-years.

A tremendous whirlwind whipped up around our feet. The sheer power of the wind dragged us off-balance without any chance to resist. I toppled, and my feet left the ground—and to my horror, they did not touch it again.

"K-Kirito!"

Asuna reached out with the free hand that wasn't holding Toto, and I grabbed it. The three of us were thrown upward by the impromptu tornado. The light blurred and rotated, and the wind caused my coat hem and Asuna's skirt to flap hard (a phenomenon that never happened with ordinary breezes in the wilderness), not that I had the attention to dedicate to it.

"Ah! Aaah! Aaaaaaah!" I screamed.

"Aieeeeee!" Asuna shrieked.

"Harf-arf-arf!!" barked the dog with great excitement.

We rose directly up into the air toward the floating log cabin far overhead.

5

"…Wh-what's the point of *you* comin' up *here*?!" were the first words out of the mouth of the player in the log cabin who'd been pleading for help.

About ninety seconds earlier…

Asuna and the dog and I were sucked up into the sky toward the flying cabin. The whirlwind took us over the roof, then down a chimney yawning at one end of it. After going through a cramped, dark tunnel, we landed on our behinds on the wood-paneled floor of the living room, where a female player looked down at us, aghast.

Once I could think straight again after that astonishing event, I looked up into the face of the cabin's inhabitant. To my shock, it was a very familiar one, but I wasn't really capable of wringing out the strength to *act* further shocked.

Instead, I said, "Hiya. It's been a while."

And that was what earned me that response.

At any rate, the first step was trading information.

But my suggestion, while met with agreement by the other player, also elicited a disappointed slump of her shoulders. She pointed toward a round table fixed to the floor of the living room. I sat next to Asuna, who was still holding the dog. The female player kept her distance and sat on the other side.

By this point, Asuna had recovered her normal wits, too. She greeted the woman, whom the both of us knew quite well.

"It's nice to see you again, Argo."

"...Hullo, A-chan. Same to you, Kiri-boy," she said with a wave and an indecipherable expression. There were three lines painted on each of her cheeks to look like whiskers. For the nearly two years since the start of this game of death—in fact, add an extra month for the beta test—she had stuck with that face paint, because it matched her nickname, Argo the Rat. She was the finest info dealer in all of Aincrad.

Asuna and I had known her since the earliest days of the game, and we'd bought and sold her info countless times since then. Even outside of business circumstances, we'd helped her and been helped in return many times, and we'd never been on outright hostile terms. It didn't sit right with me that she'd act guarded around us, but there were more pressing matters for now.

"So, Argo...what's going on here?"

I gestured with my right arm around the room, indicating the tremendously airborne building. The info dealer's eyes blinked, framed by her golden-brown curls.

"You don't know? You had to've picked it up ta get here! The quest, man, the quest!"

"Oh...r-right..."

I glanced over at the pup, who was looking sleepy in Asuna's arms. The *?* over its head was still active. That meant there was a quest in progress...

"But it wasn't as much that we *accepted* the quest as it *happened* to us..."

Asuna nodded. "That's right. I picked up this dog, and then all of a sudden, we were getting blown all the way up into this house. In fact, it was almost like someone else had started a quest and left...it...behind..."

She trailed off, and I looked over at her. I knew exactly what thought had just popped into her head:

If a quest *someone else had started* was the cause of all this, then the guilty party could not be anyone other than Argo the Rat here.

Our heads turned with a crack to stare at Argo, who hunched her shoulders guiltily and said, "Guess I'll explain from the top."

See, lately I've been pickin' up word of strange new quests bein' generated on the lower floors of Aincrad. Like masked ogres that just keep respawning, no matter how many ya kill, or fire-breathin' tortoises that do spinning jumps, or an undead woman dressed in white who comes crawlin' out of a cursed message window.

Since I'm the one putting out the Complete, Unabridged Quest Guidebook, I gotta get the scoop on every new quest as soon as I can. So the day before yesterday, I came here to the southwest region of the twenty-second floor to investigate a quest, and I found the starting point right away. But there's a problem with the content. I hopped inside this house without bringing along a key character for the quest, and all of a sudden, the whole house just shoots up into the air! I've been stuck inside this place for the last two days, just hopin' someone would come along and reset the quest for me.

At that point, Argo just threw up her hands in resignation.

Resetting a quest was an operation performed from the menu, when an active quest had been ignored for a long period of time. There were more than a few quests in *SAO* that could only be attempted by one player at a time, which was why the function existed. Of course, you had to be in the vicinity of the NPC who started the quest in the first place.

In other words, at the point that we spotted the pup named Toto under the cedar tree and noticed the ? over its head, if we had opened our menus and opened the quest tab, there should have been a quest-reset button there. But now that we had piggy-backed onto the quest in progress, neither Asuna nor I could reset it.

"...Well, I guess that kind of explains the situation...but there are still plenty of mysteries. Argo, you said there was a problem with the content of the quest?" I asked.

The info dealer adopted the same conflicted expression from before, and she glanced at Asuna—or more accurately, the little animal sleeping in Asuna's arms.

"W-well, the thing is…even I've got certain things I'm better at than others…"

"Ooh, I get it! You're afraid of dogs!" Asuna said with a smile. The whiskers painted on Argo's cheeks twitched awkwardly.

"I—I can't help it! That's my default status! As if you're perfect—I've heard you're afraid of astral-type mobs, A-chan!"

"B-but those are ghosts! Of course people are scared of ghosts. But puppies are cute! Come on—just hold him!"

"N-no! Stop! Let the dog sleep!"

I stood to the side, allowing Argo and Asuna to bicker so I could mull over the facts. Argo (despite being a rat) was afraid of dogs, and there was a quest marker open over the dog's head, which meant…

"Aha, I get it. Argo, you started the quest, but because the quest character was a dog, you ran for the house with all your Agility stat and shut yourself inside, which advanced the quest and shot it up into the air, but the dog wasn't able to keep up and get inside the house with you, so the quest got stuck, and you were trapped inside a flying building for two whole days…Ha-ha-ha, oh, the fun you get into on your own. You should write about your exploits in the *Great Adventures of Argo* one day. You'll make a fortune," I jabbed, laughing.

Argo briefly made a tempted face—"A fortune?"—but then exploded, "This isn't funny! It means that both you and A-chan are stuck here in the house now, too!"

"Oh, you're exaggerating. If we really have to, we can just use a teleport crystal to zip over to a town," I replied, chuckling—until I saw both Argo and Asuna making the same expression.

Asuna glanced at her, then back at me. "Um, Kirito…don't you think Argo would have tried that already?"

"Eh?"

"It can vary depending on the quest, but usually in forced-event quests like this, they prevent you from teleporting out of trouble. Right, Argo?"

"You betcha!"

"…Are you serious?" I asked, feeling a cold sweat break out.

Argo just shook her head in disappointment. "Well, I suppose there's always the final option of jumpin' out the window and teleporting just before ya hit the ground…but I don't have the guts to try that."

"Y-yeah, I don't think I do, either…," I said, glancing at all the space outside the window.

I gave the matter more consideration. What was this quest, anyway? You take a quest from the dog, then go inside the house with it, and it gets blown into the sky on a whirlwind? The premise just didn't make sense. *SAO*'s game server couldn't be under the control of its developer, Argus, anymore, so I doubted that anyone at Argus had written this script. So who came up with this pointless scenario? And without a function to call for GM help, how were we going to get out of being stuck…?

"…Oh…wait a second," I called out.

Asuna looked up from petting Toto's head, and Argo looked away from keeping an eye on the fearsome beast.

"If the reason the quest is stuck is that the dog, Toto, was left on the ground…then hasn't that been solved? Wouldn't that mean the quest is functioning normally again…?"

"Ah…!"

Argo snapped her fingers. She bolted over for the window with alarming speed and looked down toward the ground.

"W-we're moving! In fact, we're almost back down again!"

"R-really?! Great, then we can get back home before it gets dark," Asuna said with relief, walking toward the window, but I was not feeling so optimistic. I had a bad feeling about this.

As far as quest openings go, throwing an entire house into the sky was a drastic one. A story that began that dramatically would not end this easily. It might involve several steps, like going here and finding something, going there and helping someone…And most important, beating the quest did not guarantee this house would return to its former status as a purchasable asset. And at this rate, I didn't know when Asuna and I would ever be marri—

"Ooh!" I grunted and glanced over at Argo, who was maintaining an awkward distance from Asuna—or more specifically, the dog in her arms.

She was an old friend, but it was imperative that Asuna and I didn't let her catch on to our eloping before it happened. As soon as she knew about it, it'd be front-page news in *Weekly Argo*, and I'd be cursed to the grave by Asuna's fan club.

So the longer we worked on this quest together, the more dangerous it would be. We needed to beat it quick and say our good-byes before the Rat's keen sense of smell sniffed out what was going on.

I straightened up with a newfound sense of purpose—right as the log house came crashing to the ground in an unknown place.

6

"…By the way, what was the name of this quest?" I asked.

Argo opened her window and answered, "It's 'The Three Treasures of the Wicked Witch of the West.'"

"Sounds normal enough. Especially for one so surreal…"

The three of us stepped out onto soil again—Argo for the first time in two days, Asuna and I for the first time in fifteen minutes—while the next key character in the quest stood wavering before us.

But once again, it was not human. It was a figure with a torso made of two crossed sticks, and a round fabric head that was stuffed full—a scarecrow. It looked silly, but it was a monster by definition. Scarecrow mobs were not uncommon on horror-themed floors.

And the scarecrow wasn't the only thing greeting us. To its left was an enemy that resembled a hollow suit of plate armor. And on its right was a werelion, which had a human head on a lion's body. None of the trio were attempting to attack us. Their color cursors were yellow, indicating they were nonaggressive now.

I was just wondering what was going on when the scarecrow began to talk.

"Oh! We've been waiting for you!"

At that, the *!* symbol over the scarecrow's head turned into a *?*, indicating that a quest had initiated. The symbol over the dog's head vanished.

"You've been...waiting for us?" I asked, playing along. The scarecrow nodded its head much harder and began to tell its story. It went roughly like this.

We're Scarecrow, Tin Man, and Lion, and we're on a journey to become real humans. But the girl we were with got kidnapped by the Wicked Witch of the West. We want to rescue her, but the witch stole the stuffing from Scarecrow's head, the jewel in Tin Man's heart, and Lion's golden mane of courage. So we cast a whirlwind spell on the girl's dog, Toto, and sent it beyond the walls to find a warrior who will fight the witch for us.

"Ah...ha-ha-ha...I see..."

I glanced behind us.

According to the map, we were in the northwest part of the twenty-second floor. We were surrounded by vertical cliff walls that made it impossible to walk here. Those had to be the walls the scarecrow mentioned.

That gave me a broad idea of the quest itself, but I couldn't shake the feeling of how strange the quest was. For one thing, there was no magic in *SAO*, so things like witches and whirlwind spells didn't make sense. Plus, the scarecrow and the lion were easy to understand, but why was the living armor called Tin Man?

These were probably not the most pressing questions at the moment, but I couldn't help myself. Next to me, however, Asuna murmured, "Okay...I get it. I know what this quest is."

Argo nodded, too. "So do I. No wonder the house was flyin'."

"Huh? What do you mean?" I asked, turning left and right.

Asuna gave me a grin and said something that took me completely by surprise.

"You must have read it when you were a boy, Kirito. Some of the details are different...but this quest is clearly based on *The Wonderful Wizard of Oz!*"

"…Ohhh…Oh, now I get it!"

To be honest, I couldn't remember every part of the story. But a girl with her pet dog being blown into the air in her house by a tornado, then falling into another world where she met a scarecrow, a tin man, and a lion before finding her way back to the real world—yes, that seemed familiar to me.

Well, that explained why the living armor monster was the "tin man," but it also was a foreboding sign for the quest ahead.

"…I bet that means this one's going to take forever," I groaned. Asuna gave me a curious look, so I explained, "I mean, we'll probably have to get the scarecrow's brain, the tin man's heart, and the lion's mane in order, right? How many hours will each one take…?"

Asuna and Argo shared a look, then grinned for some reason.

"Kiri-boy, you don't really remember how the story goes, do you?"

"Uh…W-well, I suppose not…"

"Ha-ha, I don't think we'll need to collect any items. Let's just skip past all of that and head straight for the witch's castle!"

"Wh-whaaat?!" I shouted. The scarecrow, tin man, and lion also made shocked faces, although maybe that was just my imagination.

On the map, the elliptical quest area had three golden ! symbols to indicate quest checkpoints, with one other ! that was gray (the final destination, but not yet activated). Ordinarily, we would have to tackle each of the three golden symbols first before heading to the last one, but Asuna and Argo were resolute in their direction.

The two girls led the way on the road paved with yellow bricks, followed by three monsters that wanted to be human, and me, the least certain member of the group. Argo kept an awkward distance from Asuna, presumably because of the cute little dog in Asuna's arms.

Since the ! over Toto's head was gone, and it was no longer the point character for the quest, Argo and I suggested that the dog be left in the log cabin. But Asuna refused to let it go, and she pouted with the occasional snarl, so we couldn't insist. I was fine with or without the dog, but it seemed like this was going to really test Argo's resolve.

If she was actually that uniformly upset, then she had to be telling the truth about her phobia—she wasn't just role-playing for the sake of her character. Argo must have been deathly afraid of dogs in real life. But if I were in her position, would I be able to let my innermost feelings be expressed this openly? If I were her, I would be desperate to uphold the image that I'd built around me, and I'd push down my true feelings and attempt to act unbothered.

And if that was how I felt, then could I call the feelings I felt for Asuna genuine love...?

"...What do you think?" I muttered to one of our accompanying NPCs, the lion whose courage had been stolen.

Nearly all of the myriad NPCs placed throughout Aincrad ran on simple algorithms that performed some basic question-and-answer routines, which made actual conversations impossible. So I wasn't expecting the character to give me a real answer.

"Did someone take something from you, too, pal?" the lion mumbled back, which took me a bit by surprise...Well, maybe *a lot* by surprise.

"Hmm...Yeah, maybe that's true. Until this point, I don't remember ever truly falling in love with someone," I said, letting my momentum answer for me. The lion nodded, looking even more downcast. He was very shabby by the standards of the game's werelion monsters, which appeared around the fortieth floor.

"I see. The fact is, I don't know the truth, either. I can't recall if I was truly c-c-courageous before the witch took my mane away."

He sighed and hung his head, revealing a part of his mane at the back of his head that had been cut abruptly short, as though barber's clippers had chopped it right off.

With that in mind, I looked at the scarecrow bouncing along next to the lion and saw a rip in the back of his head bag that had been roughly sewn back together. Past him, the tin man's breast-plate featured a large hole that had been covered with two bandages in an X shape. These were evidence of the Wicked Witch of the West having stolen the things that were most important to them.

Of course, I couldn't remember any witch stealing my ability to love another person. If my heart had been sealed away, then it was me who had done it—I'd been keeping everyone, even my family, at arm's length ever since I was a child.

So where could I go to find that heart? If I married Asuna and lived with her, would I be able to find it? But what if the lion's suspicions were true in my case, and I never had one to begin with...?

Just then, as though psychically sensing my unease, Asuna turned and glanced at me over her shoulder. She tilted her head and smiled, just like always. Then she pointed in the direction we were going and called out, "C'mon, Kirito! You can see it just ahead!"

Argo extended the metal claws she had equipped on the backs of her hands and struck them together with a ringing sound. "If I don't know about this quest, then nobody knows about it! This dungeon is untouched! We'll find lotsa treasure inside!"

"Look...I hate to be a downer, but it's just the twenty-second floor, so it's not going to be anything earth-shattering," I said, playing the cynic about loot for once. I hurried to catch up to the girls, and as I moved, a castle came into view beyond the trees. It had several thin spires and walls such a dark gray, they were nearly black. Standing against the deepening red of the sky, it was truly worthy of being called a witch's castle.

If we found the witch deep within that castle and defeated her, the quest should be over, but we couldn't get inside at the moment.

After all, they weren't going to open the final dungeon and situate the boss inside until we completed the first few steps and returned the missing parts to our traveling companions. And to be honest, it felt just *mean* to ignore their plight...

But meanwhile, Asuna and Argo continued walking at a brisk pace and awkward distance, and within a few minutes, the castle gates came into view. They were a good fifteen feet tall, made of black cast iron, and firmly shut. They wouldn't be opening anytime soon—

Click-click-ka-ching.

It was an undeniable unlocking sound. The gates swung open smoothly and automatically, leaving me standing there with my mouth agape. The little dog in Asuna's arms barked, but obviously it hadn't caused that to happen.

The two women looked at each other and nodded with satisfaction, but I had no idea why it had happened. I glanced at the others, who were missing their parts, and gave them an uncomfortable shrug, then walked into the castle.

Instantly, there were growls all around, and four monsters popped into the front entrance of the castle. They were werepanthers, monsters with burly torsos and panther heads. Witches kept black cats as familiars, so that seemed to fit the image, I supposed.

"Gyaaaaowr!"

The panthers howled again and drew scimitars with jagged edges. The scarecrow, tin man, and lion shrieked with terror and huddled on the spot. It wasn't clear if they were inflicted with the Fear status or just normally afraid, but they certainly didn't seem like they were going to be any help against the boss later. Not that I expected much from them in the first place, however.

Shaking my head, I drew Elucidator from my back and targeted the two werepanthers charging from the right side. One-handed swords featured few single-attack, area-effect skills, but I did have one to use: Serration Wave.

The sword smashed against the ground and vibrated at a high

rate, sending jagged, saw-edged visual effects radiating outward. The effect swallowed up the two werepanthers and left them unbalanced. It was a technique for immobilizing enemies, not dealing big damage, but these were twenty-second-floor monsters. The werepanthers lost all their HP before they could recover their footing, and they burst into pieces, one after the other.

The other two werepanthers were easily handled by Asuna, despite holding the dog in one hand, and Argo, who was actually quite powerful on her own. One of the werepanthers dropped a key with a quest item tag on it, so we used it to open a small door at the corner of the castle building.

I glanced at the sky one more time before going inside; it was red going on purple now. We had an hour at best before it would be night. The castle was of a considerable size, so it seemed unlikely we would wrap it up before sunset.

But once again, Asuna read my thoughts and patted me on the back. "Don't worry. I brought plenty of food with us."

I'm not worried about food—I'm worried about whether I'll be able to marry you before the end of the day, I thought, though I couldn't say it to her face. Instead, I hesitantly agreed with her.

Argo blithely said, "Ooh, can't wait for that! I've heard the rumors that you've developed your own take on soy sauce, A-chan!"

Just ten minutes after entering the wicked witch's castle, the combined party of me, Asuna, Argo, Scarecrow, Tin Man, Lion, and dog had already reached a big door that probably belonged to the boss.

Part of that was because our combat level was far beyond the quest's difficulty, but the most gamebreaking part of it all was Argo's incredible mobility. Balconies that should have required a detour to reach, jumps that even I wasn't sure I would attempt— she found risky shortcuts all over the place and pulled them off with ease. Thanks to that, the sky was still red through the narrow windows to the outside.

"...I suppose we can hold off on eating until after the boss fight," Asuna noted, a bit exasperated. Argo agreed. The monster trio still looked a bit bothered, like they weren't sure things were supposed to be happening in this order. The scarecrow hopped forward to speak for the group, his mouth a hole in the burlap bag with a single stitch through it.

"They say the Wicked Witch of the West uses all kinds of fearsome spells," he babbled. "If only my head weren't empty, I might be able to remember what kinds..."

Ahhh...we probably should have done the subquest steps in order, I thought. But Asuna calmly patted the scarecrow's shoulder (which was just a stick) and reassured him, "Don't worry. The three of us together should be more than strong enough to rescue Dor—to rescue your friend. C'mon, let's go."

She turned briskly on her heel and pushed the door open without a moment of hesitation.

The room beyond was large and rectangular, in true boss-chamber fashion. The moment we stepped inside, candles in chandeliers hanging high overhead lit up with eerie green flames. They got brighter and brighter farther into the room, and there was a large cage near the back wall.

Trussed up on the floor of the cage was a girl. Next to her was a large bubbling pot and an old crone dressed in black, stirring with a long ladle.

"Whoa...that's the witchiest witch I've ever seen," I murmured. As a general rule, *SAO* had no offensive magic, and for that reason, there weren't any magicians. A monster of this type was extremely rare.

How is the old witch going to attack? I wondered. But the scarecrow shouted, "Oh, Dorothy! Help her! She's going to be turned into soup!"

Next, the tin man rattled forward. "Dorothy! Danger! Help! Hurry!"

Lastly, the lion spoke up, what little parts of his mane remained standing on end.

"Just you wait, Dorothy! We're comin' ta…comin' ta…"

But then the lion's mane wilted again, the tin man's armor fell silent, and the scarecrow's spine bent.

Asuna, Argo, and I stepped forward to take their place. We approached carefully—the witch's side was facing us, and she continued stirring the pot.

Just as the party reached the midpoint of the chamber, the black-robed witch looked up from the pot and over at us. Her shining yellow eyes narrowed, and she screeched, "Would you like to taste the soup? One swallow will make you youthful again, and two will fill you with strength. The flavor's delicious, too! Hee-hee-hee-hee!"

Since being careless enough to say yes would start an event scene that would end with poor Dorothy bubbling away in the pot, I made our intentions crystal clear.

"No! We're here to save her!"

"I see, I see. What a shame. In that case," said the witch, scooping up the ladle from the bottom of the pot and blowing, "I'll just have to add *you* to the soup! Heeee-hee-heeeeee!"

She hurtled the contents of the ladle at us. The liquid turned into a horrid purple mist that surrounded us.

Instantly, there was a new green-bordered Debuff icon under my HP bar in the upper left corner: paralysis.

"Ugh…"

No sooner was the grunt out of my mouth than all of us, including the trio of companions, collapsed on the floor. The fact that even our high-level resistance didn't work suggested that it was a forced paralysis event, but it was still dangerous. I tried to pull a healing potion out of my pouch—in normal paralysis, I could still move my right hand, but now it was immobilized.

"Hee-hee-hee…Well, well, well. Which one of you should I cook first…?"

The witch danced closer, using her ladle in place of a magic wand. I was getting worried that we were actually in considerable danger. I tried desperately to get to my feet, but my body would not budge.

"Hee-hee! Don't waste your time, deary. The only thing that can break this spell is the roar of a lion."

Ohhh, I get it!

It was a very obvious hint. I swiveled my eyes—the one thing I could move—to look behind us. The scarecrow and the tin man were paralyzed, just like us, but the lion was the only one without a Debuff icon. If he gave her one good roar, it should free all of us from our paralysis.

And yet…

Alas, the lion's mane was flat against his neck. He was cowering and blubbering, cradling his head between his arms. *Are you kidding me?* I thought. But then I remembered.

It wasn't his fault. The witch had stolen his courage. If we had done the subquest and recovered the golden mane that was the source of his courage, that would be one thing, but right now, he was helpless. We could have predicted this would happen, but the girls had insisted we didn't need to bother with the other steps…

"ARF! Harf-arf-arf!" the little dog barked, interrupting my thoughts.

But that wasn't the only thing that happened. The lion's trembling stopped, and his wilted bits of mane began to bulge upward again. But why?

As I watched, wide-eyed and trapped on the floor, the lion got up to a standing position. He still looked miserable, but there was a new strength in his eyes that wasn't there before.

"I'm…I'm here…to help Dorothy!" he shouted, then sucked in as much breath as his lungs could take—and let out a *roaaaaaar!* The bellowing simply obliterated the paralysis icon affecting me.

The witch tried two more paralysis attacks after that, but following the lion, the tin man got up and dispelled the effect, and the scarecrow took his turn last. Once she was presumably out of magic, the witch panicked and simply charged with the ladle in her hand.

With her long black robe and pointy hat, the witch didn't look like much of a melee fighter, but I was a bit shocked when the end of the long ladle began to glow red above her head. As befitting a resident of this world, she could apparently use sword skills of her own that treated the ladle as a poleax.

"Kweeeaaaahhh!"

She swung the ladle down with an ear-shattering screech, but my Vertical Arc easily blocked it. The skill hit the witch as a counterattack and knocked her back, leaving an opening for Asuna to switch in.

It really didn't seem necessary for Asuna to keep holding the dog in one hand, but she was talented enough that she could execute sword skills regardless. A merciless five-part thrust attack knocked the witch farther away. Before she could even hit the ground, Argo was there. With sprint speed faster than even Asuna, Argo circled under where the witch was falling and unleashed a twirling, slicing skill with both of her metal claws.

That was a trio of high-level skills in combination, but the witch was a quest boss, after all, and she retained just a tiny bit of HP. She plopped onto the ground but got to her feet right away and rushed to the cauldron at the back of the chamber. As soon as our skill delay allowed, we ran after her, determined not to let her use the mystery soup for another curse spell.

But suddenly little Toto shot out of Asuna's arms and launched itself after the witch like a cannonball, biting the black heel of her shoe. The witch lost her balance, stumbled forward, and rolled with great velocity, plunging headfirst into the bubbling pot.

A few seconds later, a massive monster death effect burst up out of the cauldron.

When freed from the cage, Dorothy hugged her precious Toto and thanked us over and over. She said that she would be continuing the journey with the scarecrow, tin man, and lion, searching for the Emerald City that existed somewhere else in the world.

Back at the log house, we watched Dorothy and her friends go. Asuna looked sadder than the rest of us (probably because of the dog), and Argo looked relieved (probably because of the dog). I patted them on the back together. The final *!* of the quest was floating over the log cabin. If we walked inside and closed the door, it should take us back to where it should be.

"Come on. There's no place like home," I said, looking to the western sky, where the setting sun was sinking behind the clouds.

7

In the original *Wonderful Wizard of Oz* story, as Asuna taught me while on the return trip, the scarecrow was searching for his brain; the tin man, his heart; and the cowardly lion, his courage—just like in this quest.

But in the end, they never found those things. At the end of the story, the eponymous wizard tells them that in the process of rescuing Dorothy from the witch, the scarecrow used his brains, the tin man expressed emotion, and the lion showed courage. In other words, they already had what they were searching for.

"…Ah, I see. So that's why you and Argo didn't bother with their parts of the quest. You knew they'd pull through in the end," I said with a wry grimace. The girls looked very satisfied with themselves.

The house thudded down onto the ground again. Outside, we were back in the same empty clearing in the forest where I originally found the cabin. Argo walked past us across the grass, then turned around and beamed at us.

"Ya pulled me outta trouble today. So I'll make it up to ya by not selling this tip. It'll be my little secret."

"Huh? Tip…? What tip?"

"You know which one!" she said, throwing me a big wink. "Many blessings to you, Kiri-boy, A-chan!"

As we stood there, rooted to the spot in shock, Argo simply vanished from sight, like a ninja. A few seconds later, Asuna started giggling, and I found myself smiling, too. The final thorn that had been stuck in my heart had come loose at last, I could feel—and I started laughing.

From the moment you took your first step, what you sought was already within your grasp.

I hoped to be with Asuna forever, and I'd proposed to her. So I'd already found what I was looking for at that very moment—love for another person.

"……Asuna."

She looked me in the eyes, still smiling.

The last rays of sun came over the roof of the log cabin, glittering in those beautiful hazel-brown eyes. Without breaking that connection, I opened my player menu, moved two tabs over, and hovered my finger over the button I wanted.

I pressed the string of text that said MARRIAGE, then touched the name ASUNA.

Her eyes broke contact, traveling down to a small window that had appeared for her. She lifted her right hand, her slender fingers tracing the edge of the window.

"……Kirito."

She looked back, right into my eyes, and pressed the OK button.

It was just a few days after this that we learned the name of Cardinal, the autonomous system that controlled the world we lived in.

But it wasn't until much, much later that we were taught about the remarkable quest auto-generation capabilities the Cardinal System possessed.

(The End)

The Day After

§ Alfheim
June 2025

1

"Have you gotten used to that avatar yet?"

The sudden question caused Asuna to look up from the window with her English homework on it.

She twirled the long blue undine hair resting on her right shoulder and replied, "Ummm...I think I need more time. It's strange...My face and figure are still the same as they were in Aincrad, with only the hair and eyes different. But there are moments when it just feels *weird*. Like my body isn't entirely connected to my mind..."

"Hmm..."

Looking concerned was a spriggan boy with his black hair standing on end. She thought of him as a boy, but the player inside of him was just one year younger than Asuna, who was going to be eighteen this year. But the avatar looked so much more youthful and mischievous than the real person that she couldn't help but think of him as a boy.

The spriggan, who was sitting next to her on the sofa, pushed his own holo-keyboard back, then rested his elbows on the table and stared at her.

"That might be a different problem than just getting accustomed...You said there was no problem with the AmuSphere's BSIS level and response, right?"

"Yes. I checked the log, and both were above average."

"Okay…"

He reached out with his left hand and squeezed her right.

"Uh, wh-what is this?" she asked, her heart skipping a beat at the surprise attack. But he looked entirely serious as he spread her palm open and drew his index finger down it, touch just barely there.

A tiny tickling in the center of her palm ran all the way up her back, and Asuna couldn't help but yelp a little bit. The spriggan still looked perfectly solemn, however, and stared at her palm.

"I'm getting a sensation of making contact. You can feel that, too, right?"

"Yes…I can," Asuna admitted.

The boy scowled. "Then I'm going to move my finger and slowly pull it away from your skin. Tell me when you feel the sensation vanish. So…do you still feel it?"

He slowly, slowly slid his finger across her palm, and the fainter sensation stimulated her virtual nerves. Her avatar twitched, and she whispered, "Yes…I'm still…feeling it."

"All right…Then how about this?"

"Mmm…Yeah…I can…"

"Haaah…Then it seems like your BSIS level really is normal…"

"Ah, I'm…I…"

At last, Asuna recognized that what she was saying might potentially be misconstrued.

Immediately, a fiery heat covered her face. She yanked back her hand, clenched it into a fist, and bellowed at the stunned spriggan:

"What were you making me say?! Kirito, you…you jerk!!"

The right hook that smashed into his face did no numerical damage, because they were in a room of an inn in the central city—but it did succeed at blasting the little spriggan over the back of the sofa to the far wall.

*   *   *

It was eight thirty PM on Saturday, June 21st, 2025.

Asuna Yuuki was in a room on the outer edge of Yggdrasil City inside the VRMMORPG *ALfheim Online* (*ALO*), doing her school homework with Kazuto Kirigaya—Kirito.

A venture capital company called Ymir had taken over running *ALO* from the now-dissolved RCT Progress. This change had brought a number of revolutionary tweaks to the game, one of which was more (if still limited) connection to the Net from within *ALO*. If you opened a browser tab in your menu, you could search the Net just like on a computer or smartphone and access your homework files from their online server. Even if a malicious player attempted to run some kind of nasty program, the Cardinal System could instantly detect it and stop any hacking attempts. So the fairy city enjoyed peace and security.

Asuna's mother did not look kindly on her decision to resume using full-dive machines, and she often said, "At least do your homework with your own two hands," but Asuna felt that her physical body and her virtual avatar were both *herself*. Plus, it was more efficient to do homework in a full dive, because she could open as many windows as she wanted (up to a limit), and she didn't have to worry about tired eyes or stiff shoulders. And most important of all, online she could study side by side with Kirito, whereas in real life, they were located far apart, in Miyasaka in Setagaya Ward and Kawagoe in Saitama Prefecture... although that might count as an impure motive.

At any rate, she had been typing away at her holo-keyboard as a fairy, lost in her homework, when Kirito suddenly started testing her senses.

The spriggan sat up from the floor, groaning. Asuna, no longer on the couch, loomed over him, hands on her hips in the scolding position.

"Look, if you want to test my sensitivity to stimuli, there are better ways to do it!"

"...But that was the simplest way to do it...Besides, you were the one who started making eroti—er, funny sounds...," Kirito mumbled in his defense. She fixed him with an even sharper glare.

"Oh...? What was that? What were you going to say? You can tell me; I won't be angry."

"Th-that's a lie! Besides, you're already angry..."

"I am not! But if Yui wasn't out at the time, I really would have let you have it," she threatened. Kirito straightened up and trembled.

Yui was a sophisticated top-down AI playing the role of a navigation pixie within *ALO*—and was their daughter. At the moment, she was out attending a monster hunt with their friends Klein and Lisbeth. The thought of her beloved daughter witnessing that embarrassing scene brought another wave of heat to Asuna's cheeks.

Kirito started smiling for some reason, and he remarked, "Asuna, your face is red."

His smile turned to panic when he saw her clench an iron fist again. She strode in his direction with disciplinary intent, when—

"...Aah..."

She came to an abrupt stop.

It was that *sensation* again. A strange feeling, like her soul had momentarily slipped out of her virtual avatar. Like she didn't know where her arms and legs were or how they were moving... Like the present was no longer present.

Kirito sensed the change in her and instantly leaped to her side to help hold her up. He looked her in the eyes, concern clear on his features.

"Are you okay?"

"Y...yes, I'm fine. I'm better now," she replied, still allowing him to support her weight. "It's just...just the tiniest bit of an odd feeling. It's not like I can't move my avatar, so I could probably ignore it...In fact, maybe it's all in my head..."

"No...we ought to look into this. It's not a sensation you felt in Aincrad, right?"

"Right. I never felt it once…At least I don't think so…?"

Kirito easily lifted Asuna into his arms and took her to the bedroom next door. Their room was a penthouse suite, so the view from the wide windows showed them the dazzling night profile of Ygg City and the landscape of Alfheim far below. The young man ignored the sight, however, laying Asuna on the large bed and sitting next to her. He caressed her pale-blue hair.

"Asuna…I'm sure it's not something you want to remember, but…"

She could tell just from the tone of his voice what he wanted to say. She smiled at him and shook her head. "I'm fine…I never felt this way when I was Titania. It's not because of the server changing."

"Okay…"

Kirito turned his head and looked out the window at last.

He'd defeated the deadly *Sword Art Online* and freed 6,149 players from Aincrad on November 7th, 2024. But roughly three hundred players, including Asuna, were not freed from their virtual prison. A man in a principal position at the electronics manufacturer RCT Progress, Nobuyuki Sugou, had held their minds prisoner in his virtual lab in *ALO* as subjects in his illegal experiments.

Asuna had not been treated as a test subject, however; instead, he'd locked her inside a giant birdcage hung from the branches of Yggdrasil, the World Tree. He'd given her the name Titania and called himself Oberon, king of the fairies.

That torment had lasted until Kirito had succeeded in rescuing her on January 22nd, 2025. It was two months of time that felt just as long as the two years in Aincrad, but at no point in that time had she felt something wrong with her bodily sensations.

"…I think…the first I felt this…well, dissociative sensation… was about a month ago…," she murmured.

Kirito's eyes flared a bit. "You remember the first time it happened?"

"Yes. Because it was when we were fighting the boss on the first floor of New Aincrad."

His black eyes blinked a few times.

"Back then, huh...? That's right—you fumbled on your magic spell once. Was that it...?"

"I'm amazed you remember that," she remarked. Her partner had a strangely accurate sense of recall.

"While I was chanting the spell words, I felt like my bodily sensations were growing distant, and I stopped talking. Then it came right back, and it only happened the one time in that battle, so I assumed it was just a fluke of my mind...but ever since, it happens from time to time..."

"Which would mean it's not just something you're getting used to. I mean, that boss fight was at least three weeks after you first dived into *ALO* with that avatar, right? If the avatar being unfamiliar was the cause, it would have been frequent right after you started."

"Yeah...exactly. But then what could it be...?" she wondered, thinking as she lay on the bed.

Kirito considered this for a while before asking, "This never happens in VR spaces aside from *ALO*?"

"Um...that's right. I don't often dive into places other than here, but I don't remember feeling the separation anywhere else."

"Then it's not just because of a difference between NerveGear and the AmuSphere, either. And...hmm...I assume you don't feel this in the real world, either...?"

"No, I told you. That would be an actual out-of-body experience."

After she said it, she was hit by a wave of dread, and she reassessed her memories, but still there was nothing that resembled that feeling in real life. But now that they'd run through the options, the cause was a true mystery. She had tried looking for information online, but she didn't see any AmuSphere users complaining of similar problems, and her symptoms were too vague and mild for her to seek specific help from RCT Progress or Ymir.

When it happened, it lasted for only a moment. As long as she didn't let it bother her, it wasn't a big enough problem to ruin her fun—but after spending this much time thinking about it, there was no way she could just forget about the whole thing.

Kirito sat on the edge of the bed, offering her a profile view of his face as he grumbled and hummed. Eventually, he seemed to reach a conclusion.

"The only thing we can do at this point is talk to Yui, I think."

"...Yeah..."

That was an option Asuna had considered after the fourth or fifth instance of dissociation but had hesitated to do yet. Yui would be terribly worried if she learned about Asuna's problem, and if Yui's abilities weren't enough to find a solution, she might only be left with the mental burden of failure.

Yui was an artificial intelligence created to offer mental counseling to *SAO* players. But when the game was locked down and turned deadly, all her abilities were frozen, leaving her helpless to do anything but monitor the negative emotions of thousands of players. That incredible burden had built up until it shattered her core program. By the time she'd met Asuna and Kirito, she was barely capable of speech.

That was why Asuna felt so desperate not to burden Yui with this news, to keep her little heart safe from pain.

But Kirito just nodded, seeing right through his partner, and reached out again. He caressed her hair with gentle but firm strokes—few players could perform such delicate motions—and said, "I know how you feel, Asuna. But...if Yui learns that we chose not to ask her for help and advice, that would make her just as sad."

"But it really isn't that bad. I'm sure I'll get over this thing and stop thinking about it altogether."

"...I'm not sure...You're very sensitive, Asuna...," he said, trailing off. Then he clamped his mouth shut and shook his head in a panic. "Uh, I mean, not in a weird way."

"Oh, I know that's not what you meant. So...?"

"So...erm, the more sensitive a player is, the more you can't afford to ignore little anomalies with what you can feel. Especially in the midst of battle. I want you to be able to enjoy this VRMMO for what it is, not being some high-stakes death roulette. And that means eliminating any kind of impediment to your experience, no matter how small. Maybe that's just a stubborn desire of mine…," he finished in a whisper, causing Asuna to reach for him.

Her hand landed on the shoulder of his tight-fitting black shirt, and she pulled him close. The high Strength stat she'd inherited from her time in *SAO* made him lose his balance, and the skinny spriggan yelped and fell onto Asuna's chest.

She held him tight with both arms, squeezing for all she was worth.

"Thank you, Kirito," she whispered. "I'm having so much fun right now. It's so wonderful being here with you and Yui and everyone else, traveling all over Alfheim and New Aincrad to the different towns and places, shopping together, going on adventures…I just want to travel all over this world with you forever."

As she talked, Kirito eventually stopped struggling. In time, his hands snuck their way around her back.

In a sense, they hadn't held each other like this since the *SAO* days. From January to late April, she'd been busy rehabilitating after being freed from the virtual birdcage. After that, she'd been trying her best to get accustomed to the real world again, new school included, after two years stuck inside a virtual experience. There had barely been any time for them to be alone in either place. The only reason they were like this today was because they both had more homework than the others. The usual study sessions were much more crowded.

But right now, Asuna was working on a little project deep in her heart—a promise to herself, one could say.

At some point in the future, New Aincrad would be opened beyond the tenth floor, which was the current limit. When that happened, she wanted to be the first to reach the twenty-second floor and buy that little log cabin deep in the woods. The log cabin where she had shared a brief but brilliant period of bliss with Kirito.

Of course, there were subtle differences in monsters, items, and even landscapes between Aincrad and New Aincrad, so there was no guarantee the same house would be in the same place. But Asuna felt certain the cabin would be there, waiting for them. She was less sure if they would need to finish the flying-house quest again before they'd be allowed to buy it.

"...Maybe...," she murmured.

In her arms, Kirito craned his head a tiny bit in response, but she changed course and said, "Nothing. Never mind," keeping her thoughts to herself.

Maybe the strange dissociative sensation was happening because her heart longed for that cabin too strongly. Because for just a moment, her mind was leaving her avatar behind and leaping to those woods on the twenty-second floor...

Her train of thought was interrupted by Kirito's voice. "Let's talk with Yui tomorrow. I'm sure she'll find some kind of issue we wouldn't have known about."

"Yeah...I'm sure she will," Asuna agreed, releasing her hold on him.

Their cheeks separated, and they pulled back until they were gazing into each other's eyes. Asuna felt something beginning to rise within her, but after a moment, Kirito broke contact and sat up, returning to his previous position on the side of the bed.

"So...what should we do now? Go meet up with the others?" he asked.

She grimaced and shook her head. "No. We're not nearly done with our homework."

"Oh...y-yeah, right..."

"And it'll be nearly ten by the time we're done with it all, so playing will have to wait for tomorrow. Agil and Leafa said they'd be available then, so we'd have more fun with everybody there."

"Fiiine," he said like a sulking child and dropped his chin to his chest. "Man…Ten o'clock was just when the hunting got good in *SAO*…"

"Don't reminisce about the bad old days! Besides, you were known for not joining in the night activities. And yet you kept popping off level-ups—they treated you like one of the Seven Great Mysteries of the frontline group," Asuna said, sitting upright.

Kirito gave her a funny look and said, "Uh…what were the other six mysteries?"

"Let's see…There was the legend of the Black Swordsman fighting with a one-handed sword and no shield…The legend of how the Black Swordsman took way too many Last Attack bonuses…"

"H-hang on, hang on. Are these all about me?"

"Don't worry—the seventh one is the legend of how the KoB commander is too uptight…But that one wasn't a real mystery…"

She was thinking of eight months ago, when the black-haired swordsman saw through the "mystery" of Commander Heathcliff, better known as Akihiko Kayaba. Kirito patted Asuna on the head.

"I didn't have any mysterious powers, either. I only kept my level up because of the encouragement and help of others… including you, of course."

He rubbed her head a few times, then stood and stretched.

"Well, let's get back to that homework…and if you could see your way to helping me *here*, too…"

"Oh, fine," she said, rising to her feet and flashing him a smile. "But when we're done, you owe me dinner at the restaurant on the ground floor!"

Upon returning from the virtual world to the real one, the first thing she felt was the weight of her physical body.

Or to put it another way, the presence of true gravity. In *SAO*, she played a speed-first fencer, so the overall feel of gravity on her avatar was light. She raced through Aincrad as a gust of wind, leaping over obstacles like a young, powerful filly. Since she had inherited that character data for *ALO*, the feeling was still light. In fact, she probably felt even lighter because of the fairy wings.

So when she opened her eyes in the darkened bedroom, the feeling of weight that covered her body was stifling. When she was trapped inside that deadly game, she'd wanted a log-out button for so long, but now the sensation of that transition was very unpleasant. She'd probably get used to it over time, she decided.

After another ten seconds of letting herself get accustomed to the new sensations, Asuna slowly rose. She took the AmuSphere off her head—the full-dive machine felt stunningly fragile compared to the NerveGear. The sensors on the ceiling detected her movement and upped the indirect lighting to provide enough to see by.

Her feet hit the floor, and she carefully got to a standing position, but she felt woozy. It was similar to the mysterious dissociative sensation she felt in her virtual body, but unlike the feeling of her mind slipping out into the sky, the real-world sensation was like being dragged to the ground. This one was much more unpleasant.

She shook her head, driving off the dizziness, and stuck her toes into her slippers before heading to the window on the south side of her room.

Through the crack in the curtains, she could see the neighborhood at night, shrouded in the heavy, damp air of June. There were white halos around the streetlamps, perhaps because of some light rain. It reminded her of the light effects from the virtual world.

"...?"

Suddenly, a part of her memory was stimulated, knotting her brows.

A city at night. Lights shrouded in mist. Flowing water nearby. She was squatting near it, holding her knees to her chest. Lonely, terrified, but with nowhere to escape...

For the life of her, she could not remember where and when

she'd experienced this. She tried to capture and clarify that vague mental image, but it slipped out of her mind as abruptly as it appeared.

But the strange note of loneliness remained, deep in her chest.

For a while after that, Asuna found herself staring out the window at the dark vista of the real world.

2

It was four thirty PM the following day, Sunday, June 22nd.

Asuna was on the top floor—the boss chamber—of the eighth-floor labyrinth tower in New Aincrad, the giant floating castle that hovered over Alfheim.

There was only one thing to be done in a place like this: fight against the boss monster.

"Kyurrrrrr!" A high-pitched warning chirped from Pina, a tiny dragon covered with light-blue down. Its master, the cait sith Silica, shouted, "Asuna! We've got more minion summons!"

"Got it! Everyone, group up!" Asuna called out, holding her staff aloft. Then she began to chant spell words.

"Ek kalla hreinn brunnr, andask brandr og eitrid!" (Come forth, sacred spring, and stop the breath of flame and poison.)

With the end of the last syllable, she stamped the bottom of the staff against the black marble floor. Ripples of faint blue light extended from the spot, and a great volume of water sprang up behind them until it formed a surface nearly thirty feet across.

"Appreciate it, Asuna!"

"Thank you very much!"

Lisbeth the mace-wielding leprechaun charged onto the water, followed by Silica with Pina resting on her head. Elsewhere, the ax-warrior gnome Agil and the katana-bearing salamander Klein followed—other friends from the *SAO* days. A moment later, Kirito the spriggan, clad in black, and his real-life sister, Leafa the magic fighter sylph, returned from the front line.

This seven-man team was the upper limit for a single party, but they weren't the only ones fighting in the boss chamber. They were in a raid with four other parties, which put the total number of players in the circular chamber at thirty-five. The only reason it didn't feel cramped was because the chamber itself was much larger than it had been back in Aincrad.

Kirito jumped onto the water's surface, which had a healing effect and increased resistance to poison and fire, and heaved a sigh of relief. On his shoulder, Yui the tiny pixie waved at Asuna.

"Mama, you're really getting good at those spell incantations!"

"Ah-ha-ha…Thanks, Yui!" she replied, just before a number of pillars of fire erupted through the water. They quickly formed spinning maelstroms, and humanoid figures that turned into little fire elementals, each about three feet tall, emerged from the middle.

Individually, they weren't so tough, but in great numbers, it was a different story. Over thirty fire elementals had just appeared in the spacious chamber. On top of that, they were just adds—additional minions that fought alongside the primary threat: the boss monster of the eighth floor.

The boss's name was Wadjet the Flaming Serpent.

From the research they'd done after the first attempt at the fight, they'd learned that Wadjet was the name of a fire-snake god in Egyptian mythology. It looked the part, too; the creature resembled a four-armed goddess and had a massive cobra for a head. Its black body was wreathed in flames, causing a fire-based damage-over-time (DOT) effect if you were within range.

At the moment, two other parties were dealing with the boss itself. It was imperative that the rest took care of the helpers while those fourteen players still had enough HP left.

Asuna held her staff against the ground and swiftly scanned the area around her.

Wadjet and the two parties were locked in fierce battle on the far side of the huge chamber. Of the other two parties, one was led by a salamander woman, and they had retreated to another water field that a fellow undine mage had created. The other party did not have any members capable of using the Purified Surface spell. Asuna raised her free hand and called out to them.

"Kite as many of the minions as you can and get into the water over here!"

Their sylph leader acknowledged her advice with a wave.

In the meantime, the sylph's six companions were busy turning the advancing fire elementals into ash. They were secondary to the actual boss, of course, but on their own, they were tough foes that neutralized half of all physical damage. Thankfully, entering the magical water field instantly weakened them significantly, so even a party with little magic ability could fight them off if they got inside.

Once they'd beaten all the nearby fire elementals, the other party jumped into the water, bringing a train of enemies with them. The thirty-foot-diameter circle was cramped with fourteen players inside, but Kirito and Klein jumped back out, taking half the extra fire elementals with them and making it possible to fight across the entire surface.

The sight of all that flashing metal made Asuna want to switch out her staff for a rapier, but she had to keep the staff pressed to the ground to maintain the circle of magic. Asuna chose to be a healing-focused mage in *ALO* because she thought it would be fun to try a support role, but also because, by the time she had returned to playing, the party was already well supplied with physical attackers.

Leafa could sense Asuna's frustration, and she came closer to say, "I'm sorry you always have to hang back and play support, Asuna."

"Oh, it's not like I'm doing it against my will. It's fun to say the spell words."

"Yes, of course! Big Br—Kirito still feels shy about that part.

You should explain it to him sometime." Leafa grinned briefly before she lifted her free hand. *"Thú fylla heilagr austr, brott svalr bani!"* (I heal thee with holy water, staving off cold death.)

She enunciated the healing magic spell loudly and smoothly. Once she was done, blue droplets showered the area from her left hand, helping recover the damage that the water field's healing-over-time (HOT) effect could not cover.

Eventually, all the fire elementals were defeated, so Asuna lifted the staff off the ground. The water vanished with a splashing spray, and one of the many Buff icons underneath her HP bar vanished.

To their right, one of the other parties fighting fire elementals had finished up as well. Once Klein saw that all the fire elementals were gone, he shouted over to the fourteen players fighting the boss, "Okay, we took care of the adds! We can switch in at any moment!"

A large imp who seemed to be the leader over there shouted back, "Got it! Take over at the next break!"

The snakelike boss raised its flared cobra head high. The dark goddess had a wide sword in one of its four hands, which it raised high.

Purple lightning bolts shot through the space around the boss, and more of the giant, semitranslucent blades appeared. The bunched-up players in front of the boss scattered; those with shields held them up, and those with two-handed weapons prepared to block the attack.

"Shugyaaaa!!" screeched the boss, Wadjet the Flaming Serpent, and it swung down its weapons. Eight phantasmic swords smashed down upon the players.

Four of the players successfully blocked the blows, while the other four found themselves knocked backward by the impact against their shields and weapons. But the effect of using such a powerful attack tamped down the flames surrounding Wadjet. Without missing their opportunity, the mages in the back unleashed the movement-binding spells they had queued up.

Nearly all bosses had high resistance to Debuffs, but if you timed it right, you could usually stop them for about ten seconds. Debuffs generated spiderwebs, silver chains, and sticky swamps, depending on the spell. When the boss was stuck, the imp team leader waved an arm.

"Fall back!"

With a guttural roar, the human players burst into motion. The four who'd been knocked back by the swords regained their footing and hurried after their companions, wailing, "Don't leave me behind!"

"Okay, we're up!"

Klein leaped first with his katana at the ready, followed by Kirito and Agil.

As she ran with the team, Asuna thought, *Everyone's having so much fun.*

It held true with the four other parties, too, not just Kirito and Lisbeth and her friends.

The majority of the twenty-eight players from the other parties were total strangers. They found the group looking for raid partners in the teleport square of Frieven, the main town of the eighth floor. After a brief round of introductions, they headed off to the labyrinth tower and rushed right into the boss chamber. In Aincrad, you could never act that fast.

In the old days, you had to do reconnaissance runs over and over before the real fight, hold strategy meetings, weigh all the risks, and go into battle with as much power as possible. In *SAO*, you couldn't afford a single casualty in battle. That was unthinkable in *ALO*, but even still, Asuna couldn't help wondering, *Are we really just going to jump right into it?* before the battle. The eighth floor of New Aincrad was the current front line, and that meant Wadjet the Flaming Serpent had not yet been defeated. If they were going to fight an unbeaten opponent, shouldn't they at least discuss strategy and formations first?

But now, nearly thirty minutes after the battle had started, she was starting to understand.

The important thing was not actually beating the boss itself but enjoying the process of the struggle.

If they did beat the boss, it shouldn't be because of the unilateral leadership of a powerful in-group, like the Knights of the Blood, of which Asuna had been the vice commander. The entire group of players had to act as one, thinking and fighting and rejoicing together...or perhaps lamenting. That was the true fun of online RPGs, and as long as you got a good helping of that, you were having fun, even if you lost.

The imp in the back line of the two retreating parties lifted his arm as Asuna passed, calling out, "We'll be regrouped and ready in three minutes! Give us that much time!"

She slapped his palm as she went and replied, "We got this! Handle the adds when they appear!"

As the group thudded off, armor clanking, she heard retreating voices saying, "Why are you chatting her up in the middle of the fight?!"

"No, you dummy, it's not like that!"

Nearby, Lisbeth couldn't help but giggle. "Some things never change, Asuna."

"Wh-what do you mean?"

"I remember in Aincrad when we used to walk around together, every now and then, some guy would—"

"Th-that's not important right now, is it?! Look, the boss is about to attack!" she said in a mild panic. Wadjet broke through its binds and began moving again.

Compared to the Deviant Gods that lived in Jotunheim, the subterranean land of ice below Alfheim, the boss monsters of New Aincrad were smaller but much more powerful. As evidence of that, over a month had passed since the first ten floors of the floating castle were implemented, but they'd beaten only the first seven floors so far. Full forty-nine-man raid parties (seven parties of seven) had attempted Wadjet many times in the past week, and every last one of them had ended in defeat.

With that in mind, the human-faced, snake-bodied monster whose curved neck reached almost to the ceiling was a nerve-racking sight, but she could put on a smile and suck it up. The important thing wasn't winning but having fun. To do her best fighting without worrying about losing…

"*Jruuah!!*" shrieked Wadjet, swinging a bishop's staff with its lower left hand.

In synchronization with that motion, the pillars lining the edge of the chamber rotated, revealing large mirrors that had been hidden on their back sides. Instantly, the two parties that had just retreated from the boss broke apart into smaller groups without waiting for orders and took places by the mirrors, which numbered eight in all.

The tip of Wadjet's staff had a crystal in it that emitted a light beam with lethal power. That was frightening enough, but to make matters worse, the mirrors on the edge of the battlefield would deflect the beam in complex ways that made it impossible to guess the trajectory it'd take.

When the boss fight was first available, the players tried destroying the mirrors when they appeared. It was possible if you struck them enough times with your weapons, but it took way too many hits, and by the time they got rid of all eight, the light beam would have eliminated several combatants already.

But now that a week had passed, they were working on a more effective tactic. The players next to the mirrors held the surface and pushed to rotate them, then promptly leaped away. Within moments, the staff in Wadjet's hand fired a dark-green beam.

It struck the mirror on the west side of the room and would normally have bounced toward a different mirror, killing any player caught in its path. But because the player had turned the angle of the mirror, it bounced back straight—directly at Wadjet. Damaged by its own light attack, Wadjet screamed and lost much of one of its seven HP bars. That only put it at halfway on its second bar, but there had been no player deaths so far. For an impromptu group that was two parties short of a full raid, they were doing quite well.

Klein, who was acting as party leader this time, seemed to agree. He whipped his katana around and called out, "We're doing well! We can do this! Everyone, charge!!"

Agil, with his two-handed ax, and Kirito, with his longsword, bolted forward, followed by Leafa and Lisbeth. They surrounded the boss's long torso with the two other attacking parties and began to slice, pummel, and thrust into it.

This time, Asuna did not hang back. But rather than whacking at it with her staff, she used magic attacks. With her skill at high-speed recitation, she put together spells and waved her staff at Wadjet's upper half. Sharp spears of ice rained down and stuck between its black scales. The self-inflicted light-beam damage had caused its flame to temporarily disappear, so a full complement of ice magic took advantage of its weak element and, combined with all the physical attacks, gouged large chunks out of the HP gauge.

Wadjet flailed with the damage, and its long body began to coil like a spring. With a better vantage point thanks to her extra distance, Asuna recognized what was happening and called out, "Tail attack! Everyone, ready to jump!"

Immediately, the attackers wailing on the boss jumped away and prepared themselves. Wadjet was more of an elemental-damage boss, but its physical attacks were also powerful, and the three-part rotation with its long tail just off the ground meant that if you didn't dodge the first one, you'd fall over and get hit with the second and third.

Asuna bent her knees in preparation for the jump along with her comrades. With its tail fully wrapped around itself, the goddess's eyes shone deep red. And...jump!

But then, at that very moment—

Asuna felt her mind being pulled upward, just before her avatar could jump. It was the dissociative sensation again.

Not now! she thought, waiting for her senses to recover. It lasted for only a moment, but in this situation, it felt like an eternity. The power coiled in every inch of the boss's body unleashed, and its tail came whipping around. It was no good...She wouldn't make it.

Just before the massive whip swept her legs out from under her, the conversation she'd had before the fight returned to her mind.

An hour before their meeting time with Leafa, Klein, and the rest, Asuna and Kirito had logged in to the same room in the inn as the day before, summoned Yui, and explained the situation to her.

Yui had switched from her more recent navigation pixie look to her original appearance. She sat between the two of them on the sofa and listened intently to what Asuna said. When the story was over, she murmured, "Your mind...dissociates..."

The little girl's eyes were wide. Asuna said, "That's right. It's hard to describe in words...but I think there's undoubtedly something wrong with my connection to my avatar."

"I had no idea you were having this problem...I'm sorry, Mama. If only I'd realized earlier..."

"No, Yui. It's not your fault." She cupped the little girl's cheeks in her hands. "*I'm* sorry. For not telling you about it earlier. At first, I thought I just wasn't used to my new avatar. But after talking with Kirito yesterday, I'm starting to think there's a different cause..."

On the other side of Yui, Kirito said, "What do you think, Yui? Anything that seems to be a likely cause...?"

"Well, let's see..."

The AI's long eyelashes pointed downward as she adopted a thinking expression, her face still cradled in Asuna's hands. After just three seconds, her face rose, but it was still clouded.

"Based on what you told me, I'm afraid I cannot specify a cause for your reaction...And with my current privileges, I'm not able to do a direct examination of the packets being traded between your AmuSphere and the *ALO* server. Although, if it happens when I am nearby, I might be able to glean some kind of data..."

"No...I understand. I'm sorry, Yui, I didn't mean to ask the impossible of you," Asuna said, attempting to apologize. But Yui grabbed her hands and squeezed. She pulled the hands off her cheeks and brought them down between the two.

"But I can make some conjectures."

"Huh...? You can?"

"Yes. First of all, I hypothesize that the cause of your phenomenon does not exist with your AmuSphere or with you. Which means the first possibility is a server problem, but as of this moment, the Cardinal System does not detect errors, and no errors on the human side are reported, either," the little girl said crisply, still holding Asuna's hands. This put a strange feeling in Asuna's chest.

Yesterday, she and Kirito were worried that this might put a terrible strain on Yui's psyche. But that concern was apparently unnecessary. Yui admitted that she did not have the ability to solve the problem right away, and she was still trying her hardest to help. She was growing, day by day.

"But I can surmise that something on the *ALO* server, something within Alfheim, is creating some kind of abnormal interference with you, Mama. I just can't determine at the moment whether that is a player or an object, or if it is intentional or incidental."

"Abnormal...interference...," Asuna repeated.

If it was a human being causing Asuna's dissociative episodes, it couldn't be just any player. There was no magic spell or item that caused such a thing, so it would inevitably have to be something with a higher authority level...a hacker or a GM, perhaps.

That line of thought caused Asuna to envision a face she never wanted to think about again. The man who had kept her locked in a birdcage for over two months. Oberon, king of the fairies—Nobuyuki Sugou.

But he was locked up in Tokyo Detention House, and it would be impossible for him to interfere with the *ALO* server. Kirito's face went hard, too, as he momentarily considered that idea, but then he shook his head. When he looked at Yui again, he was back to his usual self.

"Hey, Yui. You said that what was interfering with Asuna could possibly be an object…What do you mean by that? Is it possible that some specific item or part of the landscape can surpass the boundaries of the game system and have a direct effect on the player…?"

The young girl tilted her head, appearing to ponder how to explain. Slowly, she said, "As I'm sure you both know, I was originally developed as a test version of a mental health counseling program meant to assist *SAO* players. That would indicate that the NerveGear can read not only the wearer's senses and kinetic movement but also their emotions. The old Cardinal System monitored and collected data on the mental state of all its players…"

None of this was new to Asuna. When she first met Yui, the program was like a toddler barely capable of speech, because her core program was broken, staggered by the weight of so much negative emotion that she could not ease.

Yui looked at each of them in turn and continued, her voice professional.

"But compared to the signals for senses and movement, the ability to analyze emotional signals was slower to develop. All that could be identified was that which appeared most often in the aggregate data: anger, sadness, fear, despair. At the time, neither Cardinal nor I, its subordinate program, could analyze anything else. So when Cardinal received an input of a particularly extreme and anomalous emotional pattern, it would save that as raw data, including everything else present. That means the ID of the player who emitted the emotional pattern, of course, but also the time, place, and even items possessed."

"…!"

Asuna sucked in a sharp breath and looked at Kirito.

This was news to them. It was difficult to grasp Yui's explanation, but it probably came down to this: When it found an interest in a player, the Cardinal System, which managed the *SAO* server, would store not compressed information that had been pattern-analyzed but the raw emotional data itself. But in a sense, that might as well be copying the player's soul—or at least, the uppermost layer of it.

Asuna was wondering if current full-dive technology was actually capable of such a thing when she suddenly remembered: She and Kirito might have witnessed this firsthand.

"...Oh yeah...Kirito, do you remember? Ages ago, when you and I were investigating a murder inside the safe haven of town..."

Kirito nodded immediately; he must have been thinking of the same thing. "Yeah. After we solved the case on that hilltop on the nineteenth floor, we saw Griselda, the murder victim, standing next to the grave. Maybe that wasn't just a vision...but the heart of Griselda, stored in that grave—or in the ring buried under the soil there..."

There was no way to determine the truth of that now. Yui did not have any comments to add. When she didn't say anything, Kirito lightly placed his hand on the small of her back. Quietly and gently, he said, "What you're telling us is that inside *SAO*, when players exuded powerful emotions, those emotions tended to get stored and attached to places or objects associated with them. Is that right?"

The pixie nodded.

"Then like you said, could the object or objects that are causing this dissociative phenomenon be those?" he continued. "Like...a player's feelings are residing inside an item and interfering with Asuna...?"

Again, Yui did not react. But her silence, Asuna could feel, was less about choosing the right words and more about wondering if it was right to speak her conjecture aloud at all.

"At the present moment...I cannot bring myself to answer in the affirmative...," Yui said, her voice frail. Then she looked up and, much more firmly, said, "But through talking and adventuring with you two, and Lisbeth and Silica, and Leafa, and Klein, and Agil, and all the others, I think I've learned. I've learned that the human heart and the full-dive system possess far greater possibilities than I understand. So I cannot say that the answer to your question is no. As I first told you, I believe this supposition is a possibility—that is all."

So the cause of the mysterious phenomenon was a player—or some part of a player's mentality that resided in an item or an area of land...

That was the possibility that Yui had raised just before they fought the boss. Then it was time to meet up with the group, so they couldn't discuss it in any further detail, but on the way to New Aincrad, Asuna mulled over Yui's statements, and she came to an interpretation she could be okay with.

Perhaps someone was calling to her. Someone playing *ALO* right now—or someone who had once played *SAO*—was calling Asuna. And because of that, her consciousness was being pulled away from her avatar. If true, then he or she was probably not doing it maliciously. The phenomenon just couldn't choose the time or place, and as a result, it interfered with her gameplay. Just like at this moment.

Right as the phantom floating sensation arrived, it brought change to everything else around her.

The black marble boss chamber grew faint and distant, and a completely different room appeared much closer to her, hazy and uncertain.

There were walls of light-brown blocks placed in random arrangements, and the floor was the same color. Monsters completely swarmed the space—ore elementals (blackened rock carved into humanoid shapes) and dark dwarves, squat and menacing, with sharp pickaxes for weapons. The flickering sight was definitely familiar to her somehow, but she could not remember the time or place. The feeling was exactly the same as what she'd felt when looking out the window last night.

So did this memory belong to someone who was calling her…?

The sight of the room and its monsters lasted for only a moment. When it vanished, her mind returned to her avatar. Her eyes opened wide, just in time to see the powerful tail of Wadjet the Flaming Serpent whipping across the floor toward her.

All her teammates in striking range jumped straight upward in unison. Only Asuna failed to match the right timing—just barely, but it was costly all the same. She wasn't going to make it—

"Asuna!"

The impact came not from the front but from the side. Suddenly, her body was being lifted upward, and only the toe of her boot grazed Wadjet's tail. Forgetting to even check her HP bar, Asuna just stared into the face of the spriggan holding her.

"K-Kirito, how…?"

She was going to ask "How did you know the timing of my slipping?" but Kirito cut her off. "Yui sensed it before it happened."

The pixie sitting on Kirito's shoulder added gravely, "Eight seconds ago, I picked up a signal being sent to you. It will take a bit more time to analyze it."

"…So it's true. Someone *is* doing this to me…"

Stunned, Asuna only realized after several seconds that she'd been airborne the entire time. The gray wings extending from Kirito's back exuded a faint glow.

All nine fairy races of Alfheim, even the less air-centric ones like leprechauns and gnomes, had the power of flight. In the game's May update, the limitation on flight time from the RCT Progress days was gone, so you could fly as much as you wanted. But there were exceptions: the underground realm of Jotunheim and the various dungeons of the game. The labyrinth towers of New Aincrad were included in that designation, of course.

But even then, there was a counter to that rule. Only the spriggans, who excelled at treasure hunting, had a special high-level ability to fly for a brief time underground. It didn't last long, though you could extend it with extra proficiency, so you could use it only in emergencies. To Kirito, this situation counted as one.

"Th-thank you, Kirito..."

She wanted to apologize, but he just shook his head.

On the ground, the tail attack continued through its second and third swings. Nearly twenty players evaded it with perfectly timed jumps. Once Wadjet's wide-area attack was over, Kirito landed with his partner in his arms. The skill had worn off, and his gray wings vanished without a sound. The cooldown timer for that one was around five or six hundred seconds, so he wouldn't be able to fly again for a good long while. If she experienced the dissociative phenomenon again, he wouldn't be able to save her.

Yui hopped off Kirito's shoulder and onto Asuna's, leaned toward her ear, and whispered, "Mama, I've memorized the broad pattern of the signal, so I will be able to warn you earlier."

"Thanks, Yui. Please do," she replied under her breath, then turned to her teammates and called out, "Sorry, I just tripped! I'll make sure to avoid it next time!"

Lisbeth waved back and said, "It's cool!" Meanwhile, Kirito rushed off toward the boss, which had paused after its big attack.

"Ryaaaa!" bellowed Klein and the others, while Kirito rushed behind them without a word. That struck Asuna as odd.

During this entire battle, Kirito had been quieter than usual. In fact, he was acting reticent even before the fight, when he allowed Klein to be party leader. She was going to ask Yui about that but changed her mind before the words left her mouth. Focusing on the fight was more important.

The assault from the team that had just evaded the tail attack unharmed managed to knock the second of Wadjet's seven HP bars into the red zone. The snake-bodied goddess issued a snarl of rage, then lifted a bronze torch with its bottom right hand.

"More minions coming!!" Klein called out.

Even before he did, Asuna stepped back and started chanting the spell words for Purified Surface again. The two parties in the back would not be enough to take care of the fire elementals that would appear throughout the chamber. The salamander's team and the sylph's team should stay to deal with the boss while Asuna's party pulled away to help with the adds.

Klein reached the same conclusion, and when he turned to give Asuna the order, he grinned upon seeing that she was already casting the spell.

"Okay, let's pull back and knock out these elemen— Hey! Kiri!"

Drawn by the consternation in his voice, Asuna followed Klein's gaze to where Kirito was mingling with the other two attacking squads. After a few moments, he seemed to recognize Klein's voice and came to a stop.

When he lifted his free hand in apology and returned to the group, Asuna paid close attention to his face as she continued her spell. Normally, he would never make this kind of mistake in the midst of a boss battle.

Was he so concerned with Asuna's out-of-body experiences that he was losing his focus on the fight...?

She finished her quick chanting of the spell, held the staff high over her head, and slammed it into the ground. The chill of the holy water flooding up from the floor seeped through her boots. Unable to resist, she decided to speak to Yui again; there was nothing else for her to do while she was maintaining the spell effect.

"Um, Yui, does Kirito seem...?"

The pixie was practically waiting for her to bring it up. "Yes, Papa is not acting like himself."

"Right...I wonder what's up with him..."

"I don't know, either..."

In a sense, Yui had much more accumulated information about Kirito than Asuna did, so if she said so, he really *was* acting different from usual today. And she couldn't believe that it was unrelated to her recent issue.

When this battle is over, I need to have a proper talk with him. About the strange sights I saw last night and just now. About everything.

With that determination planted in her mind, Asuna gripped the staff and focused on the battle around her.

About thirty minutes later, Kirito and Klein, the last two left struggling on their own, finally teleported back to the save point on the bottom floor of the labyrinth tower. As soon as their avatars materialized, the samurai clutched his fists and wailed.

"Kaaaaah! Dammit! We had barely more than a single bar left to goooo!"

Agil, who had died and returned to the save point along with Asuna, just smirked and noted, "That last bar would have been the worst. They say Wadjet's like the other bosses; once you get to the last bar, there are all new mechanics."

"Yeah, I know, but once you're down that far, it always feels like you can just power your way through, ya know?"

"No! That's not how it works! It's not how it worked for *you*, at least!"

This little comedy routine elicited laughter not just among the friends but among the other four parties in the raid.

After that one time, there had been no more dissociative episodes, and Asuna fought to the best of her ability, but the group ultimately failed to defeat the eighth-floor boss. Their faces were bright, however. The sylph party leader who had invited them to the group walked over, steel greaves clanking, and spoke to Klein with a smile.

"I've gotta say, I thought we were onto something. We probably would have done it with a full raid."

"Yeah, I agree! We had some good teamwork going. If only the fire-elemental placement hadn't ended up all lopsided…"

"Well, if it weren't for your group, the lasers would have wiped us out. You guys were amazing," said the sylph, extending his right hand. Klein chuckled and grabbed it.

After their handshake was over, the raid leader thought for a moment and looked toward Agil and Lisbeth. "Say, if you're up for it, why don't we go back to town and give it another shot? Maybe we can find another two parties to fill us out."

"Yeah, I'm down! What do you say, Boss?" Klein asked Agil, who replied "Why not?" in English. The four girls in the group gave them positive answers, too.

The samurai in red grinned and started to speak for the group but paused first, one eyebrow raised. The one player who would normally be the most enthusiastic about this had remained silent. Klein looked over at Kirito, who was standing a little ways away, and said, "Hey, are you in or not, Kiri?"

The spriggan's head shot upward. He had been listening after all. He put on a smile that seemed awkward to Asuna's practiced eye and said, "Uh, y-yeah, of course…"

But his gaze wavered in empty space. His lips pursed tight and eventually opened again.

"……Actually…I've got something to do after this. I hate to let you down, but I've got to drop out here."

"Uh…sure. No problem, but…"

Klein was poised to say something else, but he stopped himself and rubbed his whiskered chin. Then he grinned and nodded. "Okay, we'll handle it from here! I'll send you a pic when we get to the ninth floor!"

Nearby, Agil offered a line that seemed oddly familiar: "I'll give you a write-up on Wadjet's loot, in under eight hundred characters."

"Looking forward to it," Kirito said with a wry smile. He bowed to the sylph leader, then turned away. For a brief moment, he met Asuna's eyes but merely blinked in apology and started hurrying off toward the exit of the tower to the south.

Asuna could feel Yui tensing on her right shoulder. She extended her foot to walk after him on autopilot but stopped herself there. She was the only magic user in the party. She couldn't just leave them now…

"Go on, Asuna," said a voice. She turned in surprise and saw Leafa behind her, smiling. She lifted a hand and pushed Asuna on the back. "I'll find two others to invite. We'll be fine. Take care of my brother."

"……But…"

She looked to her sides and saw Lisbeth, Silica, Agil, and Klein all smiling and nodding for her to go. So she took a deep breath, summoned her courage, and bowed in apology. When she rose again, she said to the other raid members, "I'm sorry! I've got to leave now, too!"

The others they'd been playing with called out things like "Thanks!" and "Let's play again sometime!" and "Good luck with whatever you're doing!" Asuna bowed once more to their kindness, then spun around to leave.

Kirito was already nowhere to be seen in the hallway of several dozen yards leading out of the tower. But Yui was on top of it.

"Papa's flying toward the southern rim of New Aincrad!"

"Thanks, Yui," she whispered back, putting her staff away into her inventory. Then she sprinted for the exit of the labyrinth tower.

3

The outside was now wreathed in night.

The day-night cycle of Alfheim was sixteen hours total, so it was not synchronized with real-world time. Outside the game, it was after five PM; being just past the summer solstice, there was still plenty of light at this hour—but in the fairy realm, the sun was long gone.

The eighth floor of New Aincrad was a forest-themed floor. The third floor had the same motif but included grassland and rocky areas, whereas the eighth floor was utterly dedicated to thick mangrove forests. For one thing, there was no actual ground. The surface of the floor was covered in deep water that you couldn't walk across. Instead, there were massive trees (far smaller than the World Tree, Yggdrasil, of course) all around, with a complex layout of hanging bridges connecting the elevated platforms that players had to travel across.

In the *SAO* days, if you fell off, you had to wade through the water until you found a tree with a ladder to climb, but that was no longer a concern here. Asuna left the giant, blackened tree that contained the labyrinth tower, ignored the spiral staircase nearby, and buzzed the wings on her back instead.

The reason the labyrinth tower and its surrounding trees were charred like this was explained as the work of the new boss,

Wadjet the Flaming Serpent. The boss in Aincrad was completely different, and the trees around here had been perfectly green. Ymir's designers had put a lot of work into redecorating this area for their new take on the original.

She levitated directly upward for about fifty yards, only transitioning to horizontal flight once there was a decent amount of visibility below. The huge trees of this floor ran all the way up to the bottom of the ninth floor, so there was no way for her to get above the canopy. In the *SAO* days, this was one of the few floors where an intrepid climber could touch the bottom of the next floor up. Of course, no one could actually dig a shortcut hole through the rock.

Yui made her way from Asuna's shoulder to the front of her shirt as the fairy girl soared and wove around huge trunks dozens of feet across.

"Where is Kirito now?" she asked the pixie.

"He'll be reaching the outer aperture any moment now. If he gets any farther away, I won't be able to detect him anymore!"

"Got it! Geez, he's so fast…"

She tucked her arms to her sides and focused on speed. She'd gotten accustomed to the unique flying system of *ALO* quickly and no longer needed the flight controller after just a few days of practice, but in terms of really pushing the limits of flight, she was still inferior to Kirito and Leafa. She did her best to avoid the obstacles, flying by the light of the lanterns hanging from the bridges connecting tree to tree.

In time, blue light appeared ahead of her. It was moonlight; she was nearly at the edge of New Aincrad. Kirito had already left the floating structure, she was sure.

Yui chose that moment to report, "Papa's rising along the outside of New Aincrad!"

"Huh…?"

Asuna's eyes went wide. Kirito had said he had something to do, so she'd assumed he was heading for Yggdrasil City atop the World Tree. But thinking about it now, if he just needed to log out, he could do so in any inn on the eighth floor, and if he was going to Ygg City, he could get there immediately from the teleport square in the Town of Beginnings on the first floor.

This meant Kirito's destination was somewhere else in *ALO*—well, higher up in New Aincrad.

But as of now, June 22nd, the eighth floor *was* as high as you could get in New Aincrad. The outer apertures of the ninth floor and up were entirely closed off. You couldn't just fly through them onto the terrain of the floors. Asuna had once gone with Kirito and their friends to fly up to where the Ruby Palace should have been on the hundredth floor, but they'd hit the altitude limit on flight at around the fiftieth floor. The only thing they could see from there was an endless slope of steel.

Kirito knew he couldn't get inside on a higher floor. So where did he think he was going...? This question filled Asuna's mind as she burst out from the southernmost tip of the eighth floor into the open expanse.

She turned back and saw an enormous full moon in the sky behind her. It was gleaming off the enclosed surface of the flying castle. Against it, just off the steel face, rose a tiny silhouette.

He already seemed to be at about the fifteenth floor. There was something desperate about the directness of his path, and it made Asuna wonder if it was right for her to follow him.

"Kirito...," she murmured, while Yui peered out from the collar of her short robe.

"Papa..."

When Asuna heard that tiny voice, she made up her mind. She bent her knees and pushed off the air as hard as she could, stretching in a straight line toward the sky, an arrow of blue.

She and Kirito were separated by the width of seven floors—about seven hundred yards. In the *SAO* days, this would have been worlds apart, but that was all in the past. Now Asuna had four radiant blue wings.

On she flew, chasing after her beloved, but she had a premonition. Wherever Kirito was heading, it had to contain the answer to the mysterious sensation afflicting her. He must have come to some hypothesis based on talking with Yui and was now trying to see if he was correct.

Kirito tore through the virtual atmosphere of the sky far above. He was past the twentieth floor and showed no sign of slowing. He didn't even stop at the twenty-second floor, where their precious log cabin would be found. In a blink, he was past the twenty-fifth floor, where the Aincrad Liberation Squad had collapsed in battle against the boss. Where was he going?

Then the black shadow suddenly flew in a sharp loop. He plunged right for the steel exterior next to him.

"Oh...!" Asuna gasped, expecting a collision, but Kirito spread his wings to slow down just before the wall. He didn't hit the surface hard enough to cause HP damage, but Asuna could detect the impact of his hands slapping the metal all the way from her location.

It was...the twenty-seventh floor.

The name of the main town on that floor was Rombal. It was a place covered with craggy rocks and boulders, where the towns and dungeons were carved right out of the mountains. It had been very popular with crafters in the *SAO* days, because many ores were available there, but Asuna did not remember it well. They'd struggled a bit with the metal-elemental boss, but from what she could remember, they'd been on the floor for only a few days in total.

That information would be the same for Kirito, who was part of the same group of players. So why was he focused on this floor in particular?

As she watched with bated breath, the black silhouette stayed still, hands pressed against the steel surface. Almost as if, by sheer force of prayer, he could will a hole to open in the wall.

But of course, the impervious, indestructible wall did not change in any way. Asuna slowed her ascent as she reached the twenty-sixth floor, until she was coasting on momentum and upward draft and arrived at the space just behind Kirito.

She didn't say anything. Yui was silent as well, sitting inside her shirt. Almost no flying monsters would appear at this altitude, so the only thing in their vicinity was moonlight, the breeze, and the fortress of steel.

At last, Kirito let go of the wall of the twenty-seventh floor. He lowered his hands, beat his wings a little, and turned around.

"...Asuna. Yui."

There was the faintest hint of a smile on his lips. It was an expression she had hardly ever seen on him in the two years and eight months she'd known him.

"Kirito...," she whispered, closing the gap a little. But she was hesitant to get any closer. There were so many things she wanted to ask, but she didn't know what to say.

He looked away from her and took in the view, then pointed down and to the right. "Let's talk there."

There was a bridge-like protrusion extending from the surface of the structure below. It was only about ten feet long, but it would serve as a bench. Asuna nodded and flew down with him, then sat on the sideways spike of steel.

Kirito sat to her left, then lifted his right hand and rubbed Yui's head where it popped out of Asuna's collar. The smile on his face seemed to contain a hint of pain.

"I'm sorry, Yui," he said. "Sorry, Asuna...I must have worried you."

In response, Yui flitted out of Asuna's clothes and sat on Kirito's right shoulder. Her big black eyes looked right at Asuna's, saying, *Go on, Mama.*

Asuna nodded back and summoned her courage.

"Kirito...what's here on the twenty-seventh floor?" she asked. After a moment, she corrected herself. "What...*was* here... before?"

But just saying those words was the key to opening the door to her memories. Asuna's eyes went wide.

Something *did* happen. On this floor. In fact, she had heard this story right from Kirito. The number of the floor itself hadn't come up, but at this point, there was no denying it. This had to be the floor…where Kirito experienced the tragedy that led him to resist grouping up in guilds and parties and stick to being the only solo player in the frontier group…

"Yeah…that's right," Kirito said with a little nod, sensing from her expression that she had figured it out. "The twenty-seventh-floor labyrinth tower…is where my first-ever guild, the Moonlit Black Cats, fell into ruin…"

Kirito had told Asuna the tragic story of the Moonlit Black Cats just two days before their marriage in front of their forest home. That was October 22nd, 2024.

They initially met Yui in the forest on the twenty-second floor a week after that, but Yui knew the general details of the story by now. This time, Kirito didn't speak about the past again, but the present.

"When Yui said that a player's powerful emotions could be saved on the *SAO* server as an attachment to a place or item, I had an idea," he said, his voice soft. "Maybe the emotions of everyone from the Black Cats are saved, too…Recorded in that hidden room in the twenty-seventh-floor labyrinth tower, their terror and despair when the ore elementals and dark dwarves trapped and surrounded them…"

————*!!*

That brought back the image she saw in the midst of the Wadjet battle with distinct clarity.

The pattern of random sandstone blocks on the wall—that was definitely from the labyrinth tower of the twenty-seventh floor in Aincrad. The room had been packed with ore elementals and dwarves. It was exactly like Kirito just said.

"……Kirito," she squeaked, the only thing she could say. When Kirito looked up at her, she tried to explain what she'd experienced. The vision she saw in the midst of the boss battle, the room that had to be the place where the Black Cats fell—and the sight of the city at night that she saw in her room after logging out yesterday. Of a flowing waterway and lights in the fog…

"……"

Even Kirito was at a loss for words after hearing about this. Eventually, he nodded and said, "Then…that settles it. The night vision was probably…the memory of one of them…Which means the phenomenon you're feeling is from her…"

He paused, then continued even more quietly, "From Sachi… calling you…But why would it be you…and not me…?"

It was more a question to himself than to Asuna. But the reply came from the one person who had been silent thus far: Yui.

"I think…it's because you're using a different account than the one you had in *SAO*, Papa…A different avatar."

"…!"

Kirito bolted up straight. He looked down at his hands, clad in black leather gloves. Asuna was aware that his palms and fingers were subtly different than they had been in *SAO*.

In starting up a new, normal online game life in *ALfheim Online*, Asuna, Lisbeth, Silica, Klein, Agil, and the many other survivors of *SAO* transferred their *SAO* account data to *ALO* as is. Kirito was the only exception, using the spunky young sprig-gan he created from scratch when he was trying to rescue Asuna from the birdcage.

If Kirito had brought back his old avatar, then the emotions of this Sachi girl located somewhere on the twenty-seventh floor of New Aincrad would be affecting him, not Asuna. If anything, he would have been the one affected by the dissociative sensation.

But why had Sachi chosen Asuna as a replacement for Kirito? And *how* had she?

She had passed away over a year before Asuna and Kirito got married. At the time, Asuna was an executive officer of the new Knights of the Blood. She'd been focused on building up the guild and conquering new floors. She saw Kirito at strategy meetings and during boss battles, but nothing more. She hadn't known that he had joined a guild called the Moonlit Black Cats or that they had been wiped out, leaving him as the only survivor. By that token, Sachi would never have even known Asuna's name.

Again, it was Yui who had an answer.

"Mama, the avatar you're using now, technically speaking, is still married to Papa's old avatar. There's no marriage system in *ALO* at the moment, so it's not shown on your character status... but it's still connected to Papa somewhere in your data."

"R-really?!" she exclaimed, despite everything.

Kirito's eyes bulged, too. After a moment, he murmured, "I see...When Sachi died...I was there. Her emotions at the moment of her death are probably saved on the server, not just in the labyrinth tower of the twenty-seventh floor, but also linked to my avatar. But since I changed to a new avatar, the signal Sachi's memories are sending could only go to the next closest thing... and that's Asuna, because of her link to the old me...?"

That all made some kind of sense, at least. But it didn't explain everything.

"...Why is it happening *now*, though?" she wondered, looking at the exterior of the floating castle to her left. "The dissociative phenomenon first happened three weeks after my initial dive into *ALO*. And they've been happening more often lately. Plus, there's more detail to them, like memories mixed in. That didn't happen at first..."

".......That's because..."

Kirito paused, then checked his window. After staring at the time readout, he took a deep breath, and in a tense voice, he said, "Sachi died...on June 22nd, 2023...That's two years ago today. And it happened at...five forty-five PM. Three minutes from now..."

"...!!"

Asuna gasped. On Kirito's shoulder, Yui sat frozen, her big black eyes widened in shock.

Kirito closed his window and looked up into the night sky, which was now full of twinkling stars. He began to speak.

"...In *SAO*...I saw...many players die. Some of them met their end by my own sword. So...I didn't want to see the deaths of the Black Cats, and of Sachi, as being special anymore. When

we were in Aincrad, I used the tree growing outside the inn the Black Cats called home as a grave marker of sorts. I would go visit it from time to time…but right now, I can't visit the eleventh floor, where the inn was, or the twenty-seventh floor, where they died. So my plan was, while we were playing today, to just observe a moment of silence when the time came and have that be the end of it…But after what Yui said, I realized it was probably Sachi's emotions saved on the server that were causing your dissociative sensation, and I had to be sure…"

He placed his arms on his knees and clenched his fists. His head hung low, and he continued his story through obvious pain.

"……If what Sachi felt at that moment…the terror, the despair, the sadness…are still saved on the server, trying to reach someone…then it should be my responsibility, as the sole survivor. But I changed my avatar and cut loose my past…and because of that, Sachi's emotions had nowhere else to go…but to you……"

"………Kirito," Asuna murmured, shaking her head over and over. There were so many things she wanted to say that she couldn't speak a single one. She felt so powerless, it was hard even to breathe.

"You're wrong, Papa!" cried Yui. She leaped off his shoulder and flitted right in front of his face, clutching her tiny fists in umbrage. "The only thing the Cardinal System saved was special emotional outputs that it couldn't classify with the patterns it knew. This might be inappropriate to say, but the kinds of fear and despair that dying players felt in *SAO* were not unique. Just two weeks after the system began recording, it stopped saving despair-based raw data. So if Sachi left an emotional record on the server…it would not have been despair or terror!!"

Kirito's head lifted just an inch. His voice was raspy.

"…Then…what Sachi left…was…?"

Asuna did not hear the end of that sentence.

At five forty-five and thirteen seconds on June 22nd, she experienced the largest dissociative episode yet.

The hardness of the steel spike they were sitting on, the chill of the high-altitude winds, the texture of her mage's equipment—all these sensations faded. She felt like she was floating. Her virtual weight vanished.

Then Asuna's mind separated from her avatar entirely. The floating black structure beside her, the starry sky, everything was overwritten by bright light.

Her soul was sucked down a corridor of light to somewhere else…

The next thing she knew, she was standing in an unfamiliar room.

It was not large. The only fixtures were a simple bed and a wooden desk. The single window provided a view of a rustic, European-looking town. Instead of a sky overhead, there was just a lid of stone and metal. This was not the real world…It was some place in Aincrad. She recognized the style of the roofs and walls of the buildings. It was probably the main town of the eleventh or twelfth floor. Neither of them was available at the present time.

It was night, and the room was dim because there was only a single lamp on the wall. This was probably a room in an inn, not a player home. Asuna circled the bed and approached the door. She tried to turn the knob, but her hand slipped through; she couldn't grip it. She looked down at herself, and to her surprise, she was not an undine mage anymore. She was wearing a knight's uniform of white and red. She had long gloves and boots in the same colors. There was no rapier at her side, but it was un-doubtedly the equipment from her time in the Knights of the Blood. Her entire body was translucent, though, like a vision.

What was happening? She looked up again—and saw the space above the bed flicker, revealing a vague outline.

It was a female player, skinny and frail. She was sitting on the white bedsheets with her back to Asuna. She wore a light-blue tunic and miniskirt. No armor. The hair cut just above her shoulders was black with just a tinge of blue. It was clear even without seeing her face that she was around the same age as Asuna.

The girl was shaking her torso left and right. She seemed to be singing—and in fact, at that very moment, a gentle song graced Asuna's ears. It was a famous Christmas song. She was singing the chorus slowly and tenderly.

As she listened, Asuna found her vision beginning to blur and sparkle with motes of light. Her eyes brimmed with tears. Powerful emotion gripped her chest. The girl's feelings were flowing into her through the melody. There wasn't a single ounce of fear or desperation. It was pure warmth, like the sunlight of spring filling her heart...

One large teardrop spilled down Asuna's right cheek as the song came to an end.

The girl stood and turned around without a sound, facing Asuna across the bed.

Because of the quavering light that filled her eyes, Asuna could not make out her face. The only detail she could see was a smiling mouth that opened to speak.

There was a voice.

You tell him for me.
   Tell him I was happy.

The brilliant light surrounded Asuna again. She was being pulled away from the girl, the room, the town.

As she felt the floating sensation drag her away, Asuna understood innately that this was the final out-of-body experience she would be having.

Slowly and carefully, she opened her eyes.

Countless stars glittered in a black sky tinged with indigo. The steel castle loomed over her, with a large full moon at its tip.

Not far away, she found Kirito's and Yui's faces watching her with concern. His hand was propping her up in a sitting position.

"...Thank you. I'm fine now," she whispered, regaining her balance and glancing at what she was wearing. It was the regular blue robe again, of course.

"Asuna," he said, concerned and plaintive. She looked at him again. She was uncertain of how to proceed but then realized that what she needed to say was already in her mind.

"Sachi was smiling," Asuna said. Kirito's eyes went as wide as they could go.

She could see the stars reflected in his black eyes grow more numerous. Asuna used all her heart to impart the words that had been entrusted to her.

Just as heartfelt as Sachi's Christmas song had been.

4

The next day: Monday, June 23rd, at nine o'clock at night. Asuna was back in Frieven on the eighth floor of New Aincrad.

The second attempt on the boss, after she and Kirito had left the raid party, had once again ended in a painful, last-minute defeat. But they also reported that after getting the boss to its final HP bar, they were able to devise a winning strategy; thus, everyone present had promised to come back together the next day for a rematch.

This time, Asuna and Kirito would be taking part, as well as the best teams from General Eugene's salamanders and Lady Sakuya's sylphs. There was twice as much heat and excitement in the teleport square as there was last time.

Klein, who was again playing the role of raid leader, said to the sylph warrior, "It's kinda freaky, right?" The man had seemed intimidated to be remaining in the leadership position when there were two fairy leaders in the mix, but with Sakuya herself giving him furtive glances and requests to take over, he couldn't possibly back down now.

"You called up Sakuya and General Eugene together? Who *are* you?" the sylph leader asked.

Klein just chuckled awkwardly. "Aw shucks, I'm nobody special, ha-ha."

Agil, meanwhile, interjected, "They weren't *your* connections," while Asuna just shook her head in exasperation.

Behind her, she could hear Kirito and Yui talking.

"Wh-what? My hair?"

"Yes!"

She turned around and asked, "What's going on, you two?"

"Well, the thing is," said the spriggan, pinching a lock of his spiky black hair in demonstration, "Yui's saying I should change my hairstyle because it's hard to sit on my head...Even though changing your hair is actually pretty expensive..."

From his shoulder, Yui put her hands on her hips and argued, "You could stand to spend your money on something other than the weapons store and the casino! Plus, the higher I can sit, the more efficient my information gathering will be!"

"I'm sorry, Yui—what did you say after 'weapons store'...?"

"Aaah! Fine, fine! All right! I'll change it right after this boss fight!" Kirito suddenly exclaimed, having changed his mind very quickly.

But Yui shook her head. "You still have ten minutes until the gathering time! That's more than enough time to go over to that barbershop and have your hair changed!"

"Fine, fine...Well, sorry, Asuna. I've got to get this taken care of right now."

"Um, sure. Have a nice trip," Asuna said, waving as they headed off.

It occurred to her that while his avatar's face and hair were different than what he'd had in *SAO*, if he flattened his hair, he might actually look a lot like his old self.

She wasn't necessarily hoping he would go back to his old *SAO* look, but the idea seemed kind of fun, so she waved to Lisbeth, Silica, and Leafa as they came out of the teleport gate.

"Hey! Come quick!"

"What? What's up?" asked Lisbeth as the trio came over, curious.

Asuna beamed and shouted, "Listen, Kirito's about to...!"

(The End)

Rainbow Bridge

§ Alfheim
July 2025

1

On the far side of the violet sky, a castle floated, shining red.

Two months had passed since New Aincrad was added to the game, but looking up at it from sea level still filled me with a very strange sensation. It was hard to believe the tiny structure up in the sky was the exact same size as the floating world I had once lived in.

Of course, if I spread my wings and rose up toward New Aincrad, it would eventually become so huge that it filled my entire field of view. I could fly through the outer edge of the first floor and be in a vast region full of mountains and lakes of its own. Walking from end to end would take the same amount of time as in Aincrad.

But even knowing that, I couldn't help but wonder.

About being trapped there for two years. About wandering the trackless wilderness, fighting deadly monsters, and meeting and parting with countless people. About fighting Heathcliff on the seventy-fifth floor in a duel, ending the deadly game. And wondering if any of it was actually real.

Or maybe…

It was landing in Alfheim in search of the sleeping Asuna, going on a brief but head-spinning journey, and freeing her from the malice that caged her. Then joining with old and new friends in a peaceful and enjoyable life between the real and virtual worlds. Was *that* part actually real?

I stared at the floating structure lit by the setting sun, my mind trapped in this cycle of questions—when there was a deafening blast like a horn, rising up from the ground all around. The chalky-gray surface under my avatar's feet trembled and shook. I raised my arms on instinct and grabbed Asuna's hand on the right and Klein's on the left.

"Nwah! Wh-what is this?!" Lisbeth yelped.

"It's not gonna dump us right here, is it?!" Klein screeched.

"If so, we can just fly away," Agil pointed out calmly.

A small hole in the ground ahead of us grew, then erupted with a tremendous geyser of water.

"Kwirrrr!" "Hwaaaaaagh?!"

That came from the little dragon Pina, who had been located directly above the hole, and Yui the pixie, who was straddling Pina's back. The water lifted them over fifteen feet higher into the air, but Pina spread its wings for balance and hovered at the peak of the jet. Yui's scream of terror two seconds ago turned immediately to delighted laughter.

I held up my arm to block the shower of droplets and turned to confer with Asuna, breaking into a grin.

"...I mean, of course it'll blow exhaust."

She nodded and replied, "It's a whale—it's what they do."

Yes: Asuna, Leafa, Silica, Lisbeth, Agil, Klein, and I were in a seven-player party accompanied by Yui and Pina, standing on the back of a massive white whale that was so big, it would send any Deviant God stampeding away in terror.

The group stood around, nodding sagely, as the blowhole blast died out. Yui descended from the air above and moved to Asuna's left shoulder.

"The whales of the real world don't actually shoot seawater out of their blowholes, however. It's just when they surface and exhale that they blow the nearby water up with it!"

"Ooh!" all seven humans exclaimed in unison.

Always happy to show off her impressive ability to memorize facts, Yui placed her hands on her hips with adorable pride.

I looked up at the castle of steel hovering in the evening sky again. New Aincrad flew in laps around Alfheim at a tremendous speed, so it was even smaller now than it was a moment ago. I stared closer at a spot about a fifth of the way from the bottom—around the twenty-second floor.

Only the first ten floors were open at this point, but eventually, we would be able to reach the twentieth floor and beyond. Only when I saw that log cabin deep in the snowy woods would I feel certain that Aincrad had vanished into the memories of the past. Only then would we be back in a world where a game was meant to be played for fun.

The white whale took us from the island of Thule off the southwest of Alfheim to the beach in sylph territory, then beckoned us to step off with a call like a massive tuba. The party jumped off its back onto the white sand under the creature's gentle eye, after which it turned back around and swam into the red of the setting sun, accompanied by its dolphin friends.

"Mr. Whaaaale! Thank you so muuuuch! Let us ride on your back again somedaaaay!" Yui called out. The white whale responded with another majestic spout of air, then began to submerge until it was underwater and out of sight. Only then did Yui stop waving her tiny hand.

I grinned at the sorrowful expression on her face. "We'll see it again. It seemed like that quest had more story left to tell."

"Yeah! That's just it, Kiri!" bellowed Klein, completely ruining the lingering emotion of our parting. He rubbed his bristled chin and continued grumpily, "What the hell was with that quest? The mermaid princess was an old man, and the old man was a giant octopus, and the giant octopus was some king of the abyss from the something-or-other gods...I have no idea what any of that meant."

"First of all, the mermaid princess was just your own fever dream," I shot back. But I couldn't really solve his problem; a glance at the rest of our party told the tale—Asuna, the demon of quest-solving; Leafa, an eager student of Norse mythology; Agil, the brainy tank; and even Lisbeth and Silica—all of them had their arms crossed as they mulled things over.

It was Friday, July 25th, 2025.

We'd decided to tackle a quest called Pillager of the Deep, which was said to involve gigantic aquatic monsters, since Yui mentioned she wanted to see a whale.

At first, it came across as a typical kind of fetch quest, when an old NPC asked us to go into a dungeon and search for an item. But in fact, the old man was the one behind the problem and was hoping to get us to pillage the treasure sealed in a temple on the seafloor—another fairly common quest pattern. But from that point on, the story went truly haywire. The old man turned into the massive octopus monster Kraken the Abyss Lord, a monstrosity with seven HP bars that, with the flick of a single tentacle, put us into a near-death state. Just when all seemed lost, a gigantic man named Leviathan the Sea Lord descended from above, and the two shared some complicated dialogue, at which point Kraken withdrew to the depths of the sea. Leviathan seized the pearl (actually a large egg) that we took out of the temple, and we got a musical fanfare and a quest-completed notice. It was hard to know what the point was supposed to be.

Stunned, we realized the rumored aquatic monster was actually just Kraken, which was disappointing. But then the man who called himself king of the sea summoned a white whale that took us back to the beach—so at least we completed our initial goal of showing Yui a whale. It was a successful outing overall, but I couldn't disagree with Klein's dissatisfaction with the whole ordeal.

After mulling it over a bit, I turned to my friends and asked, "Does anyone actually remember exactly what the octopus and the guy talked about?"

In a classic MMORPG, you could just scroll upward on your message window with the mouse to see all the dialogue from the quest, but VRMMOs did not have such a convenient feature.

There was the option of using a crystal to record the dialogue during a story event that seemed like it would be important, but we didn't have the wherewithal to do that at the time.

The other six all tilted their heads and looked upward, searching their memory, but every one of them eventually shook their head.

"Awww, this is what we get for having a party of all meatheads with no mages," I commented with a sigh. Liz made a pitcher's windup motion and hurled an index finger in my direction three times in a row.

"You have! No room! To talk!"

"...I'm sorry, ma'am."

Yui leaped off Asuna's shoulder and landed on my head like Leviathan landing upon the seafloor.

"Very well," she said, resigned. "It's cheating a little bit, but I can re-create the conversation for you!"

The party exclaimed with wonder, and the pixie puffed out her chest with delight. She began to mimic the conversation between the octopus and the man.

Leviathan: "How long has it been, old friend? You can't kick the habit of your schemes, can you?"
Kraken: "And how long will you beg for the mercies of the Aesir? You do a disservice to the name of the king of the sea."
Leviathan: "I am satisfied with being king. This is my garden. And you would knowingly come into my realm to do battle, King of the Abyss?"
Kraken: "...I shall withdraw for now. But I will not give up, my friend. Not until the child's power is mine, and I can have my revenge on those meddling gods..."
Leviathan: "That egg belongs to the one who will one day rule all the seas and skies. You must return it so that I may transfer it to a new chamber."

"...The end!"

Yui finished the conversation to a round of applause from the humans and a flutter of Pina's wings from where it rested atop Silica's head.

"Thanks, Yui," I said to my talented daughter, then proceeded to verbalize my thoughts aloud. "Hmm...the two things that stick out to me are the words *Aesir* and *child*. I feel like I've heard these together before..."

"Ooh!" clamored Leafa the magic fighter sylph, raising her hand. She had the deepest appreciation for mythology and legends, and she stepped forward to demonstrate it.

"The Aesir are a pantheon of gods that show up in Norse mythology! You've all heard of Odin the almighty, Thor the god of thunder, and the trickster Loki, right?"

"Yeah, sure, of course," the rest of us said, bobbing our heads.

Leafa continued, "And as for the child part..."

"Uh-huh?"

"I have no idea!"

We all made a slapstick slipping motion and flopped on our faces.

The next one to speak was Silica, the cait sith beast-tamer. "Ummm, so the old Kraken man doesn't like the Aesir, but he can't beat them right now, so he wants the child's power to be stronger...right?"

"If that giant octopus's insane power wasn't enough to do it, how tough do those gods have to be...?" Lisbeth the leprechaun wondered, bouncing her pink hair in a way that showed off its metallic sheen.

"Well, they *are* gods," Asuna the undine noted.

Next, Klein the salamander interjected haughtily, "That's right! You young'uns probably don't know this, but Odin's the toughest of them all! When you summon him, he goes *zwam!* and slices all the monsters in two..."

"Uh, you're talking about another game, not the actual myth," snapped Agil the gnome, eliciting laughs from everyone, including Yui.

I snorted, too, because I recognized what Klein was referring to, but I was still working on why that conversation had seemed so strange to me.

The answer came swiftly. Kraken and Leviathan were just NPCs in the middle of the quest, even if they were both boss-type monsters. Their conversation would have been written by the scenario writers from Ymir, the company running *ALO* now.

Yet all of us were acting as through the two were real beings with minds of their own.

That was probably because their dialogue was very human. When Kraken ruefully claimed, "I will not give up," it really made you think, *Man, I bet that octo's been through a lot...*

Or could it be that Kraken and Leviathan...weren't actually simple NPCs?

In the very early days of Aincrad, Asuna and I met a dark elf knight and went on adventures with her. Her name was Kizmel, and she was an NPC, but she wasn't anything like the usual mobile objects that repeated programmed phrases over and over. She had the ability to hold natural conversations with us...something almost like a will and mind of her own.

ALO operated on almost an identical architecture as *SAO*. Meaning that simply in terms of the Cardinal System's capabilities, there was the possibility that high-functioning AI NPCs like Kizmel could exist here, too.

But in that case...did that mean that Kraken was both a quest NPC and something more than just a pawn being operated along the quest's script? Was it the giant octopus's true innate will that drove it to desire the child's power to lead a rebellion against the Aesir...?

"...Nah. No way," I muttered, realizing that my thoughts were leading into the realm of the absurd. Meanwhile, Klein was getting revved up explaining Odin and Bahamut from the good old days to the others, when he suddenly erupted into a squawk.

"Aaaah! Crap! I forgot I paid to have a pizza delivered at ten!"

"Uh-oh, that's in three minutes. It'll take you a good ten minutes to fly back to Swilvane from here," Agil pointed out.

Klein put his hands to the sides of his head and arched his back in dismay. "My seafood pizza and beeeeer!"

I felt like I'd heard him say this long ago, I noted fondly. I strode up to the katana wielder and patted the sleeve of his samurai-style armor. "We'll watch you until your body vanishes. Just log out here. Make sure to pick it up at the door this time."

He blinked in surprise, then realized what I was referring to and chuckled.

"Good point. Well, I'll take up your offer and log off for today."

"Say hi to the shrimp and crab and squid and octopus on your pizza for me," said Liz.

Klein blanched, then opened his menu. "Well, my friends, so long!"

He hit the LOG OUT button, and the salamander avatar automatically sank down to one knee and closed its eyes.

In *ALO*, logging out of the game outside town left your avatar in place for several minutes afterward; it was a measure to discourage escaping a PvP battle by simply logging out. Your avatar could be targeted by monsters, of course, so there was a high possibility that doing so would mean the next time you logged in, you would be in Remain Light (dead) form.

So when logging out in a dangerous area, the common method was to do it with friends who could guard your body until the avatar eventually faded out when it reached the time limit. Fortunately, this beach didn't seem too dangerous, so I took my eyes off Klein's body to make a suggestion to the group.

"If anyone else wants to log out here, go ahead. I'll be the last one waiting around."

Asuna was the first to raise her hand, looking sheepish. "Um...I think...I'll go, too..."

I'd not yet had an audience with her, but from what I'd been told, Asuna's mother was very strict on time and other matters. I nodded and said, "Sure thing. Thanks for coming today."

"Yeah. Thanks to everybody else, too. It was fun. Take care!" she said and quickly transitioned to the log-out pose, too. Next,

Agil said he needed to prep for the café, Liz mentioned a TV show she wanted to catch, and Silica had homework to finish. They left the fairy realm all in a batch.

When Silica went into the waiting position, Pina began swiveling its head around, as though standing guard to protect her avatar. It was a very touching detail, I thought, stretching.

Then I met the gaze of Leafa, who was stretching in the exact same pose.

We both made the same awkward smile, and I looked toward the horizon to the west.

The sun was now completely gone, leaving only a deep crimson along the land. Yui went from sitting on my head to climbing down my shoulder and into my shirt pocket, where she yawned adorably.

"...That whale was really, really big, wasn't it, Papa?" the pixie said sleepily. I rubbed her head with my fingertip.

"Yup. We'll have to get another ride someday."

"Yeah..."

Yui closed her eyes, and within moments, she was sleeping peacefully.

She was an AI independent of the *ALO* game's system, so she didn't need to sleep like a person, but when she received a great amount of information input or didn't have something urgent to process immediately, she would often go into a visible sleep mode in order to tidy up her memory. In her form of dreams, she was probably reliving today's adventure already.

A little while later, Klein's avatar turned into little motes of light that dispersed and vanished, followed by Asuna, then Agil, Liz, and Silica.

I turned to Leafa and extended my hand toward her without thinking. "C'mon, Sugu—let's just pop back over to Swilvane."

My sister pursed her lips and pouted. "You know, we're not underwater now, so I can fly perfectly fine without needing to hold your hand."

"Oh...r-right. Sorry, uh, I wasn't thinking," I said, pulling my hand back, but the golden-haired magic warrior grabbed it anyway.

"But since I'm better than you in the sky, I can be the one to do the pulling!"

"…Th-thanks."

We spread our wings and took off from the beach, with purple color flooding over the surroundings.

I glanced to the northeast, where the stars were already beginning to twinkle behind the massive silhouette of the World Tree. But closer than that was a crowd of green lights, shining like jewels. It was the familiar capital of the sylph territory, Swilvane.

After I checked to ensure Yui was tucked safely in my pocket, I joined Leafa in flight, gliding on the sea breeze toward our destination.

2

"……Ho-hai-hee," I murmured interestedly in the middle of chomping on thick, chewy udon noodles.

Across the dining table, Suguha glanced at me.

"It's rude to talk with your mouth full, Big Brother."

True, eating with my chopsticks in one hand and a tablet in the other was not exactly the proper etiquette for mealtime. Nevertheless, I swallowed the mouthful I was chewing and stated with great authority, "Obviously, it's okay to eat udon while multitasking."

"…Then what about curry udon?"

"Nope."

"…And *kitsune* udon with fried tofu?"

"Okay."

"…What about *nabeyaki* udon served in a hot pot?"

"Nope."

"I have no idea where your standards lie." Suguha sighed. She took a bite from her chilled udon soup (topped with seasoned egg, steamed chicken, boiled shrimp, okra, mekabu seaweed, perilla leaf, and chopped nori) and slurped the noodles.

We'd logged out of *ALO* about fifteen minutes earlier. Our mother wasn't home yet, for the usual reasons, so we were having a late dinner. It felt like we were getting too accustomed to

this kind of meal, because it was quick to make and clean up afterward.

I was making a mental note to have a proper three-item meal tomorrow when her voice drifted over the table again.

"So what do you see, then?"

It took me a second to recognize that she was referring to my "Ho-hai-hee" statement.

"...I'm amazed you could detect that I was saying 'Oh, I see'... Er, sorry. I meant, I was talking about the Aesir."

"Oh, so you were looking that up already."

"I only just read a brief synopsis of the concept," I said, handing Suguha the tablet, which was displaying the contents of an online encyclopedia. While she glanced at it, I debated whether to split open my egg to let the yolk mix with the udon, or to just pop it into my mouth. Suguha snorted boldly.

"...What?"

"Come on, Big Brother. You can't look at this and think you've understood anything. This is the most surface-level explanation."

"Oh...it is?"

"Yes. If you really want to know more, you have to start with Odin's father, the giant Borr, and *his* father, the original god, Búri...See, in Norse mythology, the history of the world starts with a huge tear in the fabric of existence called Ginnungagap—"

"S-stop, hold on," I interrupted. "We can go over the origin of the world some other time. Eat up quick before your noodles get cold."

Suguha looked perturbed but obliged, placing the tablet down and picking up her chopsticks again. She used them to cut the boiled egg in half, sending the yolk into the noodle broth. Its creamy yellow shine was so enticing that I did the same and slurped some up with the noodles.

I felt bad about interrupting her chance to lecture, but I didn't need any knowledge that detailed at the moment. The only thing I was curious about was the possibility of a continuation of the Pillager of the Deep quest, not a hypothetical land of the Aesir that might exist in *ALO*.

Following Kraken's deceitful instructions, we pulled the Holy Child's Egg out of the underwater temple; Leviathan took it from us and said he would transfer it to a "new chamber." But I doubted that was the happy conclusion to that story line. I had no idea what the child was—and since it was hatching from an egg, it couldn't be human—plus Kraken didn't seem to have given up yet. And on top of that, I wanted another shot at fighting that giant octopus.

Maybe there was a bit of personal sentiment mixed in there. But to me, this was clearly meant to be the intro to an entire questline rather than a single quest.

In an ordinary questline, finishing one quest would automatically begin the next, along with a quest marker pointing the way forward. But on rare occasions, it was left to the player to follow the information provided by the first quest and go to some place or perform some action to reveal the next step.

If this questline was one of the latter type, there should be some hint as to what to do within the conversation between Kraken and Leviathan…but…

"…Brother. Big Brother!"

I suddenly realized that Suguha had been calling my name, and I came to my senses with a start.

"Uh, wh-what?"

"I'm sure you haven't forgotten that tomorrow morning is the start of our big dojo cleaning. We need to get to bed early tonight so we're up bright and early."

I had, of course, completely forgotten. But I didn't let that show.

"Got it, got it. I'll be asleep by one…or two at the latest."

She gave me a piercing, skeptical look, but I evaded it by taking my empty dish to the kitchen.

I lay down on my bed and glanced up my headboard to view my alarm clock upside down.

It was eleven thirty. Back in the Aincrad days, this was right in the middle of the nighttime active hour, when I would take my sword to lucrative grinding areas in search of good loot.

Of course, leveling-up your character (not that *ALO* actually had levels, technically speaking) was essential. Especially for me, because I had started over fresh after *SAO*; there was a period where I was engaging in some hard grinding in the hopes of catching up with Asuna and the others.

But of course, I would never again have the most powerful motivation of all—the prickling sense of danger, of needing to level-up to increase my chances of survival. And this, obviously, was a good thing. I did not desire to go back to that deadly world.

Still, perhaps there was a part of me that still wanted *something*. Something like a game, but not…Something that would bring a breathtaking reality to the little garden of the virtual world.

The moment that Kraken's single attack put us on the brink of death, only to give way to Leviathan's trident, felt like that *something* to me. Despite being a story event in accordance with the quest, it also seemed like it might be a completely spontaneous happening, something no human hand had written…

"…I mean, I just think that would be cool; that's all," I murmured to hide my embarrassment as I turned out the lights, preparing for an early bedtime before our big cleaning day.

Then, ten seconds later, I reached up and felt around until my hand found the AmuSphere. I placed it on my head and quietly gave the vocal command.

"Link Start."

3

As long as I get to bed by two o'clock, that's still fairly early, I told myself as I touched down in Alfheim.

It was equally dark there at this hour. However, to dedicated online gamers, these were the golden hours, and Swilvane, capital of the fairy territory, was packed. Sylphs were the majority of them, of course, but there were also other fairy races in greater numbers than before.

The view through the window of the room I rented in the inn to safely log out made it clear that the cait siths were the most numerous of the other fairy races today. That made sense, as they were in an alliance with the sylphs. The next most common group in attendance were pookas and imps, which had adjacent territory. The sylph land also adjoined the salamander territory, but they were still officially at war, so there was no red hair to be seen here.

My race, the spriggans, were not hostile to the sylphs, but our territory was on the opposite side of the world, and it was one of the least popular races on top of that. So there were no other spriggans to be seen on the streets, like the salamanders.

I decided it was best to move about without drawing too much attention, so I pulled a hooded cape out of my inventory and put it on. Then I cast the illusionary magic spell Moonshade Lurk and snuck out of the inn.

Moonshade Lurk was a spell that made it harder for others to see you when you were in any shade cast by the light of the moon, meaning it had no effect in a dungeon, where there was no moonlight. It was only a slight benefit, but that was the best I could do with magic. Fortunately, the moon was dazzling tonight, and Swilvane was rife with cramped alleyways, so I could move fairly quickly without being exposed.

After a few minutes, I reached the center of town and came to a stop in the shade.

Right ahead, there was a rotary over a hundred yards across, with the sylph lord's manor in the center—the most beautiful building in all of Swilvane. The three-story structure was surrounded by a deep moat, with bridges only on the north and south sides that connected to the road around it. The entire rotary was wide open, with no shade for me to hide in.

At the foot of each bridge stood a pair of powerful-looking NPC guardians with tall halberds at the ready. Only the lord or lady, and players on the manor's registry, could pass by them.

Leafa was registered, as far as I knew, but the list had no exceptions, even for party members of those who had access. I had wings, so you might think I could just fly high over the guardians' field of view, but things weren't that easy. The entire manor grounds were under a special barrier that nullified all the magical power of outsiders, including flight.

I wasn't going in there to steal anything, so the proper etiquette would be to flag down a staff member going in and ask for permission to enter, but I really didn't want any rumors left behind about tonight's visit.

"…!"

In that instant, I sensed that the moment I was waiting for had arrived, and I crouched low.

A black shadow began to cross the surface of the radiant moon from the right. It was a nightly occurrence in Alfheim—an artificial lunar eclipse. New Aincrad, the flying castle, was covering the moon for less than a minute. And of that time, it was only a complete eclipse for less than five seconds.

The pale disc began to wane, until finally all the light was gone—Swilvane was entirely within the shadow of New Aincrad. I bolted out of the alleyway and into the open.

There wasn't much foot traffic here, since there were few shops to visit, but that didn't mean it was empty. The cait siths shouldn't be able to see me because of the spell's effect, but I could only pray that their keen ears wouldn't pick up my footsteps as I zipped across the rotary. There was a cast-iron fence separating the road from the moat, and right in between the two bridges, I got a foot on top of it and jumped for all I was worth.

As soon as I was over the dark surface of the water, I could no longer use my wings or any magic. Rumor said that there were nasty aquatic monsters lurking in the moat, which was nearly thirty feet across, and if they caught you, they would drag you down to the bottom, where you would die and turn into a Remain Light. But the light would actually appear just before the moat, so anyone could see that someone had attempted to sneak past.

Even for a nimble spriggan, crossing thirty feet in a single jump without flight was simply impossible. But in midair, I pulled my sword off my back and reached forward as far as I could during the fall. The end of it just barely managed to catch on the stone blocks on the far side.

If it were ordinary stone found anywhere else, a sword crafted by a master blacksmith like Lisbeth would just cut right through it, but the structures in town were indestructible. I used that to my advantage, pushing down on the block with the tip of the sword and using it for leverage to hurtle myself upward.

The following hop was enough for my left hand to reach the edge. I sheathed my blade and scrambled up. There was a brief, quiet ringing when I pressed on the stone with the sword tip, but fortunately, the guardians at the bridges did not react.

Crouching low again, I hurried behind the bushes of the garden before the brief eclipse was over.

"......Whew." I exhaled in relief and looked upward at the manor before me. My destination was in the center of the top floor, if I recalled correctly. I didn't know if the person I wanted to meet was there, but if they weren't, I'd just have to wait around anyway.

There would be no protection from my spell here. I placed my weapon into my virtual inventory, prayed there wouldn't be any guardians indoors, and began to circle the building in search of the front entrance.

Five minutes later, I had finally made my way to the stately double doors on the third floor of the lady's manor. I swiveled to each side to make sure it was safe.

There were no figures to be seen in the spacious hallway. The majority of the administrative players were having a chat in the great hall on the second floor, which meant I was able to get up to the top without being seen or scolded. But if the person I was looking for was on the second floor, it would all be for nothing. Praying that my good fortune would last, I pulled back my hood and knocked on the doors.

After a moment, a familiar voice said, "Come in." I exhaled in relief, pulled the silver handle, and slipped inside through the smallest possible crack in the doors.

I shut the doors behind me right as the woman operating the territorial master's access window looked up across the desk.

Sakuya, lady of the sylphs, wore an elegant kimono-style dress. When she recognized me, her shapely eyebrows wrinkled, she inclined her head in confusion, and lastly, she pointed a finger in my direction.

"May I ask something, just to be certain?"

"Anything you want."

"You haven't been hired by salamanders to come here and take me out...have you, Kirito?"

"Uh…is that even possible? As a spriggan, can I even pass the bonus from defeating a fairy lord to a salamander?"

"It is, if you are officially hired as a mercenary. Of course, the guardians in the town would react as though you were a salamander, so you would not get more than a hundred yards inside without a pass medallion."

"Ahhh…Hrmm, sorry, didn't mean to sound interested. The answer is no, of course," I said, holding up my hands in a show of peace. "The truth is, there's something I was hoping you could tell me, Sakuya."

"…And that's why you broke into my house?"

"Well, yes…I mean, I'm not on your friends list, so I can't send you a direct message…and I didn't want anyone else to hear this…," I explained, keenly aware that I was starting to sound like a girl in a rom-com.

The sylph lady shook her head and said, "It is no matter…but I am the master of this territory. As you belong to a different fairy race, I am limited in what I can tell you—even if you did save my life."

"Oh, that won't be a problem. I'm not asking for any sylph military secrets. Plus, I'm prepared to offer you information in return, of course."

"You are? What will you tell me?"

"How to sneak into the sylph manor and how to prevent that from happening."

Sakuya blinked with surprise, then burst into laughter. I could only pray the sound didn't carry all the way downstairs.

She poured me a glass of expensive-looking wine that I sipped very carefully. Step by step, I ran through the reason for my unannounced visit.

Sakuya listened in silence until I was finished, then nodded.

"I performed the Pillager of the Deep quest about ten days ago, myself."

"You…you did? On your own?"

"I enjoy the occasional dungeon dive, too, you know. Plus,

you've seen me taking part in a number of floor-boss raids in New Aincrad."

"Ah, good point."

"But…"

The proactive sylph master downed the rest of her wine and paused to consider.

"When I and some of my cabinet members did the quest, there was no Kraken or Leviathan."

"What?"

"We found the pearl, or egg, or what have you, in the temple and handed it back to the NPC. He thanked us, and that was the end of the quest. Then he summoned a giant squid that grabbed us with its tentacles and pulled us back to the beach. It was…not the most enjoyable experience."

"A…giant squid? I wish I could have seen that…Er, I mean, I suppose that means there's a branch depending on whether or not you hand over the pearl…"

"It would seem so. But who would refuse to hand over the quest item?" she said with a smirk. I smiled back uncomfortably.

"Well, I was *going* to give it back to him…but Asuna took it away from me before I could."

"Ha-ha. I would never doubt her sixth sense," she said, pouring herself another glass of wine. "So I understand now that the quest has a branching path. And…what is it you're hoping to learn from me?"

"Well…I was wondering if you had any ideas about the 'new chamber' Leviathan mentioned…For example, were there any other buildings on the seafloor aside from the temple that seemed likely…?"

"Hmm…Not off the top of my head…"

The sylph leader thought for a bit, then opened her special menu and displayed a map across the entire surface of her desk. It was a map of all of Alfheim, several times more detailed than any that we common players could produce.

"This is a kind of state secret, I suppose, but I'm willing to show you. This map contains discovered quest locations, buildings and headstones with a particular history, and unique spots like shortcuts—everything. If we search this for 'new chamber,' then perhaps..."

Her fingers ran across the map surface, and a window with search results opened up. There were zero hits.

"Then 'holy child'...Nothing. 'Kraken'...'Leviathan'...still nothing."

"What about 'egg'?"

"That might be too vague to work...There, you see? Over a hundred hits. There are dozens of quests about finding eggs or protecting them or cooking them."

"Oh...right...Hrmm..."

I stared at the flat image of the fairy world and replayed the dialogue between the king of the sea and the king of the abyss in my mind.

How long has it been, old friend? And how long will you beg for the mercies of the Aesir? ...Not until the child's power is mine... The one who will one day rule all the seas and skies......

All the seas and skies.

"Um...Sakuya?"

"What?"

"Does that map have three-dimensional data on the unique points of interest?"

"Of course."

"Could you tell me the lowest of those points on the map? Aside from Jotunheim, I mean."

Sakuya quickly sorted the information. "The lowest coordinates are at negative three hundred and twenty-one feet. The quest name is...Pillager of the Deep."

Her eyes glittered. I bobbed my head in return and said, "Next, tell me the point that is highest. Aside from New Aincrad, I mean."

"...I don't need to search for that one."

"Huh...?"

"The answer is obvious. The mystery located at the highest point of Alfheim...?"

The beautiful leader of the sylphs jabbed a thumb at the large window behind her and grinned.

"That would be the top of the World Tree, of course."

4

Three months earlier: April 2025.

The new company running *ALfheim Online*, Ymir, unveiled a massive update to the game.

It implemented the flying castle, New Aincrad; consolidated old *SAO* accounts; and removed the limit on flying time.

Previously, the fairies had been unable to reach even the lowest branch of the World Tree on their own power, but now you could fly all the way up to New Aincrad, which hovered far, far above the ground. The first place the newly powered fairies went was not to the new flying castle, however, but the tallest place in Alfheim itself—the top of the World Tree.

But they did not reach the top of the tree, nor even see it.

The top of the World Tree was shrouded in massive cumulonimbus clouds. The ferocious gale-force winds and lightning bolts that crackled around them rebuffed any player's attempt to pass through. The result was the same if you tried to rise along the trunk. Within seconds of entering the mass of clouds, you would either die from lightning shock or get physically hurled out into the open air by the winds.

The idea had probably come from a classic animated film, but among the players, it was known as the Lightning Dragon's

Nest, and even now, there was no end of foolhardy adventurers attempting to breach the supercell…

"…Hey, Kirito," said Asuna, who stood at my side, staring up at the sky. "How many times have you died trying to fly into those clouds?"

"Um…no more than ten…I think…?"

"And who had to use magic to recover your Remain Light each and every time? Remind me again."

"You, Asuna…"

"And who helped you recover from the experience penalties each and every time?"

"You, Asuna…"

"Well, I'm glad you remember," she said, beaming. I awkwardly returned the smile.

"O-of course I do. And I've thanked you for that more times than there are total suckers on the eight tentacles of the Kraken."

"That's…not the nicest analogy…," she muttered, looking up to the sky again.

It was two o'clock on Saturday, July 26th.

There were no other players on the observation deck built at the southern tip of Yggdrasil City, the elevated city built into the center of the World Tree. In the past, countless people had challenged the storm from here, but now the supercell surrounding the peak of the tree was considered an impassable barrier, much like the dome at the base of the tree guarded by its NPC knights had been in the early days of *ALO*.

That dome was created by Nobuyuki Sugou, the previous manager of *ALO*. He'd set the difficulty to an impossible level in order to hide his personal usage of server resources and, more important, his illegal experiments. It was impossible to imagine Ymir, the new management company, having people held prisoner at the top of the tree, however.

If we couldn't get through the clouds, then, it was because we hadn't fulfilled some condition. Meaning if we cleared whatever hurdle that was, there might be a way through the howling, crackling storm...

"Thanks for waiting!" called an energetic voice from below as a green blur zipped past the handrail of the observation deck.

The figure that did a flip overhead and landed in front of us was a speed-demon sylph warrior. After logging out in Swilvane last night, she must have flown at top speed to get to Yggdrasil City.

Leafa glanced at the time readout and groaned, "I couldn't break forty minutes!" The distance between the two cities was over forty miles, so she'd need to maintain a solid sixty miles an hour to record a time that short.

"Wow, that's really impressive, Leafa. It took me and Kirito nearly an hour," Asuna remarked, genuinely impressed.

My boorish, unsophisticated sister puffed out her chest with pride and said, "There's a trick to it. The wind direction changes with altitude and time, so you have to constantly fine-tune your facing to keep following the proper tailwind."

"So you've totally memorized how the wind blows. That's amazing...Kirito fell asleep while he was flying and ended up crashing through a flock of Cyrus Medusas."

Leafa shot me a nasty look. "He logged in by himself late last night so he could do something in Swilvane. Apparently, this idea to tackle the Lightning Dragon's Nest again came from some information he picked up on, but he won't tell me anything more than that."

Even Asuna's expression grew suspicious at that point, so I coughed unconvincingly to hide my embarrassment. Suguha had learned about my late-night dive during our big cleaning of the dojo this morning, due to all my yawning. Of course, I didn't tell her anything about what I was actually doing—infiltrating Lady Sakuya's manor—but it felt like the secret was going to get out sooner or later.

Still, it was worth the risk. If I hadn't met with Sakuya and seen that secret world map, I would never have gotten the hint that the "new chamber" might be on the top of the World Tree.

And once I was aware of it, I couldn't possibly sit still. After the cleaning was done, I reached out to the usual gang—of course, it was the middle of the day, so Agil and Klein couldn't join in—and called for a meetup at this observation deck.

I was gazing at the passing clouds for no particular reason, hoping Liz and Silica would show up soon, when a tiny spirit of salvation popped out of my shirt pocket. She stretched her tiny arms, yawned adorably, and flitted upward with a sound like bells ringing, landing on Asuna's shoulder with a smile.

"Papa, Mama, Leafa, good morning! I think I slept in a little," said our daughter, who giggled to herself cutely. The women immediately forgot about their criticisms and beamed back at her.

We were reminiscing about the whale from yesterday when Lisbeth and Silica arrived from the southwest. With all members present, we were ready to hold our meeting.

"...Well, I don't really have a very fancy plan. Basically, I'm going to charge into the Lightning Dragon's Nest, so if I die, bring me back with magic, please..."

The Remain Light left behind after a player's death generally had to be physically grabbed by party members to be moved, but a few high-level magic spells and expensive consumable items could retrieve a Remain Light from a distance. Since trying a direct retrieval of a Remain Light inside the Lightning Dragon's Nest was likely to lead to additional victims, I would need to be pulled out of the clouds by magic.

Of course, after a certain amount of time, I would automatically revive at my save point, but that would come with a much harsher experience penalty than if someone else revived me. I was prepared to die once or twice, but the less I lost, the better.

When the girls heard my plan, they looked at one another, and then Lisbeth spoke for the group.

"So, um, just to make sure I have this right...You want to go to the top of the World Tree because you think that giant pearl, or Holy Child's Egg, will be there?"

"Yes," I confirmed.

Silica's triangular ears twitched as she asked, "But, Kirito, assuming you find the egg, what will you actually do with it? You aren't going to steal it, are you?"

"Y-yes," I said again, and I explained, "The thing about the egg is…I have a feeling we can get a continuation to the Pillager of the Deep quest from yesterday. I really don't think it was meant to be a one-off quest…"

Asuna's light-blue hair swayed as she considered the idea. "Maybe that's true…but when there's additional quests, aren't they usually found in the same area? On a straight line, there's over sixty miles between the underwater temple and the top of the World Tree. Even if the phrase 'all the seas and skies' is the hint, it seems like an extreme leap."

It was a very keen observation from the woman who was known as the quest-finishing demon back in the Aincrad days. Out of all the many points of interest in Alfheim, the deepest was located in the underwater temple and the highest was in the Lightning Dragon's Nest. But I couldn't bring that up here, because it was a secret of the sylph government, and I shouldn't technically know that.

If I wanted to use that as evidence to convince her, I'd have to reveal that I snuck into Lady Sakuya's manor last night…

"You know……"

That was Leafa, who was leaning against the observation deck handrail. She looked around at each of us, then started again.

"You know, I had a dream last night. A dream of a rainbow bridge coming down from somewhere very high in the sky. And I went up and up that bridge until I came to a *huge* and very beautiful gate… But before I could get there, I woke up," she said, smiling bashfully, and looked out at the blue sky. "I'm sure I had that dream because we were talking about the Aesir on the beach last night. See, in the mythology, the Aesir live in a land called Asgard…"

"Is that a land in the same sense of Alfheim and Jotunheim being lands?" I asked. Leafa nodded.

"Yes. In Norse mythology, there are nine lands in all. There's Vanaheim, where the Vanir live; Niflheim, the land of ice; and so on...Asgard is located all the way beyond the sky, and there's a rainbow bridge leading from it down to the ground. And the rainbow's name is Bifrost..."

The sylph warrior looked up again, tilting her golden ponytail downward.

"Ever since the first time I saw the Lightning Dragon's Nest... I've had this idea in my head. What if there's a rainbow bridge inside those clouds that leads to Asgard...?"

"Wow...that's so romantic!" squealed Silica, her eyes sparkling. The exclamation caused Pina to stir atop her head. "If that's true, I want to see that for myself...I mean, I want to cross it!"

Liz, Asuna, and Yui all smiled and nodded along. I considered this for myself.

Based on the conversation between Kraken and Leviathan, the Aesir could quite possibly exist somewhere in *ALO* as NPCs. In that case, their home of Asgard existed, too...But simply seen in terms of MMO construction, it was baffling to imagine an entire new region existing in the game without any announcements or hints whatsoever.

In fact, when the underground realm of Jotunheim opened, there were huge announcements all over the official site and other spots for gaming news, and they held a commemorative in-game event. If they were spending all the money and time to create a new game zone, why would they make the gate impossible to reach and ensure that no one could get there?

But on the other hand, there was no point to listing all the reasons it couldn't be true. All I had to do was get through those clouds to find out if there was a rainbow bridge inside, a Holy Child's Egg...or perhaps both.

"Then I'll go and find out what—"

"In that case, I'm going, too!" chirped Leafa, raising her hand. Then the other girls joined in, even Yui.

"At this point, we might as well all go as a group!"

"Yeah, let's go!" cheered the girls, much to my alarm.

"W-wait, wait. If we all get wiped out, who's going to get our Remain Lights?"

"Look, I want to be on the front line rather than playing backup all the time," Asuna said slightly petulantly. But as someone who relied on her to get me out of trouble all the time, I couldn't argue with her wishes.

She smiled again and pointed out, "If we get wiped out, we can go out and hunt monsters when we return to town. We'll make up for the experience penalty in no time with a group this large."

It was true that summoning them here and telling them to wait around while I exposed myself to danger was hypocritical of me. More important than figuring out the mystery of the quest was making sure everyone had fun engaging in the adventure.

"...You're right. Let's all go together, then!" I agreed.

The four of them, along with Yui and Pina, cheered in unison.

"Yeah!"

After checking over our gear, we left the observation deck and soared through gigantic branches that twisted and craned like the walls of a maze. I stayed at the tip of our V-formation and kept us moving straight upward.

The Alne highlands were clear and sunny today, without a single shred of cloud in the sky. But after a few minutes following the curve of the World Tree, curling white clouds came into view ahead. If I concentrated, I could hear the faint, deep rumble of thunder.

"We're almost there!" I shouted to my companions, lowering my speed. We passed through the layer of haze that acted as a warning zone, and then there was nothing but a huge white block filling our view—the Lightning Dragon's Nest. The sharp tip of the World Tree was surrounded by a block of cumulonimbus clouds, five hundred yards tall and across, that blocked it from sight.

I threw my wings out to come to a stop and hovered in the air.

A supercell storm in the real world could be six miles across and two or three times higher, but seen up close like this, the virtual cloud mass was every bit as terrifying. I'd flown inside many times before, but even now, I felt myself trembling with excitement.

Just on my left, Silica exclaimed, "Ooh, wow! It looks yummy—like whipped cream!"

"You're right," Lisbeth added. "I want to drop that on top of a stack of pancakes, slather it in syrup, and gobble it up."

On my right, Asuna came to a stop and laughed. "Ah-ha-ha-ha! Let's go get some when we're done here, then. I hear there's a really good pancake shop in Ygg City now."

"Really?! I love pancakes!! I'll have a ten-stack!" Leafa finished.

Should I find their confidence and excitement infectious or worrisome? And what happened to going hunting if we got wiped out and had an experience penalty?

But that was only *if* we wiped out. If all went well, we were going to charge through the clouds, find the rainbow bridge that continued the quest, and celebrate with pancakes instead.

Properly motivated again, I proclaimed, "I'll eat a hundred!"

It was time to reveal the strategy to my steadfast companions. "Based on dying in there ten times, I can tell you that dodging the lightning is impossible. Rather than trying to endlessly change directions, slowing us down, we should try to cross through as quickly as possible. There's no visibility when you're in there, so we'll need to make a star to fly straight."

"Got it!" the others chimed. Yui flew into my shirt pocket, and Pina flattened itself against Silica's back like a booster rocket.

The five of us formed a tight circle. Rather than holding hands with Leafa and Lisbeth on my sides, I grabbed Asuna and Silica across from me. The rest of them followed suit so that our ten arms interlocked in a five-sided star pattern. This was a high-level group-flying technique called a star bind. It worked only with a group of five, but it offered much sturdier support than a horizontal line or a circle while still improving speed and stability.

The problem was that flying sideways in this formation meant that at least two of the five would be flying backward, which required a lot of skill, so Leafa and I elected to do it. We moved slowly, maintaining our formation, until we reached the height of the cumulonimbus clouds, and just in case—or just for good luck—we had Asuna cast a spell of increased lightning resistance.

"Okay...I'll count us down. Five, four, three, two, one..."

Lastly, all five of us shouted in unison, """""*Go!!*"""""

Five pairs of wings shone five different colors, and we accelerated as though shot from a giant cannon.

With a thousand feet of lead-in, we reached our maximum speed and burst right into the giant cloud mass. At first, the only thing we could see was white, but it got darker very soon. The density of the air increased against our skin, slowing our speed.

"...Here it comes!" I shouted, and clenched my jaw.

Krakaaang! A piercing explosion rattled my ears as a burly bolt of purple lightning shot through the air just ten feet away from us. Liz and Silica, who were experiencing the Lightning Dragon's Nest for the first time, yelped a little, but our pace stayed firm. We held hands tight and made a beeline across the storm, which was dark as the night.

The next thing to assault us was a lateral gust of wind. Alone, we might have been buffeted head over heels and lost our sense of direction, but with the weight and propulsion of five, we withstood it.

There was another brilliant flash of lightning nearby. Then another. And another.

The path of the lightning bolts seemed random, but I didn't think they actually were. For one thing, there had probably been thousands of attempts in total on this storm, and not a single person had made it through. Every person who invaded these clouds, somewhere between one and ten seconds inside, suffered a direct lightning bolt attack and died instantly. Dodging or defending against them was impossible.

But if my suspicion was correct—then the "new chamber" Leviathan spoke of was somewhere beyond this cloud layer.

We *could* break through this storm. I had faith, if not any evidence. We *had* to be able to seize *something* in this ordained death zone…*something* capable of telling a true story in this artificial world…

Kra-boooooom!!

Yet another barrel of purple lightning—I'd lost count of how many there had been—shot toward us, twirling and zigzagging like a dragon. It just barely grazed us and continued onward. The light left me blinded, and all sound vanished. We were flying so fast that my fear didn't have time to catch up.

Were we still under ten seconds? Or had that milestone already passed? How far would these storm clouds go…?

Just on my right, Leafa shouted loud enough to be heard over the thunder. "There's a huge wind coming from below! Don't fight; let's ride it!"

Below. We were the ones facing backward, so it would be at our backs. No sooner had that registered for me than a tremendous gale buffeted us. We squeezed even harder, desperate to maintain our star formation as the forces of nature tried to tear us apart.

"………*Here!*" Leafa yelled. I buzzed my wings as hard as I could.

We went from horizontal flight to a sudden jump upward. The vibration weakened, but our flying speed reached levels I'd never experienced before. Several lightning bolts were raining down around us. If we freaked out and slowed down, they would certainly strike us.

"*Keep goiiiiiiiing!!*" I bellowed, wrenching my voice from my lungs.

The star formation held firm, as our arms were locked, not just with the two across the way but also with the arms of the other two on my sides. I could feel courage coming from where our skin intersected.

We were a comet with five multicolored trails. Four bolts of lightning struck ahead, behind, and on either side, turning my vision white again. The visual illusion of blindness did not leave so quickly this time, either. Instead, the area got whiter and whiter, even brighter...

And then the sound was gone, too.

The howling of the storm, the flashing of the lightning dragon—everything went distant. With nothing but unbelievable silence around, I opened my narrowed eyes at last.

The first thing that came into view was a vertical white wall. It acted like a screen without definition—the only detail was our shadows, rising along it.

I looked to Asuna and Silica, across from me. They were both wide-eyed. I wondered what they were seeing from their vantage point.

"...I think we're good to undo the formation now," Asuna whispered. I slowed down and carefully let go. With the star undone, Leafa, Liz, and I turned around to see.

There was a vast, spherical space bounded by pure white around us.

It had to be about a thousand feet across. A green pillar ran through the center of the area. The foot of the pillar was submerged in the white wall, but its sharp tip was visible near the roof.

No question. That pillar was...

"The tip...of the World Tree...," Leafa said, her voice raspy.

We had broken through. We were in the Lightning Dragon's Nest, which no other players had reached, inside the eye of the storm that surrounded the top of the World Tree.

"I can't believe it..." Asuna gasped, holding a hand to her mouth as she stared. We locked eyes, then smiled and sucked in a deep breath together to erupt into cheers.

But at that very moment, a pixie leaped out of my shirt pocket and cried, "Papa, something's coming!"

"...!"

The five of us tensed. I drew my sword from over my back, looking around for trouble.

The cloud dome was almost completely silent. There was no hint of the lightning that was rumbling just on the other side of them behind us. All I could hear was the gentle rustling of the tree's leaves in the breeze running under the dome...

No.

There was a tapping sound approaching, but from no direction in particular. It wasn't metallic but something both hard and soft, like a branch striking a thick pane of glass.

"Oh...there!" yelped Lisbeth, pointing up at an angle.

The sun was out of sight, but the uppermost part of the cloud dome was full of brilliance that caused me to squint against it. A small silhouette was approaching from the light. It wasn't a monster. It was a fairy like us, wearing a loose toga...No, wait, a human...?

It was a young, thin man. Despite having no wings on his back, he was creating footsteps in the air, as though walking on some invisible glass staircase. His long blue-silver hair was flared upward at the ends, and he wore a thin circlet around his forehead. I couldn't see a sword or staff on him, but there was an unbelievable intensity about him that sucked the air from my lungs. We backed away.

The young man maintained his pace until he had descended to our level, then came to a stop in the air just fifteen feet away. Though his features had a crystalline beauty, it was the piercing, golden-brown eyes that made the greatest impact.

When he spoke, a cursor appeared over his head.

"Put away your swords, fairies."

It was a voice as pure as polished steel. The name on his cursor was *Hraesvelg the Sky Lord*.

"Hraesvelg...the Sky Lord...," Leafa whispered at my side.

It felt like a name I'd heard somewhere before, but I didn't have time to go dredging up memories. Instead, I threw an elbow into my dazed sister's side.

"Oof…Wh-what was that for?!"

"Put your sword away!" I hissed quietly, slipping my own weapon into the sheath on my back. The girls made sure to remove their weapons, pulling us back from a battle footing.

Identity aside, there was no doubt that Hraesvelg here was of a kind with Leviathan. If we fought, he would prove to have such powerful stats that the wave of a finger could wipe us out.

With my sword put away, I stared over the young man's head again. But the only thing there was a cursor with his name. There was no golden *!* to indicate he was a quest-related NPC.

Was this the wrong place to go to find the second quest in the story line? Then why had Hraesvelg appeared? The sky lord, well over six feet tall, looked down upon us and hummed to himself.

"I see. I wondered how you tiny fairies managed to break through my storm. You had the protection of the king of the sea."

"King of the sea…? Do you mean Leviathan…uh, Your Majesty?" I added hastily. The lord of the sky did not change his expression at my rather forward question but merely nodded.

On the other hand, the giant old man had given us a ride back to land on a whale, but I didn't remember him casting any magic on us. When had we received his protection…? Or was that the evidence that the quest was still ongoing?

"But, fairies," Hraesvelg continued, slightly harder than before, "just because you have gained the acquaintance of the sea lord does not mean you are allowed into the sky chamber. Or are you thieves who consort with the lord of the abyss?"

"No, sir!" "Certainly not!" "No way!" "You're kidding!" "That's not true!" "*Kyurrrr!*"

Fortunately, the sky lord was capable of discerning six different protests at the same time. He nodded and said, "I see. Then you should leave here at once."

"……"

This time, we were all silent.

Hraesvelg had mentioned the "sky chamber." That had to be the "new chamber" Leviathan had mentioned.

It meant the Holy Child's Egg that Kraken was after was safely contained somewhere under this dome. I looked at the trunk of the World Tree and saw a structure on the lower part that looked much like a gate. The interior of the thick trunk had to be fashioned into a dungeon, just like the underwater temple.

A new dungeon! I want to go in there! More specifically, I want to go in and open all the treasure chests! I thought, driven by my baser instincts.

But my sister did not share them. Leafa floated in front and shouted to the sky lord, "Um...excuse me! Before we leave, can you tell us just one thing?"

"What is it, fairy girl?"

"Is there no rainbow bridge here...? There's no Bifrost leading to Asgard?!"

Those golden-brown eyes grew even sharper somehow, like the eyes of a bird of prey. "Why do you want to know that? Do you intend to cross it and seek an audience with the Aesir?"

The tension in the air reminded me of something. The conversational ability of Hraesvelg, the lord of the sky, was advanced far beyond that of a simple chat bot. He, along with Kraken and Leviathan, had to have a more developed AI with a rudimentary facsimile of self-awareness. Something closer to the dark elf Kizmel from Aincrad, or Yui, who was curled up in my pocket right now.

Had Ymir created these characters and inserted them into *ALO*? Or...was this the work of the true god that controlled this virtual world...?

Leafa was silent, too, but for a different reason. She shook her head.

"No, I don't want to meet any gods. I just...want to know. Is this the end of the world...? Or is there more beyond this point?"

It was a rather abstract answer to the NPC's question; how would he interpret it?

The sky lord smirked mysteriously and said, "It is a hope beyond your means, little fairy. I call myself the lord of the sky, and even I have not seen the very limits of the nine worlds."

"...Oh..."

"But I shall tell you one thing. The rainbow bridge of Bifrost does indeed come from Asgard, but it does not end in your land."

"Huh...?!"

All four of the others gasped, too, not just Leafa. The only other land currently accessible in the game was the subterranean realm of Jotunheim. The rainbow couldn't be passing right through the surface and ending at the bottom of the cave.

But the sky lord did not intend to give us any further hints. He just smiled enigmatically and took a step back.

"And now, you ought to return home."

"Huh...? W-we have to pass through that storm again...?" Silica asked, her voice frail.

The lord of the sky looked stern once more. "Did you break through my shield without considering that on your return?"

We all looked guilty, realizing our mistake. Fortunately, he did not summon any lightning bolts in his anger.

"In light of my friendship with the king of the sea, I will send you back outside, just this once. Listen to me, fairies: You must never come back to this place without the proper role."

"Yes, Your Majesty!" we said obediently. It felt like his lip curled just the slightest bit with mirth.

But then his expression turned stern again, and he raised a long-sleeved arm high in the air. I presumed that, like Leviathan, he was calling us our return taxi. What would it be this time—a giant bird? A dragon? A flying saucer...?

But my expectations were utterly shattered.

"Farewell, little ones," Hraesvelg said in a deep, authoritative voice, and he swung his right hand down. The arc of his hand looked like the transparent wing of a bird of prey. But the very next moment, a powerful whirlwind appeared and swallowed us up.

"Aaah! Yah, ah, *aaaaah!*"

Fortunately, I wasn't the only one embarrassing myself. The four girls screamed, too, as the vortex picked us up and spun us around. On instinct, I spread my wings and tried to escape the tornado, but there was no propulsion behind the motion at all.

Soon the sky lord was distant, and the roof of the dome was approaching. Either way, the big storm wasn't happening inside this dome, I thought. But then a small hole opened in its ceiling. Would it take us to a safe passage or back into a zone of instant, crackling death? I couldn't tell from here.

Liz grabbed Silica's hand before she got sucked through the hole. Then Leafa grabbed Liz, and Asuna grabbed Leafa.

"Kirito...!" she cried, stretching toward me. I grabbed her hand next.

Sadly, that was the end of our chain. I didn't have a sixth person to grab for help.

But as my hand scrabbled in empty space for anything it could touch, I felt something.

On pure reflex, I squeezed it tight. Tensing myself against the buffeting wind, I looked back at my hand and saw it was holding a narrow, vertical branch. There were two cute, perky little leaves growing from the end. It was the very, very tip of the World Tree.

"Rrr...rrrgh!"

I clenched the branch with all my strength, fighting against the sky lord's whirlwind. Just above me, Asuna shouted, "Um, Kirito...?!"

"It's all right! I won't...let...go!"

"No, not that...I feel like...you aren't meant to do that—!"

"Huh...?"

I looked up and saw a surprisingly conflicted look on Asuna's face. Behind her, Leafa yelled, "That's right, Big Brother. I don't think you're supposed to grab that branch!"

"Let go, Kirito! His Majesty's going to be angry!" Liz called.

"If it snaps, that's your fault!" Silica warned.

"*Kyuuuu!*" Pina agreed.

"B-but…I was trying to help you guys," I complained weakly.

Then, far below the thin branch I was holding, a shadow leaped out from a part of the World Tree's trunk.

It was not Hraesvelg the Sky Lord. It was much bigger than a human being, with two wings and a long neck and tail. Alfheim was a big place, but even then, this was the most supreme of monsters that you rarely witnessed: a dragon.

The dragon rolled, its numerous scales glittering like sapphires. The creature looked right up at us and roared like a bundle of thunderbolts. It exposed sharp fangs, which were crackling with visible electricity.

"S-see? It's angry, Kirito!" Asuna warbled. I couldn't disagree with that observation.

"F-fine! Fine! I'll let go on the count of three! One, two, thr—"

Craaack!

The branch I was holding snapped with a tremendously satisfying sound.

The thunder dragon, screeching lightning bolts at us, glared with fury smoldering in its blue eyes. But fortunately—if you could call it that—we had lost our lifeline to the tree and were sucked out of the hole in the roof with great force.

The line of us, all connected, shot through a dark, narrow tube of space at high speed. I couldn't even tell if we were going up or down at that point. With each turn to the left or right, I felt like my soul was being wrenched out of my avatar.

"Yaaaaaah!" screamed someone; I wasn't sure who.

"Yahooooo!" screamed another someone; it was definitely Leafa.

We spent at least thirty seconds on this unexpected roller-coaster ride before the tunnel ahead began to get lighter. But our speed did not slow at all as we approached the white light at the end.

Shu-pu-pu-pu-pung! We popped right out into the midst of an endless cobalt blue.

No matter which direction I looked, there was nothing but sky, sky, sky. I spread my arms and wings to steady myself and looked down. There was a pure-white cumulonimbus cloud directly below, but very far away. Even farther below that were the hazy, faded branches of the World Tree.

"Kirito!" someone said. I looked up, expecting to be scolded, and saw Asuna—

—with a dazzling smile on her face.

I smiled back at her, then grabbed the hand she stretched toward me. Leafa grabbed her other hand, then connected with Liz and Silica so that the five of us were floating in a line again. Lastly, Yui emerged from my pocket and alighted upon Asuna's shoulder.

Ultra-high-altitude gusts whistled past our ears. The falling sunlight made our hair and equipment glitter and shine.

No one said anything for quite a while. They must have been reflecting upon the strange experience we'd just had.

We did not gain another quest to follow up Pillager of the Deep. But as we'd left, the sky lord had told us that we "must never come back to this place without the proper role."

In other words, if we *did* have the proper role, we were allowed to return...I assumed. We must not have fulfilled the requirement for the quest yet. The continuation of the story was waiting for us somewhere in the world. And that meant we would find it sooner or later.

It wasn't just the quest, either. Suguha wanted to see the Bifrost, and if the sky lord was to be believed, that existed somewhere else, too.

I turned my head to the right and called out to the sylph warrior whose ponytail was whipping in the wind. "Leafa, it's too bad we didn't find the rainbow bridge. But I'm sure one day..."

"Oh...about that," she said, snapping out of her reverie and looking back at me. "Hraesvelg said that the bridge starts in

Asgard but doesn't end in Alfheim. Hearing that reminded me of something. In the myth, the Bifrost connects Asgard and Midgard."

"Mid...gard?" the rest of us repeated, unfamiliar with the name.

Leafa grinned and explained, "The land of the humans."

"...Humans...," I repeated.

At first, I didn't understand why that wasn't the place we were now—but then I understood. Alfheim *wasn't* the land of the humans. Every player and NPC, without exception, was a fairy with pointed ears and translucent wings.

But then that meant there was no place in *ALO* that could be considered the land of the humans. No place for a rainbow bridge to appear. I shared a look with Asuna, Liz, and Silica, who had all come to the same conclusion. But in the middle, Leafa did not stop smiling.

"Oh...I get it!" shouted Yui from Asuna's shoulder.

"What do you get, Yui?"

"I know where the human land is!"

She flew up from Asuna's shoulder and took a little distance so she could turn and face all of us together. The little pixie puffed out her tiny chest with pride and pointed to a part of the sky.

The navy-blue curtain stretched onward without end. There was no sign of any rainbow bridge, or even any flying monsters at this elevation...

But that wasn't true. In the far distance, at nearly the same height as us in the air, was a small floating shadow. A frustum shape with just the faintest hint of a curve along the sides.

New Aincrad.

"Oh...th-that's right!" I yelped, wide-eyed.

There were scores of NPCs living in New Aincrad. They didn't have wings, and their ears were rounded. The same thing was true of the players who once fought there.

"...Is New Aincrad meant to be Midgard in this world...?" Asuna murmured.

"That's what I suspect!" Yui claimed.

Leafa bobbed her head. "I think so, too. Of course, there's no rainbow bridge leading to New Aincrad for now…but I'm sure that at some point, maybe once we've conquered up to the hundredth floor, Bifrost will come down from the sky…"

"That's right! I'm sure it will!" Silica cried. Asuna and Lisbeth nodded vigorously.

On the inside, I couldn't help but lament, *Awww, the hundredth floor?* But I didn't let that disappointment show. I pointed at New Aincrad with the object in my hand and said, "All right, let's be the first to hit floor one hundred!"

Despite my expectations, there was no cheer in response.

I looked to the side in surprise and saw the four girls, Yui, and Pina all staring at me with a strange look in their eyes.

"D-did I say something weird…?"

"No, but…I can't believe you brought that along…," Asuna said. I looked at what I was pointing toward New Aincrad.

It was a very long stick, nearly five feet long. The surface was fine and pale, with delicate spirals near the tip, followed by two large dazzling leaves.

The highest branch of the World Tree.

"Oh…I b-brought it with me…"

I looked down at the cumulonimbus clouds below, but there was not yet any sign of a furious sky lord or dragon chasing after us.

"Ummm…what should I do with this?"

"I don't know—you grabbed it! You deal with it! I don't want to experience divine punishment on account of you!" Lisbeth snapped. So I tried to think of how to "deal with it." Alas, throwing it away, burning it, or boiling and eating it all seemed likely to invoke that very divine punishment.

"Well…maybe I'll sell it to Agil and let him suffer the consequences instead…"

"…So you're going to sell it to him, not *give* it to him."

"I mean, it's the very top of the World Tree! You can't find something like that just anywhere," I protested, then got an idea and tapped the branch with my finger.

A properties window popped up with a little jingle. I assumed, of course, that it would say something like *Wooden Branch*.

"Huh...? Wait, this name is really long. Uhhh, Crest of Yggdrasil...? Category...Two-Handed Staff?!"

I looked up and saw Asuna staring back at me with wide eyes. I lifted up the branch, which had just been revealed to be a staff, and said in a quavering voice, "I guess it's actually a weapon... and the specs on this thing are crazy...It's got to be a legendary weapon..."

"I-I've never seen a staff like that before. Does that mean it's a one-of-a-kind weapon...? H-how much would you get for something like that at the auction house in Alne...?" wondered Lisbeth, unable to resist her business instincts.

Then someone coughed. Next to Liz was Silica, whose triangular ears were twitching as she scolded, "Kirito? If it's a weapon, then there's not going to be any punishment for taking it. And what to do with it should be obvious."

"*Kyuuu!*" squeaked Pina, bobbing its head up and down.

"O-o-of course. Of course." I nodded back and let go of my grip on Asuna's hand at last. I slid forward through the air and turned next to Yui so that I was facing Asuna directly. She looked dumbfounded.

Leafa, Liz, and Silica all knew what I was about to do and fanned out to the sides.

But Asuna was still at a loss. I straightened up, then laid the Crest of Yggdrasil flat across my hands and offered it to her.

"Use this, Asuna. I'm sure it will be a big help for you."

"Uh...Y-you want *me* to have it...?"

I inclined my head to confirm, and she hesitantly took the staff. It looked just like a tree branch, but that merely gave it a graceful beauty. It was the perfect match for an undine healer.

I glanced at the others to send a signal, then took a deep breath and announced, "Asuna, thanks for always having our backs!"

""""Thanks!!!"""" the other girls chorused.

Asuna clutched the branch from the World Tree to her chest and flashed a dazzling smile.

5

As we gradually descended toward Yggdrasil City, I glanced up one last time at the white clouds atop the World Tree.

We didn't find the continuation of the quest I wanted or the rainbow bridge Suguha was seeking. But perhaps those two goals were actually the same thing.

Based on the conversation between Kraken and Leviathan, the quest was just the start of a grand narrative encompassing the unseen Aesir. In that case, the day would eventually come when we crossed a multicolored bridge and visited Asgard beyond the sky—far in the future, of course.

There was a vision in my head that put a small but undeniable flame in my heart: of beating the hundredth floor of New Aincrad and seeing Bifrost touch down upon the ground there.

There's no end to the adventure. There's always something else that comes next. Even if I grow into an adult and leave ALO behind, I'll always be able to find that rainbow bridge if I just look up into the sky.

"Hey, Kirito!" said Asuna excitedly as she paced alongside me. "Remember that dungeon we couldn't beat because my healing abilities couldn't keep up with the damage? Let's all go try it again tonight! With this staff, I think we can finish it this time!"

But then Lisbeth turned back and called out, "We have to eat pancakes in Ygg City first! I wanna see you reach a hundred, Kirito!"

"Uh…c-can we drop that down to fifty…?" I replied. The girls laughed.

Leafa turned and flew nimbly in reverse. There was a mischievous smile on her lips. "That can be arranged. But in return, you have to admit what you were doing in Swilvane last night!"

"Oof…"

Should I attempt a hundred pancakes, knowing I'd have no appetite for dinner? Or should I give up and admit my sins in infiltrating the sylph manor?

Either choice made for a pathetic finish to our two-day adventure. I couldn't make up my mind, so Yui spoke from my shoulder with a brilliant way out.

"Don't worry, Papa! If you cook up a hundred pancakes' worth of batter at once, then you only have to eat one big one!"

"…Ah, I see. That's a good idea."

I gave a gentle fingertip rub to the head of my daughter, who was clearly going through a fascination-with-big-things phase. One day I'd have to show her a real whale.

Up ahead, the city built around the giant tree was coming into view. I put all my strength into my back, vibrating my wings as hard as they could go.

(The End)

022-04

Sisters' Prayer

§ *Serene Garden*
May 2024

The memories of the very first day connecting to the original Medicuboid test prototype were still vivid.

Test Unit One was a rather artless combination of large headgear and a prebought gel bed. Dozens of colorful cables spilled down onto the floor, with gobs of monitors and tools arranged all around. There wasn't an official code name yet, just MFT1, for Medical Full-Dive Tester One.

She was a little afraid the first time she lay down on the bed, in part because the *SAO* Incident had started just three months ago and was still unsolved. But her big sister, Aiko, was there to hold her hand, and Dr. Kurahashi promised her it was absolutely safe and wouldn't hurt. So she withstood her nerves and waited for the moment to arrive.

An electronic contraption like a huge helmet came down from above and fit over her head, plus her entire face. She closed her eyes and gripped her sister's hand.

"You'll be fine, Yuu," said a faint voice, and the hand squeezed back. There was a strange whistling, rushing sound, and the feeling of her sister's hand and the pressure of the gel bed faded away. Eventually, there was a colorful ring of light before her eyes, despite the fact that they were closed. And then Yuuki Konno was in a VR world with a new body.

It was a year and three months after she'd developed multidrug resistant AIDS. She was twelve years and nine months old.

1

"Ah…!" cried Ran.

The sound roused Yuuki from the hillslope where she'd been napping.

"What's wrong, Sis?"

"Oh…I didn't mean to wake you, Yuu. I just saw a news article that surprised me…"

Her sister was holding a thin, partially translucent board that looked like carved crystal fitted into a silver frame. That was an information screen used for browsing the external Net while you were inside *Serene Garden*, the VR hospice program.

"What's the article?" Yuuki asked, leaning forward. Ran hesitated, then offered her the crystal.

The moment she read the article at the top of the daily news for May 11th, 2024, Yuuki yelped with surprise. In a large font, it said, *Police department looking into forced rescue of SAO Incident victims*.

Already a year and a half had passed since the start of the Incident, an unprecedented situation in which ten thousand people were trapped inside a virtual world. Initially, the government led a plan to free the victims through software means, but they found no way through the comprehensive trap set up by the incident's perpetrator. It had seemed there was nothing they could do but helplessly watch.

"Forced rescue...how?" Yuuki murmured, reading the article. She couldn't go to middle school, but she was able to continue her studies in the virtual world, and she always liked reading, so news articles like this weren't out of her ability to understand.

"Hmm...the police are investigating the possibility of externally destroying the NerveGear that the seven thousand surviving victims are wearing...?"

At that point, she paused and let out a wordless exclamation. Yuuki looked up from the tablet to her sister and asked, "But the perpetrators made it so that if you try to destroy the NerveGear, it electrocutes the brain, right?"

"Not electricity—electromagnetic waves," Ran corrected in a teacherly tone. Still, her face was grave. "Based on this article, they're hoping that instantly destroying the battery might prevent the device from creating a pulse strong enough to damage the wearer's brain...but..."

"Hmm..."

Yuuki gazed at the photo of the NerveGear attached to the article. The bulky headgear that Medicuboid Test Unit One used was modeled after the NerveGear, so the resemblance was rather close.

She was currently using—no, inside—Test Unit Two, which was very different in size and shape, but the thought of physically destroying VR headgear that someone was wearing gave her the chills.

"...How do they instantly destroy it, physically speaking? They can't just blow it up or smash it with a hammer, I assume," she said.

"Good point...Maybe they're using a precision drill to open a hole in the exterior shell, then hoping to snip the positive electrode line? But knowing how thorough the culprit was, I bet there are secret backup circuits that would still work."

"Uh-huh..."

"Plus, I seem to recall that in the culprit's message, there was something about how if we tried to destroy the NerveGear to save a player, it might compromise the safety of the others. Meaning the plan to free them all would have to be done absolutely simultaneously with seven thousand different NerveGear units. I'm not sure that's possible."

"It sounds…difficult," murmured Yuuki, although the truth was that she didn't understand what her sister was saying anymore.

Usually, she'd stop trying to process what Aiko was saying and think, *She's so smart.* This time, however, Yuuki looked back at the crystal tablet. She'd heard that some of the *SAO* Incident victims were being kept in their hospital, under the same roof, so she couldn't help but be curious.

"…Ran, why do you think this Kayaba guy did this?" Yuuki asked.

Aiko's avatar, Ran, just looked ahead without answering. Yuuki looked up, too, out toward the ridge of the horizon, faded and blue with distance.

The two girls were sitting in a place on the eastern side of the spacious *Serene Garden* called Teal Hills. The hills themselves were gentle and covered with greenery. Blue lakes and delicate little villages were nestled between them. It was so beautiful, she could sit here and watch forever.

Beginning in September of 2023, *Serene Garden* was a VR hospice, a virtual world meant to provide palliative care to terminally ill patients. The majority of the system resources went into creating a beautiful and pleasant world. When the AmuSphere was released in June of that year, all its games revolved around adventures or shooting things, but *Serene Garden* replaced the concept of combat with carefully and intricately designed landscapes with striking views. The eastern part of its large map was full of green hills; the north, snowy fields; the west, tall mountains; and the south, deep woods. Sitting in the center of the map was a capital city designed to look like a European-style town. If you wanted to walk to see every part of the world, it would take you an entire week.

Yuuki and Ran's parents died at the end of last year, one after the other. The direct cause of death in both cases was pneumonia, but they'd suffered from a number of opportunistic infections and had to be given powerful pain suppressants to ease their suffering. By the end of the fall, they were asleep around the clock.

There was one single time in which their parents used Amu-Spheres to visit "the garden."

The pain-canceling function of the AmuSphere wasn't powerful enough to eliminate their suffering entirely, so they could be together for only about an hour. But that hour took them on a stroll from the center of town to the grassy fields outside, a precious memory that would forever remain in Yuuki's and Ran's hearts. Their father ate the lunch they prepared and marveled over how delicious it was. Their mother's eyes brimmed with tears at the sight of the beautiful landscape, and she sang the children's songs and hymns the sisters loved so much.

If not for full-dive technology and virtual reality, this experience could never have happened.

And this technology was almost entirely created by Akihiko Kayaba, the man behind the horrible *SAO* Incident.

The precious memory with their parents wasn't the only thing he enabled. Yuuki was using a Medicuboid developed by a medical company, but Ran had to use a modified version of the Nerve-Gear, one with a smaller battery and other safety limitations. So it was thanks to the worst criminal of the century that the two sisters were able to interact in the virtual world.

Ran rubbed Yuuki's back, sensing there were some conflicted feelings to be smoothed out.

"I don't know, either. But you don't need to worry about that, Yuu. You're testing the Medicuboid so that it works right and helps as many patients as possible in the future."

"......Yeah..."

Yuuki leaned against her big sister's shoulder.

Ran (Aiko) was Yuuki's "big" sister, but the truth was that they were twins. However, for as long as Yuuki could remember, she'd always looked up to her sister and relied on her for help. Ran had always doted on her and protected her.

The reason Yuuki was the test subject for the Medicuboid was because of her sister's strong insistence. The Medicuboid, a very delicate and complex piece of machinery, was installed in a biological clean room at Yokohama Kohoku General Hospital, where the girls were hospitalized. The interior of the room had far fewer germs and viruses than outside, meaning it minimized the risk of opportunistic infections—the greatest danger to a person with AIDS.

Being a tester meant going into the clean room, extending your time to live. Ran knew this and withdrew from candidacy to let Yuuki take it. A year and three months had passed since then, with Ran staying in an ordinary long-term hospital room. Her condition had deteriorated slightly more than Yuuki's in that time. Even now, Ran was living with the fear of disease that the NerveGear couldn't prevent.

When Dr. Kurahashi proposed going into the clean room to be a Medicuboid test subject, Yuuki could have said, "I'm fine. You go in, Sis," but she didn't. Ran said that instead, and she said it without a moment's hesitation: "You take it, Yuu."

Yuuki bit her lip and squeezed hard with her teeth. Suddenly, Ran shot to her feet.

The wind blew her long hair as she stretched her limbs. Their avatars were automatically generated by the game based on photographs, but even still, Ran's avatar was surprisingly accurate to her real self. The girlie shirtdress she was wearing looked great on her.

She grabbed Yuuki's hand with a smile and exclaimed, "C'mon, Yuu, let's pick some herbs. I have a feeling we're going to find that ultrarare one today."

"……Okay!"

Yuuki squeezed her sister's hand back.

2

There might be no combat in *Serene Garden*, but that didn't mean sightseeing was the only activity to do.

The biggest gameplay aspect was housing. Users were given a specific area of land in Serenity, the city at the center of the world, where they could build and design their own homes. The exterior was limited to the varieties of colored bricks seen elsewhere around the city, so most of the customization was interior decoration.

You could purchase or order the materials and furniture for interior decoration from the NPC shops around the town, which required points called currens (which was apparently short for *currency*). But currens couldn't be shared between people; the only way to earn more was by collecting. That meant going around the world map to locations where harvestable plants, minable ores, and catchable bugs and such would appear, then taking them to a shop in town where you could exchange them for currens based on their rarity level. You could also use those items to craft other items directly, or raise the bugs to participate in the Insect Battle Tournament. There was a surprising amount to do.

In Serenity, Yuuki and Ran shared a house that they'd been customizing for the last six months, but they were far from finished. At the moment, they were saving up points to put a large standing hearth in their living room. They were about 70 percent of the way there.

The good thing was that collecting was fun on its own, not a pain. An hour or two would simply vanish while they walked through the picturesque meadows looking for special herbs. Every single person using *Serene Garden* was already battling the pressure of wondering how much time they had left to live, so the relaxing effect of the collecting process and how it helped the time pass made it very popular. There was an old woman Yuuki was friends with who was so dedicated to scouring the entire world map and acquiring items that she had built herself a four-story mansion that loomed over part of Serenity.

The twins weren't going that far, but if they were going to build a hearth where they could roast potatoes, they couldn't take a day off. From the hillside where they were resting in the sun, they went to their favorite secret collecting spot: the banks of a little pond nearby. Yuuki eagerly peered around the area for herbs, basket in hand.

"...Ah," her sister said.

"What is it?" she asked. Ran was a bit farther away and motioned for her to be quiet. Her older sister was frozen in a half crouch. Yuuki tried to follow the angle of her eyesight but couldn't tell what Ran had spotted to cause this reaction.

She set the basket down and snuck as quietly as possible to Ran's side, then squinted, searching the grassy thicket...

"...Ah," Yuuki said, too, when she saw it.

On the trunk of an aged, leafy tree standing at the side of the pond was a stag beetle colored a deep, vivid blue. It seemed to be nearly four inches long, with two massive mandibles and an extremely long horn jutting from its thorax. Yuuki had seen its picture in a book of all the insects in the game.

"Doesn't that beetle look valuable to you?" her sister asked.

"It's more than valuable. That's a royal triton stag beetle," Yuuki replied immediately.

Despite the nerves and excitement, there was a clear note of annoyance in her sister's reply. "I can't believe you even know its name."

"If you raise it right, it can be the strongest of all the stag beetles!"

"...I didn't know you were interested in bug battles, Yuu."

"A-actually, I kinda like it. A lot," she whispered back.

In the meantime, the blue beetle was slowly climbing the trunk of the ancient tree. There was a stream of golden sap ahead of it, and that seemed to be the beetle's destination.

"Did you bring a net, Sis?"

"I was only expecting to pick herbs today, so I just brought the basket."

"Same here..."

The storage space for users of the garden was quite limited. If you were out collecting for hours at a time, there was no room for anything you didn't absolutely need to bring. Yuuki and Ran were plant experts, and the only times they caught insects were when they found one that was worth a lot.

But this one sitting less than twenty feet away was the royal triton, the rarest of them all. If they cashed it in at the insect shop, they'd be able to buy their hearth with change to spare. They *had* to catch this bug.

"I'll just grab it with my hands," Yuuki whispered. Ran looked shocked and sucked in a sharp breath.

"Yuu...you're going to touch it with your bare hands?"

"......"

That's right. She's like Mom—she hated bugs in real life. If I caught a grasshopper in the yard and brought it inside, they'd both scream and run around, she recalled fondly.

"The bugs here are totally fine. They don't bite you or sting or shoot gross liquid. Just wait here," Yuuki said, patting Ran on the shoulder. She took off her sandals and crouched low before proceeding forward.

She'd never told her sister, but she was secretly engaging in a fair amount of bug hunting on her own time. There were three ironclad rules of catching rare bugs. One, don't move too fast. Two, don't approach from the front. Three, don't make any unnatural sounds.

She was moving through knee-high grass, so there was some unavoidable rustling. The trick was not to move too fast, so the sound would get lost in the blowing of the breeze.

The rare stag beetle reached the place where the golden sap was seeping from the trunk and came to a stop. Feeding time was the best opportunity to catch an insect, but from personal experience, Yuuki knew that the rarer the bug, the shorter the window was. In about fifteen seconds, it would spread its wings and buzz off into the air.

Less than ten feet to the tree. If she kept waiting for the breeze to blow before moving, she'd never get there in time. But if she charged now and made a lot of noise, the beetle would easily escape.

What should I do? How can I move without touching the grass...?

Yuuki briefly glanced to her sides and caught sight of something. Along the water in the pond, just to her right, was a sequence of wooden posts spaced about three feet apart. They were taller than the grass, and if she hopped from post to post, she wouldn't make any noise.

The problem was that the posts were only about two inches across. If her balance was anything less than perfect, she'd topple into the grass to the left or the pond to the right. And she didn't have time to carefully judge each step.

...Just gotta do it! she told herself and moved sideways with the next breeze. She waited for the right timing, stood up, and leaped onto the narrow stake.

Here goes!

Silently, she hopped from post to post. By the time she got to the last one, somehow managing not to fall off, the stag beetle had finished its meal and spread its jewellike elytra, revealing the clear hind wings that would enable it to fly away.

Bzzz! It took flight, wings buzzing.

"Yaaah!" Yuuki shouted, no longer bothering to remain silent, and leaped for all she was worth. The tips of her fingers caught the long horn of the beetle.

In the real world, grabbing the back of a huge, powerful insect like this wouldn't be the end of the struggle. But this was a virtual world designed with usability in mind. The instant she had a hold of the rare insect, a triumphant fanfare sounded, and the stag beetle folded its wings and acquiesced. She landed in the grass with a soft thud.

"I did iiiiit! I caught the royal triton stag beetle!" she cried, thrusting her left fist into the air.

Ran approached carefully, her expression four parts surprise to one part fear. "Th...that was amazing, Yuu. You really caught it with your bare hands."

"Nee-hee-hee! I'm surprised, too. Here, want to hold it?" she said, extending her hand with the giant beetle.

Ran backed away slowly, shaking her head. "N-no, I'll pass. But congratulations, Yuuki. What are you going to do with it? Sell it? Keep it?"

"Hmm...*Hmmmm*..."

She brought the now-docile stag beetle, horn held between her fingers, to her face for a better look. When trying to catch it, she was only thinking about how many points it was worth, but after six months of harvesting items in *Serene Garden*, she'd never found something as rare as this. Plus, as she looked at the beetle's face, its big black segmented eyes looked kind of cute to her...

The problem was that raising insects in this world cost money for food, just like in real life. If the bugs were good enough to win the bug battle events, they could make back that money on their own, but just being able to participate in those events required clearing lots of hurdles.

"What should I do...?" she worried, staring at the beetle as its mandibles waggled back and forth.

"Aaaaaaah!!" Suddenly, there came a scream from her left, and she found herself toppling in the other direction.

"Wh-what?!" she yelped along with Ran. Together, they saw another girl standing there alone, a bit farther away. Of course, it was just a girl's avatar, but changing gender was impossible in *Serene Garden*, and an avatar's appearance was based on real photographs, so this was certainly very close to what the girl playing the avatar looked like.

Her long green hair was tied into a ponytail (hairstyle and color *could* be customized), and she wore a brown camo-pattern T-shirt and cargo pants with many pockets—the look of an insect hunter, if there ever was one. A long bug-catching net trembled in her left hand, and her right index finger was pointed right at Yuuki.

"There! That royton! I was chasing after that for an entire hour!"

It took Yuuki a full three seconds to realize that *royton* wasn't the beetle's name but an abbreviation of *royal triton*. She quickly hid the beetle behind her back and argued, "W-well, I caught it."

The rules of *Serene Garden* said that whoever picked up an item, whether plant or ore or insect, got to keep it. You might argue, "This is my collecting spot" or "I saw it first," but those statements held no real power. The girl in the camo shirt knew that, and she clammed up briefly, but she wouldn't remain silent.

"You don't look like a bug hunter to me, though. You don't have a cage. How are you going to take it back home with you?"

Now it was Yuuki who had no answer.

She had a point: Without a special insect cage like the one attached to the girl's waist, she couldn't put the beetle in her inventory. And with it stuck in her hand right now, the beetle was slowly but surely weakening. It would heal right away if put in a cage with food and water, but it would take twenty minutes at the quickest to reach the nearest town. Yuuki didn't know how much of the stag beetle's life would be lost, but if she ended up killing the precious insect, she'd never stop regretting it. The only reason Yuuki hadn't taken part in the bug battles was because she was afraid of losing her pet through a careless accident.

Ran put a gentle hand on Yuuki's shoulder and said, "Yuu..."

Yuuki understood what her sister was telling her. She pulled the hand holding the royal triton stag beetle out from behind her back, said a silent good-bye to her catch, then held it out toward the bug-hunting girl.

"Here. You can have it."

The ponytailed girl's eyes went wide with surprise. "Uh... I can?"

"You said you wanted it, didn't you?" Yuuki said, taking a step forward. But the girl looked down at herself in a panic.

"B-but I don't have anything worth exchanging for it..."

You couldn't trade with other players using currens in *Serene Garden*, only barter with items you were carrying. No players walked around with items worth the value of a superrare insect.

Yuuki smiled and said, "It doesn't have to be a trade. I bet this bug would be happier if it was raised by someone like you, who works really hard to be a proper bug hunter."

"......"

But the girl's initial boldness had all but melted away. She didn't move or speak. She'd probably said that because she was incensed that someone else had caught the thing she was chasing, but she hadn't actually considered that the person might give it to her anyway.

Yuuki was wise enough to read this in the other girl's body language but not wise enough to know the right thing to say now. Instead, Ran said softly, "Then how about you trade by allowing Yuu to give the bug a name?"

The girl's face lit up, and she nodded repeatedly. "Y-yeah! Yeah! That's good! You name it!"

"Huh...? Me?"

Yuuki was in a panic. She knew she wasn't great at coming up with names. When creating their avatars for *Serene Garden*, Aiko had gone with Ran because it was an alternate reading of the *Ai* kanji in her name, but Yuuki just went with her regular name.

If she gave up now, it would be a waste, so she did her best. But after at least a dozen seconds of thinking, she came up with…

"…Ummm…how about…Roy…?"

It's the same thing!!

But despite her fears, the ponytailed girl just smiled and nodded.

"That's nice! I like simple names like that. Then I'll register this bug's name as Roy!"

"Okay!"

Yuuki said a silent farewell to her stag beetle, then presented it to the girl again.

The girl cupped her hands to accept the beetle, then gazed, rapt, at the beautiful royal-blue luster of the beetle's carapace. Then she carefully transferred it to her insect cage, opened her player window, and put the whole cage in her inventory. The stag beetle's life value couldn't drop anymore after that.

The girl picked up the net she'd dropped and put that in her inventory, too, then she straightened and performed a deep, courteous bow.

"Thank you so much for giving it to me! I've been looking for that insect forever since coming here, so I'm really, really happy to have it!"

Yuuki understood that when she said "coming here," she wasn't talking about Teal Hills but *Serene Garden*, the VR hospice program. She asked her, "How long have you been here?"

"Since just after it started, so it's been about eight months—oh, gosh! I never even told you my name. Hello, I'm Merida. Nice to meet you!"

Merida grinned and stuck out her right hand, which Yuuki accepted and shook.

"I'm Yuuki! Nice to meet you!"

Ran took Merida's hand next. "I'm Ran. I'm Yuuki's big sister. It's nice to meet you, Miss Merida."

"Just call me Merida. I'm only slightly older than you two, if anything. It's really nice to meet you. I hope we can be...good... frien..."

Merida's voice unexpectedly wavered, then vanished. Her green ponytail fluttered as she suddenly lurched to the side, and Yuuki had to reach out with both hands to steady her.

They moved her over to the shade under the tree where Yuuki had caught Roy the stag beetle and sat her down on the grass. Merida quickly recovered after that.

She blinked a couple times, then noticed Yuuki's and Ran's concerned looks and hunched her shoulders with guilt.

"...I'm sorry. I was so excited about getting Roy that I think I got a little too carried away," she said, giggling guiltily. Yuuki smiled back at her but couldn't fully contain her worry.

The people engaged in *Serene Garden* weren't called players, and that was for a reason. Accordingly, users avoided saying that word for the most part. People weren't coming to this world simply because it was fun.

The point of the VR hospice program was to provide palliative care—easing the suffering of their illness and improving quality of life. Without exception, everyone found here was dealing with a very serious disease. In fact, you couldn't even connect and make an account unless it was through the facilities at a hospital. That meant Merida was connecting to this world through a hospital located somewhere in Japan.

They didn't know Merida's condition yet. But if her avatar within the VR world collapsed, that meant it wasn't just dizziness or anemia but a condition afflicting the brain itself, which was connected through the AmuSphere.

Of course, if the situation were bad enough, the AmuSphere would automatically disconnect, and her avatar would disappear. Since Merida recovered right away, she had to be right that it was just a temporary problem. But on the other hand, Merida was so relaxed about it that it conversely amplified Yuuki's concern. She was *used* to this phenomenon. It was something that happened all the time.

Merida could feel Yuuki's state of mind through the hand on her back, so she smiled reassuringly. "Ha-ha, really, I'm fine. If I stay still for a moment, I'll be better again…There. I'm completely fine now."

She hopped up onto her feet and bounced into the air. Her agility was so smooth that it spoke to how much experience she had here. But the fact that she'd been in *Serene Garden* since nearly the point it started meant that she'd needed this palliative care for that long of a period already.

Mindful of Merida's symptoms, Yuuki stood up, too. But the other girl took a step back and gave them a piercing glare.

"Wh…what is it?" Yuuki asked, wondering if the matching dresses she and her sister were wearing didn't look good after all. But Merida just flashed a cheerful smile.

"Sorry, didn't mean to stare at you like that. Those dresses are very cute, but they're not really suited for bug hunting. I was just thinking how impressive it was that you caught the royal triton dressed like that. They fly away as soon as they hear a single footstep. How did you move so quietly through the grass?"

"Ummm…" Yuuki stopped to think, trying to remember what exactly she'd done.

Ran giggled and explained, "Yuu didn't go through the grass. She jumped from stake to stake, standing in the water over there. She went *boing, boing, boing!*"

"Oh, I see."

Yuuki chuckled, embarrassed that she couldn't remember what she'd been doing barely fifteen minutes ago, but she wasn't expecting Merida's smile to vanish.

"Whaaat?! On those tiny posts?! You can do that?!"

"Um, y-yeah. I guess. You can just call me Yuuki, by the way!"

"Oh…w-well, Yuuki, can you stand on one foot for me?"

"Huh? Okay…"

Yuuki did as Merida asked and bent her left knee so that she was only standing on her right leg, though she had no idea where Merida was going with this. She held out her arms a bit for balance and said, "There's no muscle fatigue here, so I can stand on one leg for forever. So can you, right, Sis?"

"I…I dunno…I've never tried it," said Ran without much confidence. She rose up on one leg, too. There was a brief wobble at first, but soon her body was stable.

Until they had to leave school in fourth grade, Yuuki and Ran had taken normal physical education. They grew at nearly the same rate, because they were twins, but when it came to running speed, throwing control, and even test scores, Ran was always just a bit better—a source of secret frustration for her sister.

I at least want to show I can beat her at standing on one leg in the virtual world! Yuuki swore to herself. But after about a minute, Merida suddenly burst into rapturous applause.

"Yuuki, Ran, that's amazing! I've never seen anyone who can stand on one leg for so long on this side!"

The sisters were taken aback; it seemed like a bit of an exaggeration. Merida clasped her hands together with consternation.

"If your FC numbers are that high, you could be incredible insect hunters! Say, why don't you switch over to being hunters?! I can teach you all about it!"

Even as she balanced on one foot, Ran lifted her hands in a placating motion, trying to calm down the excited girl. "Merida, what is FC?" she asked gently.

"I've never heard of it, either," said Yuuki.

Merida took a deep breath to slow herself down, realizing that she was confusing her audience. "I'm sorry for getting carried away," she said. "I'm always like this. Well, FC stands for Full-Dive Conformation. It means how well you adapt to the virtual world. Standing on one leg is the simplest and quickest method of testing it. The sense of balance and gravity is slightly different here, so it's hard to stand on one leg for an extended time unless your body is able to adjust. I'm sure my total time spent here is much longer than yours, but I can only manage about forty seconds at best."

"Oh, I didn't realize…," said Yuuki.

Startled by the breadth of Merida's knowledge about full-dive systems, Yuuki looked down at the foot she had planted on the ground. She could remember being a little confused at the fine differences from the real world when she first used the Medicuboid, but once she got the chance to run and jump around the vivid, exciting virtual world, she got used to it right away. She couldn't remember Ran complaining about a difference in sensations, either.

"…Meaning there are personal differences in this FC thing?" Yuuki asked nonchalantly.

"That's right," Merida said gravely. "It's rare, but sometimes the first connection test gets you an FNC, meaning you don't conform to full-diving. It has to be a shock to spend all that money on a Ner—on an AmuSphere and get told it won't work for you. But there are more places out there now where you can test it before you buy one."

"Hmm…"

Upon learning this, Yuuki was relieved that she and her sister hadn't gotten an FNC. Medicuboid Test Unit Two and Ran's augmented NerveGear were provided by the hospital, of course. Dr. Kurahashi said it wasn't even close to proper atonement for how the two got sick, but when they interacted with other people in *Serene Garden*, Yuuki was always left with a particular thought: She and her sister wouldn't be able to visit these places ordinarily without buying two of those very expensive AmuSpheres.

In fact, while her sister might have excellent physical reflexes, maybe the only reason Yuuki could stand on one foot for minutes on end was because she got to use the much more advanced Medicuboid.

The moment this thought popped into her head, Yuuki felt bad for engaging in this competition with Ran and started to lower her leg.

But before it touched the ground, Ran shouted, "Aaah, I can't do it anymore!" and clung to her side. They both tumbled to the grass.

"Hey, what was that for, Sis?"

"You touched the ground first, Yuu, so I win the balance competition!"

"Hey, no fair! I could have kept going!" she protested, forgetting her brief resignation just seconds before.

Merida watched it happen, wide-eyed, and burst into bubbling laughter. "Ah-ha-ha, you two are so close. I wish I had a sister to be friends with…"

Suddenly, she clammed up and stopped smiling. It must have occurred to her what it meant that the two sisters were in a VR hospice together.

Yuuki wanted to tell her not to feel bad about it but couldn't find the right way to say it. Fortunately, Ran did.

"I'm sure you'd be a great big sister, Merida. You're very cool and very knowledgeable," she said, pulling Yuuki up from the grass. "You seem to know a lot about full-dive games. Do you play others aside from *Serene Garden*?"

"Mmm, *SG*'s my main game for now. I'm too busy catching and raising bugs," she replied, the smile returning but a bit more tempered than before. "Before *SG*, I played a different game…but they found my disease before it officially launched, so I was too late to start."

"Oh? What game?" asked Yuuki with great interest; she didn't know much about other VR worlds.

Merida's smile seemed to be cradling some source of pain. She answered with another question: "Do you have more time to talk?"

"Ummm…"

She looked at the clock readout in the lower right of her field of view. It was three thirty in the afternoon. There was a fair amount of time before dinner at six, and they didn't have any tests or meetings on the schedule today.

"I think we have another two hours," Yuuki said.

The bug hunter nodded. "Then why don't we go back to the village and talk over some tea?"

3

In addition to the capital of Serenity, there was one village or town in each of the four cardinal directions. The village in the eastern region of Teal Hills was called Leute. There was a teleport gate in the square at the center of town that would take you instantly to the capital.

Merida passed through the town gate first and turned back to face the sisters. "Which do you like better, crepes or ice cream?"

They instantly said "Crepes!" in perfect harmony. Merida gasped.

"Y-you didn't hesitate a moment."

"Hee-hee-hee."

The sisters chuckled and shared a brief look. Crepes were their late mother's secret best recipe. They could eat her homemade crepes every single day: *crepes sucrées*, which were baked golden brown and folded around whipped cream and fruit; *crepes salées*, which were savory with cheese and ham; even *crepes suzette*, which were served with a sweet orange-citrus sauce on top.

Even in the hospital, they had the chance to eat crepes in the cafeteria, although they weren't quite as good as their mother's. Since going into the clean room, that was no longer an option for Yuuki.

Ran, on the other hand, got to have normal hospital food and could visit the cafeteria. But in a show of solidarity with Yuuki, she was only eating crepes in the virtual world, she said. Yuuki scolded her and said Ran should have some with her real body, but her sister claimed, "It doesn't taste good if I eat them alone."

Merida had no idea about any of this, of course, but she seemed to sense it was a special thing for them. She pounded the chest of her camo shirt and said, "Then I'll show you to the best crepes around!"

"Huh…? There are more places to eat than the restaurants in the square?" Ran asked. Merida just grinned and started walking.

The village of Leute was placed atop a little hill. The stone-cobbled main street ran past brick houses that looked like they belonged in some mountain village in the Alps. At most, *Serene Garden* could support about a thousand connections, and because the total number of hospice patients in the nation was around thirty thousand, it was far from ubiquitous. But since there were only five towns in this world, the number of players strolling the main street felt rather high.

Merida took them off that crowded road packed with businesses and down a maze of alleys, turning them left and right and back and forth.

Serene Garden had no in-game map function. Her ability to steer them around with absolute confidence spoke not just to her complete knowledge of the complicated layout of Leute but her familiarity with existing in a virtual space itself. Yuuki followed, feeling more and more curious about whatever game Merida had been playing before this one, and was just losing her sense of direction entirely when they came to a more open space again.

There was a small terrace jutting out of the western slope of the hill that gave them a clear view of the meadow below, sparkling in the afternoon sun. Faded into the distance was a series of folds in the land as the island met the sea in fjords. That was the edge of the world.

There was a single table on the terrace with a parasol overhead. Behind it was a tiny café exuding a sweet smell.

"Yay, the outside table is empty!" Merida said with a smile. She circled behind the sisters and pushed them into the chairs that overlooked the meadow. Then she sat across from them and slid them menus from the table.

"This is my favorite place to eat in Leute. This one's on me. Order whatever you like!"

Yuuki and Ran were briefly arrested by the beauty of the sight below them, but this comment got them to look up and shake their heads.

"Oh, no. You've already shown us this wonderful place—we couldn't ask you to pay for our food, too," said Ran, getting up from the chair, but Merida waved her back down.

"What are you talking about? The crepes here don't even begin to match the value of the royal triton stag beetle. It's the *least* I can possibly do!"

"Well…if you insist…"

Ran sat down again; Yuuki was already looking over the corkboard menu. The virtual refrigerator had no limits on what it could hold, but even still, the number of words on the menu was astonishing. There were five types of batter, ten types of cream, twenty varieties of fruit, thirty sauces, and fifty toppings, all of which were available to combine. The possibilities were essentially endless.

"Amazing…but how am I supposed to choose…?" Yuuki wailed.

Luckily, Ran spurred her on with a cheery smile. "Then I'll go with smooth honey for my batter, milky whipped cream, ruby strawberries and fresh mandarins for my fruit, rich chocolate sauce, and toppings of fresh pistachio and caramel crunch!"

"……"

Yuuki stared at her older sister, aghast, as she tapped the items on the touch pad menu. Even Merida looked shocked. There were many ways in which Yuuki was inferior to her sister, and foremost among them was the ability to make decisions. She couldn't recall ever seeing Ran waffle between options in her life.

When her order was in, she looked up and asked, "What are you having, Yuu?"

"...The same as you, Sis," she said, waving the white flag. Merida chimed in with "Me too!"

Ran bumped the number of orders up to three. "All right, it's your treat, as you said."

She handed the menu over to Merida, who pushed the button to complete the order and paid the currens for three crepes. Barely ten seconds later, an NPC waitress came rushing out of the building with three plates.

The crepes were folded in the familiar cone shape but were much bigger than they expected. Gobs of cream and fruit popped out from the pale-yellow pancake, and the sauce and toppings glittered among them.

"Ooh, it looks so yummy!" exclaimed Yuuki, clasping her hands before her chest in a very brief prayer before accepting her crepe. In the real world, it would be nearly impossible to eat such a thing without it falling apart, but here, as long as she didn't let go of it, there was no worry about the cream or fruit spilling out and landing on her clothes.

"Here goes!" Ran said, speaking for the trio, and she opened her mouth as wide as it could go for a big bite. The smooth, thin crepe broke with just the right amount of texture, giving way to fluffy light cream and a large, fresh strawberry.

Right when they'd first visited this world, it felt very strange and wrong to "eat" food that wasn't actually real—but that soon became normal to them. There was a bit of a trick to chewing and tasting the same way as it worked in the real world, but if you closed your eyes and chewed without moving your tongue too much, the sensation of tasting wasn't too different.

The crepe, cream, and strawberry melted together and vanished when she swallowed, creating a brief descending sensation in her throat. Then Yuuki opened her eyes and shouted, "Merida, this crepe is a-*mazing*! It's completely different from the kind at the shop near the teleport gate!"

Her brand-new friend beamed with pure delight. "Right?! I think there must be more data to process, so they put this in a more out-of-the-way spot. I've had to work really hard to learn the way here without getting lost. What do you think, Ran...? Is it good?"

Ran looked up from her crepe, finishing her third large bite. She bobbed her head deeply and said with grave importance, "I've decided that I will continue visiting this shop until I've eaten every crepe they make."

"Ah-ha-ha-ha! That'll be tough—good luck! I've been coming here for half a year, and I still haven't tried half the combinations."

"Tell me your recommended flavors for next time, then."

Meanwhile, Yuuki was busily shrinking the surface area of the bountiful crepe. Unfortunately, she couldn't say it was more delicious than her mother's crepes—those were something that would never exist again. But just being here and eating the crepe with the girl she'd randomly met and become quick friends with made it feel many times more delicious than the actual taste data of the item itself.

Before the disease presented itself, when she was still in elementary school, Yuuki had many good friends. She always longed for the lunch period, when they would slide their desks together and eat the same items from the cafeteria.

But that daily treat was lost forever from the moment the rumor that she was HIV positive got around. No longer would any of her classmates slide their desks over to hers. Yuuki had to eat her lunch alone in a corner of the room every day. All her favorites, like pork curry and glass-noodle soup and milk pudding, suddenly didn't taste so good anymore.

In a sense, this was the first time she'd eaten anything with a friend since coming to the hospital. Even if it was a virtual crepe she was holding, and her friend was a stranger whose real name and face were a mystery, and they were eating in a virtual café in a world that didn't exist, the feelings of pain and warmth that wrenched at her heart were very, very real.

"......Yuuki."

The sound of Merida's voice snapped Yuuki's eyes open again. She realized they were welling up with tears as she ate, so she quickly put down her food and rubbed at her eyes. But the tears wouldn't go away. As Ran had told her before, the virtual world tended to overemote what you were feeling, which made it hard to hold back tears.

"I-I'm fine, just a bit...a bit...," she mumbled. Ran gently patted her on the back. Thanks to her years of experience being comforted by her sister, Yuuki quickly felt the tears dry up.

"...I'm sorry for bursting into tears like that, Merida. The crepe just tasted so good, and I was having so much fun that..."

She beamed at Merida, who seemed to be holding back something herself. Yuuki tossed the last bit of crepe into her mouth, swallowed it, and exhaled.

"To tell you the truth," Merida said, "I found myself crying alone a lot until recently. In fact, I still feel sad when I remember. Sad, frustrated, angry, ready to cry like a little baby."

Her voice was soft, and her gaze pointed out across the meadow below. The sun was much weaker now, and its light was golden and fading on the vast field.

"...Are you thinking of the game you played before coming here?" Ran asked.

The deep-green ponytail swayed. "Yes. I only got to play it for a month...and it was only a beta test, not the full release. It was August of 2022, about a whole year before *SG* started up. I wore NerveGear, not an AmuSphere, and got to play the world's first VRMMORPG..."

After a brief time lag, the meaning of her words sank into Yuuki's mind. She recalled the news article Ran had shown her before they started on their herb-collecting run. The name left her lips, which felt cracked and dry.

"...*Sword Art Online*..."

Merida's head barely moved. She still wore that sad little smile. "Yes. I played the *SAO* beta test and got into a midsize guild. It was really fun...and that month passed by in a blink. On the final day, I made a promise to everyone that we'd meet up again when it launched in November. It was just after that when they found the tumor on my brain. I couldn't play these games anymore. They took away my NerveGear."

"...But...that means...," Ran murmured.

Merida understood what she was going to say. "That's right. Because of the tumor, I didn't get trapped inside that game. The tumor saved my life, the doctors and my parents said, so it's sure to heal very soon. But...the world isn't that kind. My brain tumor was in a place where it couldn't be removed. I've been doing chemotherapy and radiation, but it just won't disappear. I've been dealing with it for a year and a half already."

She chuckled and pressed her fingertips against her temples, as though feeling around for her brain. Neither Yuuki nor Ran seemed to know what to say.

So Merida's collapse at the tree where they caught the stag beetle was because of a brain condition. Malignant tumors, a kind of cancer, weren't an unfamiliar thing to the sisters. As their immune systems fell to the point of reaching AIDS, the lymphocytes in their blood were at increased risk of developing cancer. The regular testing hadn't picked up signs of tumors in Yuuki or Ran yet, but even being in a clean room wouldn't prevent Yuuki's cells from becoming cancerous.

Merida lowered her hands, leaned against the back of her chair, and gazed up at the sky, which was a blend of blue and pale yellow.

"I can never tell my parents this," she said, searching for the words, "but there are times when I think...if I'm just going to die from this tumor, I'd rather have been trapped in Aincrad. At least then, I could be fighting alongside my friends..."

""...!""

Yuuki and Ran gasped. Aincrad, from what they understood, was the name of the flying castle that was the setting of *Sword Art Online*. When the game launched, ten thousand players were trapped inside and placed under severe rules: Logging out was impossible, and if the player fell to zero HP, they would *actually* die. Over the year and a half that this situation continued, three thousand of those players had died. In terms of fatalities caused by a single person's actions, it was surely the greatest total in the history of Japan—perhaps even the world.

They couldn't ask Merida why she would want to be inside such a terrible game.

The five-year survival rate for malignant brain tumors was about 30 percent on average. In other words, of all the patients who came down with the tumors at the same time, about 70 percent would be dead within five years. That was vastly worse than *SAO*'s 30 percent rate.

"...That's a good point," Ran murmured. Yuuki glanced over at her sister and saw the usual calm look on her face. But those dark-blue eyes were just a little brighter than she was used to seeing. "If I were a beta tester of *Sword Art Online*, I might have thought the same way you do, Merida. My only choice with disease is to withstand and resist it—but at least monsters, I can fight with my own power."

Merida looked surprised by this. She glanced down at the empty plate on the table. It was completely clean, as though there had never been a crepe topped with dollops of whipped cream resting upon it.

"...Yeah. If I'm just going to wither away and die on a hospital bed...I'd rather jump right into *SAO* and die to save someone else. At least that way...I might feel like my life...had meaning......"

With a soft splat, a clear droplet fell onto the plate. It caught the fading light of the sun as it fell, shining brilliantly before it simply vanished.

A life with meaning.

The phrase stabbed Yuuki deep inside her heart.

There was something she'd asked herself, over and over, for much of her life—something she'd never said to her late parents or to her sister. Why was she alive? She was going to die before she grew to be an adult, leaving behind only agony for her father and mother, and trouble for her teachers and friends at school, achieving nothing. What was the meaning of it all?

She hadn't found the answer to that question yet. Maybe she wouldn't find it until the very end of her life. But Yuuki couldn't bring herself to agree with Merida. She breathed in and out, trying to work out how to mold the feeling bubbling up in her chest into words. Then she felt Ran's hand on her back, warm and gentle. At last, she found her voice.

"Don't say that...don't say that, Merida! If you did such a thing, you'd never see your mom and dad again. You shouldn't put them through that heartache...At least...at least..."

At least you can still see them. Not like me and my sister.

Merida seemed to pick up on what she didn't say. She lifted her head, face streaked with tears, and stared right at Yuuki with big wet eyes. There was the barest hint of a smile on her lips.

"...Mmm...You're right. Yuuki, Ran, I'm sorry. I'm being weird."

She rubbed her face like Yuuki did earlier, wiping away the tears, then beamed, dimpling her cheeks.

"I'm all right! I'm going to take good care of Roy, because I have a big goal now: to win the next Insect Battle Tournament! Plus... it's not like I can even get into Aincrad, anyway. There's no playing *SAO* without NerveGear, and the only addresses it will accept are the ones from the IPs of the players already connected."

That made sense; aside from the NerveGear being worn by the Incident's victims, all other NerveGear had been seized, and she hadn't heard about a single person logging in to *SAO* on their own after it started. Yuuki relaxed a little and smiled back.

"I'll cheer you on in the tournament. You have to win it!"

"Don't worry!" said Merida, pounding her chest. As she stretched, she remembered something: "Oh, right. What other VR games do you play?

Yuuki had just stuck the rest of her crepe into her mouth, so Ran answered instead.

"This is the only one we've ever done."

"Awww, that's a waste! Especially when you can stand on one leg for so long. I'm sure you would do great in any action-based game..."

Yuuki and her sister shared a look.

They knew that more and more VR games had come out for the AmuSphere in the last year. Around the same time that *Serene Garden* started, there had been a popular MMORPG called *ALfheim Online*, where the players were all fairies that could fly. There were also zombie-based horror shooters, action-adventure games about exploring ruins, and other traditionally popular genres.

But she and Ran had never even brought up the idea of playing a different game. That was probably because she felt guilty about the idea of using the Medicuboid to simply "play around." Ran had been provided with the modified NerveGear for free, so she would feel the same way about it.

But how could they explain that to Merida? Ran grinned and said, "It's nice of you to suggest, but AmuSphere games are pretty expensive, right? We can't buy them on our allowance."

That, at least, was true. A little while after their parents died, the girls talked it over and decided to minimize the allowance they received from their inheritance. They wanted to donate as much of that as possible to nonprofit organizations supporting children suffering from severe diseases. It was hard for them to feel good about buying a video game that cost nearly ten thousand yen.

But Merida just looked surprised and shook her head. "Oh, that's no problem! There are games that are free to play, and you can make money just by selling items."

"Huh...? You don't have to pay for the game itself?!" they asked in shock.

She nodded more firmly this time. "Yes! You just download and install the game, and you can play it. If you want to buy helpful items for convenience or get really cool-looking gear, it'll cost real money, but I don't spend anything at all."

"Ooooh…what kind of game is it?" Ran asked, unexpectedly hooked by this pitch. Merida reached toward her left side and made a show of pretending to grab something, then whipped her hand across the table.

"I haven't been in there in a little while, but it's a Japanese-style MMO called *Asuka Empire*. You turn into samurai or ninjas or shrine maidens to fight each other. It looks completely different from *SG*, too…There are unbelievably huge castles and gorgeous temples. It's really fun."

"…Fight…," Yuuki mumbled.

Of course there was fighting; it was a game. But she felt intimidated by the idea of fighting with other players in a virtual setting using swords and guns. It wasn't like watching your character move around on a screen…The opponents were avatars, but they were *real*. She couldn't imagine physically performing the violence of swinging, striking, and punching other people that way.

But to her surprise, Ran simply said, "That sounds really fun."

"Right?!" Merida leaned over the table, her eyes sparkling. "Hey, would you want to come check out *Asuka*? I'll show you how it works!"

"Hmm, well…"

"I'll take pictures of you wearing your miko outfits or samurai armor or whatever! You'll look great in them!"

"Hmm, well…"

"Also, there's all kinds of traditional sweets you can eat! Like *anmitsu* and *oshiruko* and *warabi mochi*!"

"……!!"

Yuuki didn't miss the little twitch of Ran's shoulders. She knew that after her mother's homemade crepes, the one thing that Ran loved most that she couldn't get inside *Serene Garden* or from the hospital cafeteria was *oshiruko*, a dessert of hot, sweet red bean soup, with a big chewy mochi rice cake dipped inside.

She could see that her sister was trapped between guilt about enjoying a game for its own sake, yearning for a new and mysterious world, and temptation for the flavor of sweet red beans. So to help with the final push, Yuuki added, "Since Merida's inviting us, we should just go with her, Sis! I'm sure the doctor will let us!"

Ran looked back at her in mild surprise, then gave a rare full smile and nodded. "Yeah…let's check it out!"

"Yay!" Merida cheered, clapping her hands over her head. She glanced upward. "Today's…probably a stretch. I'll send you a message to your *SG* account about how to install *Asuka Empire*. How about we meet up at one o'clock tomorrow?"

"Sure, that works," replied Ran. Merida hopped to her feet, ponytail bouncing, and stuck out both hands toward the sisters.

"Yuuki, Ran, I'm so happy I got to meet you and become friends with you. I think we're going to have a great time!"

Feeling the joy and the light in her eyes and words, Yuuki joined her sister in standing and grasped the hand of the first friend she'd made in ages.

4

May 12th was a Sunday.

There was no outpatient service on Sunday, so the hospital felt quieter than usual as a whole. Of course, the only time Yuuki would even be aware of that was when she was out of the Medicuboid for tests or to wash up.

Yuuki couldn't stay in a shared room in the hospital ward due to the high risk of infection, so there was a special pod-type bathing apparatus installed in the sterilizing room adjacent to the clean room. The tub was extremely cramped, so she felt more like she was being washed than bathing. Still, it felt very good to be able to dunk her body and head in hot water.

Serene Garden had its own huge bathhouse that was more of a spa resort. But the sensation of the hot water wasn't quite the same, and she felt resistance to the idea of getting naked around other people, even if it was just a virtual body. Ran always laughed it off and said, "You're too sensitive!"

Feeling nice and fresh after her Sunday afternoon bath, Yuuki sterilized her body and put on the examination outfit she used for pajamas, then returned to the clean room, where she lay down on the high-density gel bed of Medicuboid Test Unit Two. Unlike Test Unit One, which was known only by the appellation MFT1, this had the proper name of Medicuboid because it was a cubical structure with medical applications. The body of the device was shaped like a huge box. Test Unit Three, which was in production now, was even larger, apparently. Yuuki didn't know if she would ever see it.

She was lying on her back and pondering this when a little voice sounded in the back of her head.

I suppose that would mean I found a reason to live...

A reason to live.

Most of the elderly players in *Serene Garden* were shockingly active in the game, which shouldn't have been a surprise, because they were choosing to come and experience the VR world. Still, there were times when she heard them say things that sounded regretful or negative.

If I can't get better, then I'd rather just die.

Nothing good's going to happen. There's no point to living.

Every time she came across one of those people, Ran did her very best to cheer them up. But Yuuki couldn't do what her big sister did. She felt that same kind of emptiness in her core, too.

Until half a year ago, she could have fought through the sorrow, just because she didn't want to make her parents sad. No matter how bad things got, she could always be cheerful in front of them. She would do anything she could to put a smile on her mom's and dad's faces. But now they were gone.

She still had her big sister at her side for now. She never wanted to say or do anything that would make Ran sad. But if—on some small chance—Ran took the journey to see their parents before Yuuki did, she couldn't imagine how she would find a reason to keep going.

But no. Ran would never leave her behind like that. As long as she was alive, Ran would be, too, and vice versa.

This was pointless. Merida was going to show them a new game, and she didn't want to go into the experience with dark feelings.

She installed the client for the VRMMO *Asuka Empire* with Dr. Kurahashi's approval—and his stern reminder that she must not tell anyone that she was a Medicuboid test subject—and created her avatar. After checking the time, she placed her head against the headrest and pulled down the headgear.

Yuuki closed her eyes and heard a faint machine whirring, then spoke the start-up command that the Medicuboid shared with the NerveGear and AmuSphere.

"...Link Start!"

In the app launcher, instead of her usual *Serene Garden*, she chose the new icon belonging to *Asuka Empire*. Yuuki's mind plummeted into digital darkness.

A glowing ring appeared below her feet and rose upward. When she passed through it, there was suddenly light all around.

She blinked as her feet touched ground. Yuuki looked up and experienced a rich color palette filling her vision.

Red, yellow, crimson, and orange: The square space was surrounded by a breathtaking tapestry of leaves rustling in a light breeze.

The sky was so blue, it seemed crystal clear. There was rounded white gravel on the ground, so each step caused light skittering sounds. Before her was a huge torii gate, painted a shade of red even deeper than maple leaves, through which the gravel path led.

"Yes...there's nothing like *this* in *Serene Garden*," said a nearby voice. She turned to see a girl wearing a simple but cute kimono. Her face was slightly different from how it looked in the real world and in *Serene Garden*, but the hair, voice, and general demeanor instantly told her it was Ran. There were no other players around.

Yuuki looked down to see that she was wearing the same kimono in a different color pattern and said, "Yeah. It feels so... traditional!"

"It really does. I think I'm looking forward to this now."

"Looking forward to the *oshiruko*, you mean?"

"Of course!"

Suddenly, there were quick, light footsteps running toward

them from the far side of the gate. It was another girl, this one with a long ponytail, running with an extreme forward slant.

Once through the gate, she jumped high in the air, doing multiple flips before landing directly in front of the sisters.

""Ooh!""

Yuuki and Ran applauded as the girl, dressed in a very ninja-esque light-green outfit, gave a very theatrical bow. After Yuuki focused on her for a few moments, the character name *Merida* appeared over her head. That was a feature that didn't exist in *Serene Garden*.

"Thanks for waiting! Welcome to *Asuka Empire*!" Merida explained, lifting her head. Her avatar, which looked a little bolder than the one they saw yesterday, leaned back slightly to assess their appearances. "You're both very good at avatar creation! You look so cute, and you're still very similar to your *SG* avatars."

"Y-you think so...? I just took what was on the default setting and tweaked it a little bit...," Yuuki mumbled. It was at this point that she noticed something new in the upper left corner of her vision.

There was a narrow blue bar resting above a narrow green bar, below which was the name *Yuuki*. If she looked at it long enough, letters floated inside the bars, with *LP 350/350* inside the green one and *SP 100/100* inside the blue.

Merida could tell what she was looking at from the direction of Yuuki's eyes, and she held up a pointer finger to explain. "This is probably your first time seeing that, since you've only played *SG* before. The green one is your life points, which is your health, and the blue one is your soul points, which you use to do jutsu and techniques and stuff. You're still neophytes, so you have the same numbers, but when you do an initiation quest in town and select a class, one of them will shoot way higher."

"Uh-huh...And what's your class, Merida? Well, I can guess based on your clothes," Ran said.

Merida grinned, then clasped her hands together and ran them through a series of complex arrangements. They looked very familiar.

"Hah!" she shouted, and suddenly, her body was surrounded in pale smoke, then was gone. Yuuki and Ran looked around, but there was no sign of her anywhere. The only thing they could hear was the faint sound of footsteps on gravel. It seemed to be in the distance behind them—and then instantly, someone hugged Yuuki from behind.

"Gotcha, Yuuki!"

There was another puff of smoke, and she saw arms grabbing her around the midriff.

"Aaah! I'm not a stag beetle!" Yuuki protested, struggling. Merida grinned, let go, and returned to where she was initially standing.

Ran stated, "So you're a ninja?"

"Bingo! Technically, ninja is the advanced version of the thief class. Every neophyte has to pick from either swordsman, thief, or mage, and from there, you rank up into advanced classes like samurai, archer, ninja, shrine maiden, monk, and so on."

"Ooooh…What should I be, then?"

"Making that decision is part of the fun of playing MMOs!" Merida said with a dimpled grin, then pointed toward the torii gate. "C'mon, let's go! The capital of *Asuka* is up there!"

The setting of *Asuka Empire* was a fantastical, fictionalized version of the ancient Yamato court that ruled over the central and western regions of Japan, if it had lasted for over a thousand years. The capital, Kiyomihara, was a castle city laid out like an enormous Go board and was at least three times larger than Serenity, the central city of *Serene Garden*.

The number of concurrent players was second only to *ALfheim Online*, the most popular of all the VRMMOs. On a Sunday afternoon, the city was packed with players dressed in traditional garb. Yuuki and Ran had never seen this many players in a virtual space, so after they passed through the great southern gate, they simply stood there in silent awe.

It wasn't just the numbers. It was the activity, the chaos, the *energy* in this place that was unlike anything they'd experienced before. The main street was no less than a hundred feet wide and full of groups of people engaged in lively chats, gangs arguing and itching for a fight, and even item sellers setting up shops on the sides of the path.

"Wow…there are so many people," Yuuki marveled.

"Right?" said Merida.

She began walking and motioned for the sisters to follow. As they moved forward, she lowered her volume and explained, "Right after the *SAO* Incident started, everyone was afraid of VR games, and they were talking about outlawing full-dive technology…but I think there's something to this world that isn't found in traditional video games. Once you get hooked, you'll never be able to go back to a monitor and controller again…"

Yuuki understood what she was talking about. She didn't know if they were going to keep playing *Asuka Empire* after this, but she knew that if they couldn't go back to *Serene Garden*, life would feel much blander. Having a place to visit with Ran where they could eat good food, search for items, and study together was a joy she got to experience on a daily basis.

While their world might be different, thousands of people in *Asuka Empire* had to feel the same way. It wasn't a simple time waster or an escape from reality for them. And Merida was one of that group. The fact that she'd worked her way up to an advanced ninja class was evidence that she'd found something important here.

But yesterday at the crepe shop in Leute, Merida intimated that she wanted to go back to *Sword Art Online*. She said she might find a reason to live there—and shed tears. That probably meant *Asuka Empire* didn't have what Merida was really searching for. So what was different between *Asuka Empire* and *Sword Art Online*? They were both VRMMOs…

"Look! There's the initiate hall!" Merida cried out, rousing Yuuki from her thoughts. Up ahead on the right side of the street was an especially large building with three separate entrances.

"Okay, you two. Which do you want to be: swordsman, thief, or mage?"

"What's the difference?" asked Ran, who didn't know that much about video games.

"A swordsman goes in front, fighting with weapons or martial arts and getting hit by enemy attacks," Merida explained. "A thief zips around quickly, confusing the enemy and doing lots of other activities. A mage stays in the back and casts magic to attack enemies or back up their friends."

"Uh-huh. I see," muttered Yuuki, giving this some thought along with Ran. After five seconds, she said, "Then I'll be a swordsman!"

"And I'll be a mage."

Merida chuckled when she heard their answers. "I had a feeling that's what you'd pick. In that case, Yuuki, you go in the middle entrance, and, Ran, take the right. Inside, you'll be able to accept a quest. I'll help you finish them, so let's take care of these initiation quests!"

"Yeah!"

Yuuki pumped her fist into the air and glanced over at Ran before running for the doorway.

The act of holding a weapon in her hands and swinging at realistic monsters was a major shock.

At first, she ran and screamed whenever the dog-sized rats charged at her. But once she learned their bites didn't hurt (it was just mildly unpleasant) and that there was no blood when she slashed them (just a spray of red light), she stopped being afraid and was able to fight. Ran showed no fear of the rats at all, though, and dispatched them easily from the start.

With the help of their experienced ninja friend, they spent two hours finishing the five-part initiation quests. Yuuki was now a swordsman, and Ran was a mage. When Merida invited them to get something to eat in celebration, Ran immediately requested *oshiruko*, of course.

"Fwaaaah…," Ran moaned the moment the steaming, lacquered cups were brought out. "It's amazing, Merida. It's perfect. The grilled crisp on the chewy mochi, the texture of the mashed beans, the contrasting taste of the salted kombu, the style of the establishment—it's all perfect."

"I…I'm glad you like it."

"If I'd known they had such delicious *oshiruko* here, I would have come much sooner," Ran said, lost in reverie. She brought her hands up in prayer, then lifted her painted chopsticks.

Yuuki waited for her sister to start eating first, then lifted her *oshiruko* to her lips. The gentle sweetness and flavor of crushed red beans filled her mouth, followed by the scent of the mochi. She wasn't as obsessed with sweet red beans as her sister, but this was very delicious.

The trio ate in almost total silence until they exhaled in blissful satisfaction at the same time. Ran set down her chopsticks and took a sip of tea.

"…That was wonderful. Thank you for bringing us here, Merida."

"I'm glad you liked it."

"Anyway…is this Kiyomihara place supposed to be set around the real-life Asuka region?"

"That's right. Why?" Merida asked. Ran pointed at the menu on the table.

"When this dish is made with chunky beans rather than blended, only the Kanto region around Tokyo calls it *oshiruko*. In the actual Kansai area where Asuka is, the ones with whole red beans are called *zenzai*. They only call the thinner soup with fine bean paste *oshiruko*."

"Ohhh! Does that mean they call the finer bean paste *zenzai* in the Kanto region?"

"Actually, they call it *oshiruko* whether it's chunky or smooth. *Zenzai* is used to describe solid crushed red beans without any liquid, like the kind you dollop over mochi or rice dumplings."

"Oh, wow! I'm from Tokyo, but I had no idea about the difference. Well, we ordered *oshiruko* and got something with the beans crushed, so I guess this restaurant must be Kanto style," Merida narrated, fascinated.

Ran grimaced and shook her head. "Actually, not necessarily. They might have simply reversed it, like you guessed…"

Yuuki suddenly realized what was going on, gave her sister a piercing look, and shouted, "Oh, I get it! You keep talking about different regional styles—but you just want to order the *zenzai*, too!"

"Heh-heh-heh, you got me." Ran stuck out her tongue, and Merida laughed.

When they ordered the *zenzai*, they received neither a bowl of finely filtered sweet bean paste nor a solid mash but another soup of crushed beans with chestnuts in it. Despite the confusion, however, it was delicious, too, so the trio ate with gusto. By the time they left, the sun was much farther down in the sky.

"Ahhh, here I've gone and eaten two bowls of *oshiruko* at this hour. Will I have any appetite for dinner?" Merida grumbled, rubbing her stomach. "It's so strange how this virtual food really makes you feel full."

"Yeah, seriously," Yuuki agreed. "From what I hear, when you're eating, the full-dive machine stimulates the chewing centers of your brain, and it's so tightly related to your fullness centers that they feel the illusion, too."

"Ooooh! …Hey, why am I the one gushing over everything? You guys are too knowledgeable about stuff!"

"No, I'm just repeating what was explained to me," Yuuki said with a shrug. For a brief moment, Merida looked like she was waking up from a dream. She must have understood that Yuuki wasn't talking about a teacher at school but the doctor at the hospital.

They left the sweets shop, which was a special hole-in-the-wall place just like the crepe shop yesterday, and headed out into the lonely backstreet. Ran's wooden geta sandals made sad little clacking sounds on the stone pavement.

After a little while, Merida murmured, "So...your doctor knows about how full-diving works."

"Yeah..."

After all, it was Dr. Kurahashi himself who had recommended that Yuuki be a test patient for the Medicuboid. The young doctor had high hopes for the use of full-dive tech in improving terminal care. But Yuuki was sworn to secrecy, so she couldn't tell Merida about that.

"What about your doctor?" she asked.

The other girl shrugged, the ash-green fabric of her ninja outfit rising and falling. "My doctor...doesn't think very highly of it. I had to ask a bunch of times before I got approval to register for *SG*. He doesn't seem to think that VR-based palliative care improves QOL."

QOL was an abbreviation for *quality of life*. Palliative care was meant to improve the patient's quality of life by focusing on easing physical, mental, and social pain caused by their condition. The AmuSphere had a function that canceled bodily sensations up to a point, meaning it could ease a sick person's pain and therefore might be a useful substitute for painkillers, which had side effects and dependency problems.

On the other hand, patients in the midst of a full dive were essentially just lying prone on a bed, so there was a strong counterargument that it wasn't improving the patient's actual life. Merida's doctor had to share that opinion, then.

Yuuki didn't know which side was right. *Serene Garden* and *Asuka Empire* were both enticing worlds, and the time she spent with Ran in them felt extremely valuable, but at this point, she spent no time together with Aiko in the real world. Every now and then, she thought that being able to interact with her sister all day in the virtual world, rather than being stuck in her clean room, was the happier option.

While Yuuki was lost in these heavy thoughts, Ran said, "I don't think you can blame anyone for being negative about full-diving while the *SAO* Incident is still ongoing. But…I want to believe in the possibilities of this place. We met you because of *Serene Garden*, and I think we'll meet many more people after this. Even if the connections are only online…I think the things we're feeling are real."

"Yes…that's right," Merida agreed, putting a hand to her chest. "I'm so happy I met you two. The memories we've made together will always be here…not in my avatar's heart but in *my* heart."

Her tone of voice was light, but the word *memories* felt heavy and sad in the lonely evening alleyway. She'd said that a year and a half had passed since starting treatment for her brain tumor. She must have spent all that time thinking about how much she had left before the end. That was why Merida was searching in the virtual world for a meaning to her life.

"…I'm happy, too," Yuuki murmured, grabbing Merida's hand as they walked side by side. "Since starting in *Serene Garden*, I never got too close to anyone other than Sis. I was afraid of hurting them or getting hurt myself…But yesterday, you gave us everything you have. And that's how we were able to become friends so quickly."

Merida's eyes briefly widened. Then she beamed for all she was worth and squeezed Yuuki's hand back.

"Thanks, Yuuki! It makes me feel good to hear that! But that enthusiasm yesterday might have been because I was thinking about the beetle so hard…"

"Turnabout is fair play. Yuuki and I have just been thinking about crepes and *oshiruko*," Ran said, laughing and reaching for Merida's other hand. The three girls laughed and laughed and laughed. Yuuki could feel a comfortable breeze blowing through her heart that made her feel light and warm.

If she could laugh like this, then maybe it didn't matter whether this was a real world or a digital one.

She wanted to laugh and smile as much as she could in the time she had left. She wanted to hurl all of her being at someone else the way Merida had done for her.

It was the first time since she'd been hospitalized—since she transferred elementary schools, even—that Yuuki had felt something so strongly.

5

"It's almost your birthday, isn't it?" said Dr. Kurahashi out of nowhere as he lowered the stethoscope. Yuuki looked down and to her right out of sheer reflex.

But this was the real world, where there was no clock in her view. Nor was there any calendar on the clean room wall. So she looked up at the doctor and asked, "Um...what day of May is it?"

Dr. Kurahashi smiled, though it was hard to see through the thick mask of his clean suit. "The sixteenth. You and Aiko were born on the twenty-third, right?"

"Yes, that's right," said Yuuki, fastening the buttons on her dustproof examination gown.

The doctor paused for a moment. With a wistful tone, he said, "You're going to be fourteen already...You've grown so much."

"What...? Actually, I wish I would grow more."

"Ha-ha-ha. Don't worry—you've still got plenty of room to grow," he said kindly, patted her on the head, and stood up. "Well, see you next week."

"Good-bye, Doctor."

She watched him go back through the door of the sterilizing room, then lay down on the gel bed.

She'd come to Yokohama Kohoku General Hospital just after

her birthday the year before last. It had been almost two years. Over half of that time, Yuuki had spent here in this clean room.

Until recently, she'd grappled with an urge during her weekly meetings with Dr. Kurahashi to rush after him and leap out the door, just so she could be sure the outside world still existed as it had before. But in the last few days, she suddenly felt much less confined by this off-white room.

That was certainly because of her meeting with Merida four days ago and the interactions she'd had with all those players in their new world. It was just simple greetings, in towns and in wilderness, no more than a few words each time, but she felt the warmth coming from them nonetheless. Despite the *SAO* Incident, there were so many people in that place enjoying the VR world, going on new adventures every day, giving birth to countless personal stories.

She shifted herself up on the bed to lay her head on the headrest. *I'm going to get that upgrade to the higher class today*, she told herself, closing her eyes and lowering the headgear.

"Jarrruooooo!"

The oni-type ogre, a good ten feet tall, rumbled toward them and swung a crude giant katana, howling eerily. The horns that split its rough, shaggy hair shone with a dark light that extended to cover the thick blade.

"Yuu, here comes a skill!" Ran called.

"I've got it, Sis!" Yuuki shouted back, holding her katana up high.

The final boss of the class upgrade quest, Akuro-ou, was a fearsome foe who could employ five different kinds of wide-area skills with its oversize *nodachi* katana. Merely attempting to avoid the attack itself only helped so much; the splash damage that followed would hit you anyway and leave you unable to switch to counterattacking.

So the role of the swordsman, as the party tank, was not to avoid the attack but to block it as best as possible. To do that as a weaker new character in her primary class, Yuuki couldn't just block it with her weapon. She had to use a skill of her own to counteract and neutralize it.

She had a window of less than a second to do this, between the start of Akuro-ou's swing and when the force of its attack skill engaged.

Yuuki opened her eyes wide, held her breath, and glared at the enemy's sword. There was a high-pitched sound like ringing in her ears, and the enemy's movements felt slower. This feeling often came over her lately when she was concentrating her hardest. The pause in the giant *nodachi* ended, and the blade began to move—now.

There!

Yuuki's left foot stomped on the ground.

Asuka Empire used a system called ground circles for its skills and spells. If you stomped on the ground with your weapon readied, your available skills or spells would appear arrayed in a circle at your feet. Stomping a second time on the icon you wanted would choose and activate it.

At first, she would have to look down at the ground, see what she wanted, and then step again. But after practice, she was learning how to do it without looking.

"Yaaaaah!" she roared, getting the hang of her battle cry, and pressed an icon with her right foot. She launched herself upward and activated the antiair skill Himukai, which turned her katana orange.

"*Ja-jaaaa!!*" Akuro-ou bellowed again. But Yuuki's antiair skill had already struck the middle of its *nodachi*. The flash of orange tore the blackish-blue effect in two and dispersed it. The *nodachi* jolted backward, pulling Akuro-ou's giant body with it.

"Sis, Merida, now!" she cried as she fell. A strip of white paper—Ran's magic seal—flew up from the rear and stuck to Akuro-ou's forehead. The seal shone and created a series of complex magic circles, then exploded in a huge fireball.

The boss groaned and faltered, right as three silhouettes rushed toward its feet and sliced with countless shinobi blades. That was Merida's special Body Double skill. Huge chunks fell from the boss's LP bar, leaving just a few pixels left.

Akuro-ou recovered from the delay caused by canceling its attack skill just as Yuuki's cooldown ended. She held her katana at her left side and stepped on the floor again. As soon as she sensed the ground circle had appeared again, she stomped on the icon directly in front of her.

"Haaaaah!"

The quick-draw skill Suminagi had a tremendous reach, enough to hit the horns on the boss's forehead—its weak point. It sliced them off, and the boss's LP gauge was empty at last. Akuro-ou's giant body turned into eerie blue flames and fell apart.

The battle had taken over twenty minutes to finish. A victory fanfare played in their ears as they cheered and shouted.

After turning in their quest to the NPC in Kiyomihara, Yuuki and Ran were promoted to the advanced classes of samurai and miko. Once they were outside the building, they spent some time examining their new looks.

These weren't anything like the simple clothes from *Serene Garden*; instead, they were fancy and flashy RPG outfits. They felt both excited and bashful about them, and they giggled together. Suddenly, a familiar voice called out from above their heads.

"Yuuki, Ran, congrats on the promotion!"

They looked up and saw Merida sitting on the edge of the building's extended roof, waving at them. She hopped down, flipping in the air, and landed just in front of where they were standing.

"You did really well. Getting to the advanced classes in just four days is remarkable!"

"Only because you spent hours each day helping us out, Merida. Thanks," replied Ran with a big smile. Yuuki added a "Thanks!" of her own. Merida giggled and shook her head.

"Well, it was my idea to invite you to *Asuka*, so it's my

responsibility to help you out…Besides, it was fun for me, too. I don't usually play with parties."

There had been lots to learn in the last four days of *Asuka Empire*, so they were aware now that ninjas like Merida were considered the best advanced class to use if you were a solo player. Yuuki could imagine why she'd chosen it.

Befriending people you met when partying up, and joining guilds after that, meant increasing the likelihood of talking about life outside the game. If other people asked them about their real lives, Yuuki, Ran, and Merida would have some very painful choices to make. Do you tell them about your terrible disease and that VR games are just a means of making the time left more enjoyable? Or do you lie? Telling the truth might make things very awkward for the other person, and lying was just as painful.

Yuuki prayed she could have the courage to be honest with others, the way Merida was with her. But that wasn't easy. Merida had to be fighting with her own walls even now, walls her heart had built to protect herself.

Ran patted her sister on the back to cheer her up. "Come on, Yuu. Merida wants to celebrate our promotion."

"Huh? Oh…right! I want to go back to that place again!"

"Okay! There are plenty more things for you to try out there!" their friend said, grinning, and took the lead down the path.

At the sweets shop, Yuuki ordered a sweet *anmitsu* bowl with cream, Ran got the *kuzumochi*, and Merida wanted a matcha parfait. They took turns tasting one another's items until they were done and washed down the sweetness with hot mugs of tea.

"Ahhh, this is bliss…Traditional sweets and green tea really are the perfect combination," said Ran, closing her eyes. Yuuki and Merida nodded without comment. Coffee, black tea, or milk all went well with crepes, but none of them felt like the superb complementary pairing of sweet red beans and green tea.

"Speaking of perfect combinations, I can absolutely believe

you two are sisters. Your teamwork in battle is impeccable. I can't believe you're newcomers to VRMMOs," Merida said out of the blue.

Yuuki and her sister shared a look, then shrugged.

"I-I'm just swinging my katana around. Sis is the one who times everything to match me...," Yuuki said—right at the same moment Ran claimed, "I'm just casting spells from the back, so I have a good view of Yuu..."

The combination caused Merida to spit up and nearly choke.

"You see? You're perfectly in sync! But that's not the only remarkable thing about you. You're able to use your skills without looking at your feet, right? It took me a month to be comfortable with doing that!"

"Well...that's because *Asuka Empire* is our first VRMMO experience. You played other games before this, Merida, so it was probably harder to learn how to do things differently, right? Or do all VRMMOs have the same fighting system?" Ran asked.

Merida chuckled and started to nod, but then changed her mind and shook her head. "Well, maybe there's a little bit of that...The battle system was completely different."

She glanced around the sweets shop to make sure there were no other players around, then continued in hushed tones.

"Like the name suggests, *Sword Art Online* only has weapon battles, no magic. You execute sword skills just by holding your weapon the right way. And unlike in *Asuka*, they're not all single-use attacks."

"Not all single-use...?" Yuuki repeated, not grasping what that meant.

Using the long parfait spoon, Merida swung it up, down, then to the side.

"Yes. Meaning combination attacks. In *Asuka*, you can keep swinging afterward with regular attacks, but the power of the skills in *SAO* was completely different. When you take the right pose and activate the sword skill, your body just moves all on its own. So your sword will go *sli-sli-slice!* and hit three or four times in a row superfast. In *Asuka*, you ready your katana, stomp on the ground to make the circle, stomp again to select the icon, and *then* it makes a single-attack skill. When I started, it felt sooo sloooow. I think half the reason I chose to be a ninja was so that I could move faster," Merida explained with a smirk. Yuuki and Ran chose to laugh with her, rather than ask the other half of her reasoning.

"Ah-ha-ha-ha. Yes, you really do zip around," said Ran. "One second you're over here, and the next you're coming from the other direction."

Merida joked, "It's the fundamental style of any ninja!" But her smile did not last long. She blinked slowly, reflecting on the boss battle earlier, and said, "Actually...what I think is amazing is your ability to ascertain. Like today...Yuuki, you totally saw Akuro-ou's last area attack before it happened, didn't you? Even among the best players, you don't see many people who can stop the boss's big attack over ten times in a row. I guess it wasn't a coincidence that you managed to catch that royal triton stag beetle in *Serene Garden*."

Yuuki's mouth fell open; she wasn't expecting to hear that.

In situations like these, it was always her sister who received the praise. Test scores, art skill, even running speed—Ran was always better. It should have been the same way in the virtual world. If Merida saw Yuuki as being superior to Ran, there could only be one reasonable explanation: The specs were higher on the Medicuboid compared with Ran's NerveGear.

"N...no, Merida, it's not like that," she protested, shaking her head. "It's just because I'm not using an AmuSphere. I'm on a—"

She gasped and caught herself there. Dr. Kurahashi said she could play *Asuka Empire* only so long as she didn't tell anyone about the Medicuboid.

Merida waited for the rest, looking stunned, but Yuuki just fell silent without finishing her statement. It was Ran who came to her rescue.

"Listen, Merida," she said softly, "we have something to tell you, and we hope you'll forgive us for not saying it before. Yuu was about to say that we're not using regular AmuSpheres. They're augmented NerveGear the hospital staff gave us."

Yuuki understood that she had no choice but to say it. But even that was half a lie. Whatever you might say about Test Unit One, there was no denying that Test Unit Two was a far cry from the adapted NerveGear.

She regretted that her slip of the tongue forced her sister to tell a lie. She clenched her fists in her lap until Ran's fingers gently brushed her hands. *It's all right*, she was saying.

Merida didn't seem to notice what the sisters were doing under the table. She was wide-eyed, and her voice escaped barely louder than a whisper. "Nerve...Gear..."

She blinked a few times, then continued, "When you say augmented, do you mean...made safe?"

"Yes...that's what they tell us. The battery capacity is smaller, and there are limits on its functions so that it can't transmit dangerous EM waves. The hospital recommended that we make proactive use of VR for palliative care, and they arranged for the headgear for us."

"Oh...I see...," said Merida, nodding a few times as the shock wore off. "You know...when I first tried on an AmuSphere, I noticed that the response was a bit slower than the NerveGear, and the sensory information wasn't as clean. But you can't fight that well just from having higher specs. You two are special."

She beamed at them. At this point, they couldn't keep arguing against it. Instead, the sisters fell into an awkward silence, prompting Merida to smile even wider.

"At any rate, congrats on the class change! If you have more time, we should go to the imperial palace to take pictures. You look great in your new gear!"

"Yeah, good idea. Let's go," said Ran the miko enthusiastically. At last, Yuuki felt like smiling again.

*　　*　　*

Before they said good-bye for the day, the three girls went to the glamorous palace where the emperor lived in order to take screenshots—not that there was any "screen" in a VR game per se.

The three girls continued to enjoy *Asuka Empire* after this day. Sometimes they'd go back to *Serene Garden* to see how the stag beetle was coming along or to eat crepes at that special little café. Once or twice, Merida had bouts of that dizziness again, but she was always cheerful and smiling regardless.

Time passed in a blink when it was so fulfilling. Soon it was May 21st, just two days before Yuuki and Ran's fourteenth birthday.

That was when Merida popped a very unexpected suggestion on them.

6

"This place is so dreary. You could at least put in some walls and a ceiling," Ran commented upon visiting Yuuki's private VR "room."

The data for this space was contained in the main memory of Medicuboid Test Unit Two, and only Yuuki and Ran could access it right now. There were no features in the room aside from the flat, artificial floor. That was if you considered an endless dark space with nothing but a few windows floating in the air to count as a "room" at all.

Half the windows displayed various status updates from the Medicuboid, while the rest offered an assortment of news sources and TV channels. The largest window, right in front, held a real-time stream of the clean room from the camera on Test Unit Two. It was her window from the virtual world out into the real one.

Yuuki was lying on the hard floor in her pajamas, looking up at Ran, who was wearing the same thing. "It's fine like this! If I spruce this place up like our home in *Serene Garden*, I'm going to have a hard time remembering if I'm in the real world or the virtual world."

She patted the empty space next to her and pleaded, "C'mon, Sis, sing to me. Like old times."

"Oh, fine. You're so needy, Yuu," her sister said with a smile and knelt down on the ground. Yuuki placed her head on Ran's lap and closed her eyes. She relaxed, letting the tension leave her limbs. She felt gentle hands caressing her head and heard a whisper-soft singing voice in her ear.

It was a Mother Goose lullaby called "Hush Little Baby, Don't Say a Word," which their mother had often sung to them. It was a strange song about buying a baby all kinds of gifts to make them stop crying, such as a looking glass, or a billy goat, or a horse and cart. But that was what they liked about it.

Their avatar voices, like their faces, were synthesized from samples of their real-world voices, but it didn't feel off at all. Ran's singing was as soft and enveloping as a gentle wave at the shore, filling the infinite space that surrounded them.

So hush, little baby, don't you cry.
Daddy loves you, and so do I.
Daddy loves you, and so do I.

After Ran finished the last repeated line of the song, she continued caressing Yuuki's head for a while. Yuuki was just starting to drift off to sleep—it was after ten at night—when a finger flicked her forehead and took her by surprise.

"Don't go to sleep here, Yuu. We haven't talked about what we need to yet."

"*Unyu*...Oh, right..."

She did her best to lift her heavy eyelids and sat up. Once she was facing her sister, she folded her arms and muttered, "So... what should we do, Sis?"

Even Ran, who was normally so decisive, didn't have an answer ready.

Earlier in the evening, Merida had a very sudden suggestion. She said that two days later, on the twenty-third, she wanted to pay Yuuki and Ran a visit to celebrate their birthday. Not in a virtual world, of course, but at Yokohama Kohoku General Hospital.

Merida's hospital was in Shinagawa Ward in Tokyo, which

was less than an hour away by car. Of course, she'd have family escorting her, so it probably wasn't the biggest problem on her side.

But Yuuki and Ran couldn't tell her she was welcome, not right on the spot, at least. For one thing, Yuuki's test usage of the Medicuboid was confidential, so she couldn't meet with Merida. She couldn't even tell her why.

Even if they couldn't meet in person, the idea of Merida coming to the hospital was wonderful. Yuuki knew that she would be very happy just hearing about the experience from Ran after it happened.

But what if Merida didn't take well to the answer that she couldn't see Yuuki...? What if she was so hurt by it that Yuuki lost this precious friend she'd finally made...?

"...Let's trust Merida," Ran said at last, breaking the silence.

"But...Sis..."

"I'm sure Merida will understand you have reasons why you can't see her, even though you want to. I can't imagine she'd be mad about it. Besides...if she brings her AmuSphere and dives from my room with me, we'll be able to come here together, won't we?"

"Y-you're going to bring her *here*?!" Yuuki shouted, though she didn't mean to.

Ran gave her a mischievous grin. "I'm sure Merida would be very happy to throw a birthday party for us in your room."

"Ummm...W-well, maybe I can try to decorate it to make it a bit more girlie," she murmured, looking around the dark void that screamed *virtual*.

Ran patted her on the shoulder and said, "Better be quick, then. It's in just two days. And let me be clear: I'm not helping you."

"Awww..."

"Just do what you want, Yuu. Whatever that is, it's bound to delight Merida. Well, I'll be leaving now. I'll tell her we'll be happy to see her, okay?"

"...Yeah!" Yuuki agreed vigorously, getting to her feet. Better to just go full steam ahead, rather than worrying about hurting others or being hurt. That was the lesson Merida had taught her, wasn't it?

Ran waved good night and left the space, which Yuuki surveyed with fresh eyes. If they were going to have a birthday party, they'd at least need a table and chairs. But first, walls and a ceiling.

Even if it was going to get reset in a day, this was a makeover meant to host their good friend. She was going to put all her energy into customizing the space, she decided. Yuuki headed toward one of the status windows hanging in the air.

At two o'clock on Thursday, May 23rd, Merida arrived at Yokohama Kohoku General Hospital in her mother's car.

She was sitting in a wheelchair because the brain tumor had rendered her unable to use her legs. But after leaving her mother to wait in the hospital's café, she made it all the way up to the eighth floor of the sick ward to Ran's room on her own. She brought a large tote bag containing two wrapped birthday presents and her AmuSphere. From there, the plan was for them to dive to Yuuki's private VR room from Ran's bed.

But neither Yuuki nor Ran realized what lurked in Merida's heart of hearts.

Ran used the restroom before her dive and came to her room to find a handwritten note on the bed. Next to it lay Merida, already in a full dive. Her head, bald from chemo, donned not the AmuSphere she'd brought but Ran's NerveGear.

The note simply said, *Ran, Yuuki, I'm so sorry.* And in the slot of the NerveGear was a game card with the title *Sword Art Online.*

"What...?!"

It took Yuuki several seconds to grasp what this meant after Ran showed up in her decorated VR room and explained what had happened.

Merida hadn't used her AmuSphere; she'd used Ran's Nerve-

Gear. And that was because the AmuSphere couldn't play *SAO*, presumably. Merida's stunt wasn't on a whim. She had brought the *SAO* card with her to do this from the start. She'd made an intentional choice to leap into the game where virtual death meant real death.

Ran's NerveGear was modified with safety features, like a smaller battery and output limitations. But the NerveGear still used a power cable. The power that *SAO* used to destroy the wearer's brain when the avatar's HP reached zero came from the wall outlet. They couldn't let Merida be the test case to find out if those safety features worked or not.

"S-Sis! We have to take the NerveGear off Merida!" Yuuki shouted, suddenly feeling the virtual temperature drop. Ran, who was diving here with Merida's AmuSphere, just shook her head.

"We can't…I'm not going to pull it off her head—just in case the worst happens."

"Why not?! Your NerveGear has a smaller battery, right? If you turn off the power and then take it off her, it shouldn't be able to emit those deadly waves…"

"Merida has a brain tumor. If she's exposed to any kind of abnormal EM waves at all, there's no telling how that might affect her. We can't pull it off her on our own."

"Then we need to tell the doctor at once…," Yuuki protested, feeling even more childish than usual in the presence of her ever-calm sister.

But Ran didn't agree to this, either. Instead, she placed her hands on Yuuki's shoulders in a calming gesture. "I think we should do that, too," she whispered, "but before that, give me five minutes…well, three."

"What…? What are you going to do in three minutes?" Yuuki asked.

Ran just stared her right in the eyes and replied, "I think there's still time. Come with me, Yuu."

They brought up the door that acted as the app launcher from the VR room hub and walked through it into a blinding curtain of sunlight that made Yuuki squint.

It was Leute, the village in the eastern region of *Serene Garden*. A band of NPC musicians played cheerful background music while players sat on the benches in the center of town, chatting happily. Ran rushed through the scene, her dress making her appear as a blue blur. Yuuki hurried after her.

She had no idea where her sister was going or why they were in *Serene Garden* at all. Merida was already in Aincrad, the setting of *Sword Art Online*, wasn't she? And there wasn't going to be any teleport gate that would take them from *Serene Garden* to *SAO*.

But Ran's path was absolutely determined. She took them through the village gate and out into the undulation of Teal Hills. They ran along the brick road for a while but eventually curved left off the path and across the green, grassy fields.

Yuuki only realized where her sister was taking them once they had crossed a number of hills and come within sight of a small pond glittering in the sun.

The water was only sixty feet across or so, and the bank was lined with short pegs that stuck up out of the surface. A solitary tree stood near the edge.

This was the place where Yuuki had caught the royal triton stag beetle.

The place where they'd first met Merida.

To Yuuki's shock, there was also a small figure crouched at the roots of the tree. The breeze rustled a green ponytail that shone in the sun.

Lost in emotion, Yuuki sped past her sister, running along the edge of the pond and shouting the figure's name, right as it got to its feet.

"Meridaaaaa!!"

There was shock on her friend's face when she turned around and then a strange smile that seemed likely to turn into tears. She spoke their names, and her voice sounded more fragile than any they'd ever heard.

"...Yuuki...Ran..."

Yuuki slowed and came to a stop a short distance away from Merida. Within moments, Ran was there, too.

Merida had put the NerveGear on to go into *SAO*, so why had she dived into *Serene Garden* instead? The answer was at her feet.

Resting on the ground was a bug cage with its door open, and sitting on top, a lapis-lazuli-blue stag beetle. The insect was larger than when they'd first seen it, and its antennae were waving about, as though asking its owner for answers.

Merida followed Yuuki's gaze and looked down at the beetle, smiling like a child trying to hold back tears.

"......Roy just won't fly away. I wanted to give it back to you, Yuuki, but once an insect has an owner, you can't give it to someone else. So I thought...maybe if I let it go free here, you would catch it again someday..."

Her voice cracked. When Yuuki saw the large tears pooling in Merida's eyes, she felt something hot and painful surge up within her chest. Ran sounded like she was going to cry, too.

"Roy's not going to fly away, Merida," she said. "You took such good care of him every day. He's going to win the big tournament, too—I just know it. Please, Merida...come back home with Roy and us. Me and Yuu are the only ones who know for now."

At last, Yuuki understood why her sister didn't go straight to Dr. Kurahashi to tell him. Assuming he made the decision to take off the NerveGear and it actually worked, he still had a responsibility to tell Merida's parents. And she would be forbidden from using an AmuSphere for VR care from that point onward. They would never see her in *Serene Garden* or *Asuka Empire* again. Ran made a bet that they'd find Merida here and be able to convince her to be reasonable.

Yuuki took a deep breath and followed up with everything she could say to her friend. "Please, Merida...don't go to *SAO*. I want to go on so many more adventures with you. I want to go to different places and see different things. Please...don't go...!"

But Merida looked at the ground rather than meet her eye. Bit by bit, she said, "I'm sorry, Yuuki…I'm sorry, Ran. I've ruined your special birthday with all of this…I'm so sorry. I can't ask you to forgive me. But I…I just had to…"

Her shoulders tensed beneath her shirt and trembled. Her voice was as frail and tense as thin glass, trickling over the afternoon fields.

"I saw in a news article a while ago…that the police are setting up a plan to remove the NerveGear from all the victims of the *SAO* Incident. But I don't feel like that plan can possibly work. It's going to cause so many deaths…"

It was just over ten days ago that Yuuki's sister had shown her that article, on the hillside nearby. Ran had been concerned about it in the exact same way as Merida.

"…I told you about how there were several people in the guild I joined during the *SAO* beta test. I was supposed to be there when it launched. And then I was spared from that because they found my tumor…but the truth is, that was really, really hard for me. If I…if I could go to Aincrad right now, I could use the rest of my life to help them, I thought. At least then…my life might have added up to something meaningful…"

"…Merida…"

Yuuki took a step forward. But Merida shook her head and backed away. The motion cast her tears aside, shining golden with the reflected light of the sun.

"Please, Yuuki, Ran…Let me go to Aincrad. There are *SAO* victims in this hospital, so I can get through the IP filter. I'm sure my parents will be sad, but they'll understand. I just…I just want to find it. To find the reason I was born this way…"

Her painful confession melted into the breeze blowing across the meadow and dispersed into the virtual atmosphere.

Merida said the same thing the day they'd first met her. And like that day, Yuuki was unable to find the right thing to say. Finding a reason to live, a positive meaning in life—that was something Yuuki wished she could do as well.

Ran silently came forth to stand next to Yuuki. She crouched and gently plucked Roy from the top of the cage. The stag beetle was calm and obedient in her palm. She lightly traced its brilliant carapace with her fingertip and said gently, "There are many, many reasons for you to live, here in *Serene Garden*, in *Asuka Empire*, and in reality. Look how well you've raised Roy. You brought me and Yuu to a brand-new world. There will be so many other wonderful things for you to do."

"……"

Merida's eyes, brimming with large tears, fixed on the stag beetle resting in Ran's hand. Eventually, a tiny smile appeared on her lips, and the girl who was just a bit older than the twins said, "If I've managed to give you anything, then I'm happy to hear that. But…what I really want is something I won't find here or in *Asuka* or in the real world. I want…to fight. I don't want to wait in my hospital bed for the end to arrive. I want to use my own two hands to fight against something bigger than disease—like fate or the world itself—and burn up what life I have striving against it. Please, Ran…just let me go."

"…Merida…," Yuuki heard her sister whisper. And then she understood.

Ran—Aiko—had a much stronger ability to empathize than Yuuki did. She could bring herself closer to another person's pain and sadness, understand it, and accept it.

And that was why Ran could feel and empathize with how Merida felt right now. She felt it so keenly that she wanted that desire to be made real.

But.

But…

If she let Merida go, Ran would regret it immensely later. She would be pained by what she said and the choice she made and bear that decision on her back like a sin that could never be cleansed.

It was crucial for Yuuki to speak up now. She couldn't let her sister handle everything this time; she had to use her own words and her own will to hold Merida back.

She clasped her hands, squeezing so hard, she felt the very core of her being trembling, and shouted, "Merida!!"

The girl's eyes bolted open in surprise. Yuuki stared into those emerald-green pools and continued, "I'll find it for you! I'll find something that will make you want to burn up your life for it, Merida! Please...just please don't go!!"

Merida blinked again and put on the faintest hint of a smile.

"...And how are you going to find that, Yuuki?" she asked quietly.

Yuuki didn't know why she gave the answer she did. But they were words that would determine her own fate.

"Go into *Asuka Empire* and fight me, Merida. I'm sure you'll understand after that."

7

Merida put Roy back into the insect cage and returned it to her item list, then logged out of *Serene Garden*. But there was no guarantee she would do as Yuuki hoped and log in to *Asuka Empire* rather than *Sword Art Online*.

But Yuuki could do nothing except head to the large cedar tree on the outskirts of Kiyomihara to wait and trust.

The area around the tree was a flowing meadow, rather like the area in Teal Hills, where they'd just been. But a short distance away was a large growth of pampas grass rustling in the chilly wind, a species that didn't exist in *Serene Garden*.

A few minutes later, she heard the familiar sound of quiet, quick footsteps approaching and turned to face them.

It was a ninja wearing very familiar light-green garb, but unlike when they usually met, this time she was already wearing her face-covering mask. She slowed down and came to a stop about five yards away from Yuuki and Ran, saying nothing.

"......Merida..."

Yuuki wanted to thank her for coming, but she couldn't. There was a sharp, fierce aura exuding from Merida's being, an invisible force that pressed down on the sisters.

To this point, Yuuki had no experience in a player duel. She knew you could do it, of course, and she'd watched some sporty competitions between guild partners on the street, but she felt a strong aversion to the act of fighting her hardest against another player's avatar, the representation of their physical body.

This duel, however, was something Yuuki wanted.

Merida wanted to go to *SAO* so she could sacrifice her life for something worthwhile. Whatever it was, it was something that existed in the virtual world but wasn't an artifice. A kind of truth that existed virtually, where even the extremely sick could be just as mobile as any other player.

In the deadly environment of *SAO*, thousands of players were fighting in the space between life and death. Merida had been a beta tester, and she was willing to become a prisoner of the game if it gave her the chance to fight for her old friends…for all the survivors still in there. Yuuki understood a tiny bit of this feeling.

But at the same time, she strongly felt it was the wrong choice. If she wanted to talk about destiny, wasn't it Merida's destiny *not* to be inside *SAO*, because doctors had spotted her tumor?

And even on this side of the virtual divide, there were things she could and should do. Yuuki didn't know what those things were, but they existed. She was fighting, not speaking, to get her feelings across.

She let out the air in her lungs over time, then sucked in a deep breath of cold virtual air and waved her right hand to bring up the player menu.

There was one button in the menu she had never touched until just now: the DUEL button. It displayed a list of players in the area who could be challenged, so she selected Merida's name and pressed OK.

Merida's eyes strayed away from Yuuki and moved lower. Her arm rose, operating a window that only she could see. Yuuki's window displayed a message saying that her duel challenge had been accepted, and then the whole thing vanished.

A thirty-second countdown began in the space between them. Yuuki gripped her katana in a sweaty palm and drew it from her left side. It was named Suminagashi, or Ink Washer, from the *uchigatana* category. It had a black Damascus pattern on the flat, and while it wasn't particularly rare, it was easy to use.

A moment after that, Merida readied her weapon. It was Akezuki, or Scarlet Moon, from the *shinobigatana* category. It was a rare weapon with a straight, deep-red blade, smaller than Yuuki's sword, but more powerful overall.

When the shinobi blade's sharp tip pointed in her direction, Yuuki felt something within her chest shrivel up.

There was no way she could avoid all of Merida's speedy ninja attacks. In just moments, that weapon was going to pierce and slash Yuuki's body. And Yuuki had to attack her good friend with her own katana, too. There was no real pain in the virtual world, and they were only wagering temporary numerical HP—but all the same, this was a real fight.

Could she do it? Could she put up a proper fight against Merida on her first try?

This duel was her idea, but now her heart was shying away from it. Her breathing became shallow, and her vision narrowed.

"...!"

She shivered and was about to falter backward—when she received a push in the right direction from Ran, who was watching from several yards away.

It's all right. She'll understand how you feel. It'll work if you give her your all.

"...Sis...," she murmured, and the shivers stopped.

Their chances of winning were honestly higher if Ran fought, rather than Yuuki. As a shrine maiden, she wielded a variety of magic seals with keen accuracy and mastered close combat with a Shinto staff called an *oonusa* that she used to bludgeon opponents. Her combat ability was easily higher than Yuuki's. Of course, Merida's character level was higher than both of theirs, but *Asuka Empire* was scaled in a way that a higher level didn't amount to a major statistical advantage.

But if Yuuki relied upon her big sister like she so often did, Merida wasn't going to feel Yuuki's true emotions, even if Yuuki won the fight.

That was right—she had to relate her feelings, her will, everything that was inside of her.

When the countdown reached five seconds, it flashed much brighter. Yuuki watched the numbers descend: *four, three, two, one.*

At zero, the numeral expanded outward as a circle of light and vanished.

"Iyaaaaaaah!!" Yuuki roared with all her strength as she pushed off the ground. A samurai's agility was inferior to a ninja's, but there was one case in which she had better propulsion: when charging with a slice attack. She crossed the five-yard gap with a single jump, right at Merida, and swung her katana down from overhead.

But the moment she caught sight of those green eyes behind her face mask, eyes the same shade as in *Serene Garden*, Yuuki's arms seized up against her will. The ink-colored blade wavered and slid off-center to the right. Against a monster, that kind of variation wasn't a problem, but Merida was too much of a veteran to let that opportunity pass.

With a whip of torn air, Merida evaded to the left with teleport-level speed. Yuuki's slash cut empty air, leaving only a faint visual effect behind.

Then a fierce shock ran through her left shoulder. Yuuki was knocked right off her feet, and she tumbled to the ground. Out of the corner of her eye, she saw nearly a tenth of her LP disappear. She rolled into the momentum, using the opportunity to get farther out of range before standing up.

Once in fighting position again, Yuuki saw Merida extending her left palm, rather than the shinobi sword in her right.

Ninjas had martial arts skills, but when she realized that a bare-handed attack through her shoulder armor had done so much damage on its own, Yuuki's breath caught in her throat.

She was tough—not that it was a surprise.

Or maybe she just *thought* she understood that. In all their time together, Merida had been more of an adviser or instructor to Yuuki and Ran. By spending as little time as possible attacking monsters, she made sure the sisters got as much experience as they could.

She'd seen only a tiny glimpse of Merida's true ability. That knowledge alone was enough to freeze Yuuki in her tracks.

"It was the same way for me at first," said a soft voice coming from behind the face mask. A hint of a smile could be heard in the voice. "The first time I dueled another player in *SAO*, my arms locked up, and I couldn't hit them at all. It's not like attacking a character on your monitor. You can tell yourself that it's not a real person, that it's just a digital avatar, but your body can't keep up with that knowledge…It took me two weeks to have a decent duel at last."

"…How were you able to fight?" Yuuki asked her ninja opponent.

Merida glanced at the cloudy sky above, as though consulting her memories. "When I was fighting another person using a one-handed sword like I was, they said that dueling isn't just trying to kill the other person. It's a dialogue between two swords. That's true for traditional online games, VRMMOs, and maybe even sporting competition in the real world. So when you said we should fight, I was just the tiniest bit surprised."

Yes—there was something Yuuki wanted to say to Merida. She couldn't put it into words, but it was there, hot and writhing deep in her core. She'd challenged Merida to the duel in the hope that clashing sword against sword might help that message get across.

If her arms shrank back like they did at first, no messages would be getting across. She had to push past her fears and hesitation and move forward. Forward, forward, always forward… right to where Merida would feel it.

"…There are some things you can't get past without confronting them," Yuuki whispered to herself. But Merida heard and nodded.

She flipped the shinobi blade around to hold it backhanded and brandished it diagonally. Yuuki raised the katana high again.

This time, it was Merida who moved first.

She leaned far forward, transforming into a gust of light-green wind as she charged right for Yuuki. She wasn't going to make it easy this time. Yuuki had to defend against the ultrafast ninja slash or evade it and turn that into a counterattack. She was staring, focusing on the dull reflection of sunlight on the deep-red blade, when she thought she heard a voice.

Don't look at the weapon—look at all of Merida, Yuu!

Instantly, Yuuki's eyes were open wide, expanding her vision.

Merida's right hand held the *shinobigatana* in front. Her left hand was obscured behind the blade, but she could see something shining within her clenched fist.

The sword is a feint. The first attack will come from her left...a shuriken!

The second Merida's other hand blurred, Yuuki brought down her katana directly toward the instant of reflected light she saw.

There was a high-pitched *clang!* and a shower of white sparks. The cross-shaped shuriken, deflected by Yuuki's swing, flew rotating back toward Merida. This was the effect of the samurai-class skill Parry.

"...!"

The ninja exhaled briefly, then smacked the shuriken with her shinobi sword. The reflection from the shuriken vanished off and up to the right, where Yuuki need not pay any more attention to it. She lunged toward Merida, who was now off-balance.

Her range was good. No more hesitation.

She wasn't attacking out of hatred, or the desire to win or kill. She was swinging to show Merida what could exist beyond the skills she'd taught.

"Rrraaaah!" she bellowed, flipping her wrists and slashing up from below. Despite Yuuki's awkward stance, the black blade slid through Merida's torso as she tried to jump backward and out of the way.

Zassh!! There was firm feedback in Yuuki's hands. The follow-through of the swing left her arms high, sending crimson illumination high into the air. Above Merida's head, her LP bar dropped about 15 percent.

Going by the theory of combat against monsters, this was the time to open a ground circle, activate a skill, and deliver major damage to an enemy under a movement delay. But Merida wasn't likely to leave herself that open, just from a single hit. Her follow-up should be a normal attack—but with everything Yuuki had riding on it.

She raised her katana overhead for the third time.

Merida used the momentum of that upward attack to perform a backflip in the air.

Yuuki launched herself forward, aiming for the moment when her opponent hit the ground.

"Haaaaah!!" she roared from the very bottom of her gut, preparing to deliver her best swing.

Wham! The air burst.

While airborne and looking down at Yuuki, Merida jumped *off the air* with both feet. That was the ninja-class skill Double Jump.

"Cheyaaa!" she shouted for the first time in this fight and plunged. The shinobi blade in her right hand was a flash of crimson, heading straight for Yuuki's throat.

The slashing speed advantage belonged to Merida for being a ninja, but Yuuki had started earlier. So at the moment, their timing was equal. But if Yuuki gave in to fear now and gave anything less than full dedication to the attack, she would get hit by the counter.

What did Yuuki want to tell Merida?

That she would get much, much stronger.

The world was endlessly expanding beyond the walls of the closed-off, deadly *SAO*. There were so many people to meet, discoveries to make, and stories to experience, in worlds virtual and real.

I'll take you wherever we can go.

I'll find you a new destiny, Merida.
Just don't leave...
"...Aaaaaaaaaaaaah!!"

Bright light expanded outward. Shining particles burst away from her avatar like stars. The resistance of the compressed atmosphere against her blade reached a maximum, then gave way as she broke through.

Yuuki's katana swung downward, a pure beam of light, in absolute silence.

An instant later, Merida's shinobi blade brushed the left side of her neck as it went past.

At the end of her swing, Yuuki couldn't move. Once sound returned to the world, a crimson damage effect spurted noisily from her neck wound. Over 20 percent of her LP disappeared.

Stumbling, she turned to see Merida, frozen at the end of her follow-through. Suddenly and silently, she split from the shoulder of her ninja garb through her back, and a huge visual effect sprayed from the cut. From its total of 85 percent, Merida's LP gauge rapidly decreased, stopping only when it had gone just under 50 percent.

Da-doom! With a taiko drum booming, a window appeared, announcing the end of the duel. Yuuki gasped with surprise. She blinked several times, wide-eyed, but nothing changed what she was looking at: a message that read, *Winner: Yuuki.*

"B-but why...? We're not...," she stammered.

Merida stood up straight and turned around, sliding her *shinobigatana* into the sheath at her waist. She smiled.

"In *Asuka*, you can duel to the death in showdown mode or simply go down to half your LP in bout mode. I chose bout mode when you challenged me, so this one's all you, Yuuki. You won. Congratulations...You were really tough. You stunned me."

"Um...I..."

She was going to deflect it, to say that she still had so far to go, but that was when it truly hit her.

She'd won the duel. But she didn't know if she'd gotten her

message across. Her friend was standing there smiling at her, but she still looked so fragile, like she might melt away in the sunlight. Yuuki was so preoccupied with her thoughts that she didn't even remember to sheathe her sword.

"If I'm really that strong," she said, letting the words come to her in the moment, "then it's thanks to you, Merida. I got stronger because you taught me so many things. I said I'd help you find something that you could burn your life away doing. I don't know what that is yet...but I promise you. I'm going to be even stronger...and I'll never stop...I'll just keep getting stronger..."

She tried to mold the thoughts she had in battle, to form them into words, but her voice gave out. In and out she breathed, trying to collect herself, but it wasn't happening.

Instead, Merida lowered her mask and beamed. It was the exact same smile she made when they first met in *Serene Garden*.

"I heard you, Yuuki."

"Huh...?"

"I could feel how you felt through your sword. And not just your feelings about me...I felt all kinds of things from you. Um... I'm not that smart, so I might not be saying this right. But your strength...No, something bigger than that. Ummm..."

Now it was Merida who was mumbling, searching for the right word.

"...Your possibilities," said a soft voice that drew the two girls' attention.

The speaker was Ran, who had been watching their duel from beneath the large cedar tree. The shrine maiden smiled, warm and gentle, like she always did, and glided over to the duelists.

"You meant possibilities, didn't you, Merida?"

"Yes, that!" she said, snapping her fingers and nodding furiously. "There's so much that's packed inside of you, Yuuki. Your strength in the duel was just a tiny part of it...You're going to be so much stronger and bigger than you are now. To the point that people are going to know your name in all kinds of worlds one day."

"...No...I'm not that special...," Yuuki mumbled, staring at Merida in numb shock.

There was no longer any hint of desperation in her expression, although the translucent fragility was still there. Yuuki wanted to ask her if she'd reconsidered her plan to go into *SAO* or if she was still resolute.

But then Ran came up on her right and rested a hand on Yuuki's shoulder. "Merida, Yuuki, I want to tell you something I've been thinking about," she said.

"...What, Ran?"

"I want the three of us to make a guild. And bit by bit, we can add new people...new friends, and make our little circle bigger."

She reached down and squeezed Yuuki's hand. Then she held out her other arm toward Merida, who was standing a little farther away. Without thinking, Yuuki extended her other hand toward Merida, too.

Merida looked at their hands but hesitated, confused. "But, Ran...we're..."

Yes. That was on Yuuki's mind, too.

The three had met in a VR hospice. They shared the reality of terminal illness. They could start a guild in *Asuka Empire* and recruit new members, but they couldn't keep the fact of their condition a secret forever. One day, they would have to explain the truth. Or perhaps the truth would arrive before they could tell that story.

The closer they got to other guild members, the harder that moment would be. The guild itself might fracture and fall apart. Ran would know that, of course.

"One day...one day, we'll overcome this disease and keep the circle expanding...as far as it can go, I hope...," Ran whispered, then collected herself. "I think that at first, we should recruit people in the same position as us. I think there are others in *Serene Garden* who want to see the outside world like us, to go farther. We should invite them to our guild and go to the very limits of the virtual worlds out there. The same way you pulled the two of us to join you, Merida."

Her hand was still extended, firm and unwavering. Merida's eyes were flared with surprise, fixed on Ran.

A breeze rustled the needles of the massive cedar tree. There was no lasting sign of their duel on the field any longer. The blue sky, a different shade from *Serene Garden*'s, held trailing wisps of clouds that slid quietly along. A hawk circled, calm and regal, high above.

The world map of *Asuka Empire* was based loosely on what was today known as the Kinki region. On the east end was Mount Fuji, and on the west end were the Kanmon Straits separating Honshu and Kyushu—although all the places in-game had fictional names. In the next major update, however, they were supposed to be adding the Kanto region around Tokyo, and the island of Kyushu. The world was getting larger here, and it would probably do the same in other places, like *ALfheim Online*.

I'm sure we'll find what we're looking for, Merida. New places for us. New friends for us. And a fate worth fighting for.

The words passed through her mind as she reached for all she was worth.

At last, Merida's emerald-green eyes rippled like water. The pure, shining light turned into droplets that ran silently down her cheeks.

Unlike everything else, these tears *were* the exact same shade as those in *Serene Garden*. Merida's voice emerged, hoarse with emotion.

"...Well...I guess that settles it...After a speech like that... there's no way I can leave you two behind..."

Her right foot, covered in a thick ninja *tabi* sock, ground itself against the grass a few times. Then she made up her mind and pushed forward.

One, two, three steps...Slowly but resolutely, she approached the twins. Merida lifted her hands and grabbed Ran's and Yuuki's. Her grip was firm and strong.

"It's a very small circle," she said, smiling tearfully.

Yuuki squeezed back with all the strength she had. "But it's so much bigger than the circle of just me and Sis."

She smiled, and tears of her own poured from her eyes. She couldn't wipe them away if she wanted to, so they just dripped and dripped without end. Through her blotted, colorful vision, she could still see the smile on Merida's face.

"Ha-ha...Yuuki, you look incredible. If you cry that hard, you're going to come out with tears on your cheeks in real life."

"That's fine. I'm just so happy."

She tried to blink the virtual tears away, until Ran finally had mercy on her and let go so she could use the sleeve of her miko robe to rub Yuuki's face.

"You're so strong and yet still such a crybaby, Yuu," she said, although her cheeks were shining, too. Yuuki squeezed Ran's hand again and looked up at the sky.

The hawk had flown off somewhere else, but the sky itself was still beautiful. It felt like it connected to the sky of *Serene Garden*—and the sky in the real world, too.

Let's go—wherever we will, hand in hand. For the sake of the worlds and the people to come.

Yuuki could feel the door in her heart, closed ever since the unwanted school transfer in fifth grade, finally opening a crack.

She didn't know how much time she had left. But if her life was shorter than average, that just meant she needed to run faster and bolder. In the real world, she might be confined to her bed, but in the virtual world, her possibilities were endless.

"...It's time to go back now," said Merida. She squeezed Yuuki's and Ran's hands one last time to dispel their anxieties, then let go. "I told Mom I'd meet her back at the café by three o'clock. Yuuki, Ran...I'm sorry for ruining your birthday like this. I feel terrible."

Merida tried to bow in apology, but Ran grabbed her shoulders. "You don't need to say sorry, Merida. It's been a wonderful birthday. I mean, you came all this way to visit us, didn't you?"

Yuuki added, "I was...I was really happy, too! Please...please, Merida, come meet me on the other side!"

Ran turned and gave her a look of surprise, but Yuuki continued talking.

"Listen, for my own reasons, I'm in a clean room right now, but you can see me through the glass from the monitoring room next door. I can't hold your hand, but I still want to be able to see you."

She was still sworn to secrecy about the Medicuboid, so she wasn't sure Dr. Kurahashi would allow her to have a meeting, even through glass. But she had a feeling he wasn't going to refuse them. It was her fourteenth birthday, after all.

"...Okay! Once I'm back out, I'll go right over to see you, Yuuki," Merida stated, nodding forcefully.

There was no longer any hint of fragility in her expression.

8

"Are you ready, Yuuki?"

Yuuki replied to Dr. Kurahashi through the speaker with a crisp "Ready!" The adjustable glass that separated Yuuki's clean room from the adjacent monitoring room promptly went translucent.

In the monitoring room, which was as cramped as a hallway, Dr. Kurahashi was wearing a white lab coat rather than his usual outfit. He was joined by Ran in her pajamas and a girl in a wheelchair who looked slightly older.

"…Happy birthday, Yuuki!"

Merida's real voice was a bit hoarser than how she sounded in the virtual world. Under the light-green beanie she wore, her face was sunken, and her skin was pale. But her big eyes were shining and strong.

"Thank you…thank you, Merida," Yuuki said. She was forbidden from touching the glass, but she could get as close as possible short of that. Merida wheeled her chair a foot or two closer, until her face was nearly touching the thick glass, and then she smiled.

"You and Ran both look almost exactly the way you do over there. I'm sorry…I brought flowers for you two, but they can't put them in your room."

Sure enough, there was a small bouquet of flowers on Merida's lap.

"It's fine. I'm just happy that I can see them from here! They're so pretty…Thank you so much, Merida," Yuuki said hastily.

From below the bouquet, Merida extended her hand toward the window. Her frail fist was holding something small in it. Yuuki stared closely, trying to see it.

"Yuuki, Ran…listen. Instead of giving you presents, I'm going to make you a promise. I'll never say I want to go to that place again. This is the proof."

Merida lifted her other hand and plucked the small, rectangular object she was holding—a memory card.

Printed on the card was a tiny label with a logo the size of a rice kernel, but Yuuki could recognize it clear as day.

Sword Art Online.

Merida closed her eyes and moved her lips. The mic didn't pick up the sound, but Yuuki clearly heard her voice saying "Good-bye."

She tensed her fingers to the point that they trembled—and then the little plastic memory card snapped in two.

In the end, the police department's planned operation to forcefully disengage all the *SAO* Incident victims' NerveGear did not happen. The deadly game was beaten before they could move their scheme out of the planning stage, returning six thousand survivors to the real world.

That was about half a year after Yuuki and Ran's fourteenth birthday. The day the Sleeping Knights were formed.

(The End)

AFTERWORD

Thank you for reading *Sword Art Online 22: Kiss and Fly*.

This is the first short story collection since Volume 8, *Early and Late*, and all the stories in this book were written as bonus pack-ins for Blu-rays and DVDs of the anime series. I feel sorry for those readers who bought the discs for these stories, but it's a very steep price for students and young people to pay, so I asked to have the pieces that have already been available for several years collected in this volume. I beg your forgiveness!

I have a little note about the title, too. A kiss-and-fly zone is the name for a special parking zone at Western airports, meant for people to share a quick kiss before they leave. Of course, there are no airplanes or airports in this book. But I used *kiss* to refer to the warm and romantic moments of Aincrad, and *fly* to refer to the soaring adventure in Alfheim. Overall, the phrase suggests a brief farewell until we meet again.

Upon reading over these stories again, I realized that I kind of... *don't* hate writing short stories. Overall, I don't think I'm good at ending things, which is why the main series is always "to be continued," but when you have to set up, execute, and conclude a story in thirty or fifty pages, I find it all comes together the way it's supposed to. Maybe that's because I think of each *SAO* short story as a single quest. That could be a literal quest within a game or some challenge in the real world—but it's never more evident to me that depicting characters leaping over a hurdle is the very foundation of a story.

I'm sure that Kirito and Asuna, their friends, their author, and even their readers will be faced with endless challenges, but I believe that with patience, perseverance, and courage, all these challenges can be defeated. I'm sure that my editor checking over this afterword has his own challenges in the schedule ahead, but I wish him the best of luck in surpassing them! (I can hear his voice now, saying, "This is all your fault...!")

Lastly, I'm sure that some people are wondering, "If this is Volume 22, what happened to the story you started in Volume 21, *Unital Ring I*?!" Have no fear. In the coming Volume 23, we will return to the world of *Unital Ring*. I hope to see you there!

Reki Kawahara—September 2019